PENGUIN

Third Time Lucky

Pippa Croft is the pen name of an award-winning romantic novelist. After studying English at Oxford, she worked as a copywriter and journalist before writing her debut novel, which won the RNA's New Writers' award and was later made into a TV movie. She lives in a village in the heart of England with her husband and daughter.

Also by Pippa Croft

The First Time We Met
The Second Time I Saw You

Third Time Lucky

PIPPA CROFT

PENGUIN BOOKS

PENGUIN BOOKS

Published by the Penguin Group
Penguin Books Ltd, 80 Strand, London WC2R ORL, England
Penguin Group (USA) Inc., 375 Hudson Street, New York, New York 10014, USA
Penguin Group (Canada), 90 Eglinton Avenue East, Suite 700, Toronto, Ontario, Canada M4P 2Y3
(a division of Pearson Penguin Canada Inc.)
Penguin Ireland, 25 St Stephen's Green, Dublin 2, Ireland (a division of Penguin Books Ltd)
Penguin Group (Australia), 707 Collins Street, Melbourne, Victoria 3008, Australia
(a division of Pearson Australia Group Pty Ltd)
Penguin Books India Pvt Ltd, 11 Community Centre, Panchsheel Park, New Delhi – 110 017, India
Penguin Group (NZ), 67 Apollo Drive, Rosedale, Auckland 0632, New Zealand
(a division of Pearson New Zealand Ltd)
Penguin Books (South Africa) (Pty) Ltd, Block D, Rosebank Office Park,
181 Jan Smuts Avenue, Parktown North, Gauteng 2193, South Africa

Penguin Books Ltd, Registered Offices: 80 Strand, London WC2R ORL, England

www.penguin.com

First published in Penguin Books 2014
001

Copyright © Penguin Books UK Ltd, 2014
All rights reserved

The moral right of the author has been asserted

Set in 12.5/14.75 Garamond MT Std
Typeset by Jouve (UK), Milton Keynes
Printed in Great Britain by Clays Ltd, St Ives plc

PAPERBACK ISBN: 978-1-405-91706-3

www.greenpenguin.co.uk

For Broo, Liz and Nell

Chapter One

The Easter Vacation

'How is he?'

The nurse scribbles a note on a chart and hooks it over the end of the bed before replying. 'His condition's stable for now but we'll know more when he comes round from the anaesthetic.'

I clench my fists to disguise my shaky hands. 'And he *will* come round from the anaesthetic?' I ask nervously.

'Yes, we think so, but when he does come round, he's going to feel pretty sorry for himself.'

I look at Alexander's battered face, thinking miserably that it doesn't look anything like him. How I wish it wasn't.

The nurse gives me a professional smile. I'm sure she's seen it all before, and then some, but this is new for me. New and so far out of my comfort zone I'm still struggling to believe it's really happening. That yesterday I was living it up at a party after the Oxford and Cambridge Boat Race and then one phone call from the military ward of a London hospital has turned everything on its head.

'We should hopefully see some signs of improvement in a few hours, but like I say, it's a waiting game.'

'Should' and 'hopefully' are not really the words I want to hear right now; however I've no choice but to try and keep a hold on my emotions. I'm no good to anyone if I fall apart, and Alexander's sister Emma is going to need me to hold it together – though I've only just started to process the shock of hearing he'd been seriously injured on a mission myself. When I arrived at the hospital, I could hardly take in what the medical team were telling me: severe blood loss that needed to be stemmed . . . severe damage to the muscles and tendons of the upper left bicep . . . almost cut to the bone . . . half an hour longer and that would have been it . . . the potential for sepsis to set in.

'What will I tell his sister?' I ask, dreading the moment when Emma Hunt gets here, which could be any time now. She's barely seventeen and Alexander is all she has since their father died in a riding accident in January. I called her school as soon as I'd spoken to his consultant, and Helen, the family's housekeeper, has gone to fetch her and bring her to the hospital.

'I'll ask the consultant to speak to you again. He'll advise you, I'm sure.' The nurse touches my arm briefly. 'I can't tell you not to worry because Captain Hunt's condition is serious, but assuming he does wake up, he's going to need a lot of TLC and patience.'

TLC? I don't know whether to laugh out loud or scream in frustration because Alexander Hunt is a stranger to patience, and as for Tender Loving Care, there hasn't been much of that between us since I crashed into him in the cloisters of Wyckham College six months ago. But it's a good sign, isn't it, that I feel angry with him? It has to be a million times better than facing the possibility I'd never see him again.

Never in my life do I want to make another journey like this morning's, staring out of the windows of the taxi cab, trying not to throw up or burst into tears. Even now I know things aren't as desperate as they were a few hours ago, I'd give almost anything to see him sit up, throw off the sheet and demand to know why we're all making such a bloody fuss.

The nurse removes the saline bag from the drip-stand and replaces it with a fresh one. I reach out to touch his forearm, but let my fingers hover an inch above the skin, as if I'm half afraid he'll break. That's crazy, because nothing breaks Alexander; or at least he thinks it doesn't. I stroke his arm gently, surprised – I don't know why – to find his skin as warm as it always is.

While the nurse adjusts the drip-valve, I force myself to focus on his face again and to try and get things in perspective, but the sight of him isn't helping. His eyes are slits in a mass of puffy flesh. His cheeks and fore-head are criss-crossed with cuts, some patched with Steri-Strips. Purple and yellow bruises bloom on his chest like grotesque flowers and most of his left shoul-der and arm is swathed in bandages. Is this really the man who's occupied my thoughts and shared my bed

3

so many times for the past six months? The one who's made me laugh and cry and want to beat the pillow in frustration? The one I'd decided emphatically to stay away from?

The nurse rejoins me at his bedside.

'I still can't believe this has happened to him. I don't know what . . .' I murmur.

While she waits for me to finish my sentence, she tilts her head to one side a little, possibly to let me know she's really listening to me – probably it's just her training. For some reason, it makes me even more anxious. 'I don't know what I'd do if anything happened to him . . .' I say, then realize how ridiculous that sounds considering he's just been beaten, tortured and stabbed.

She touches my arm briefly. 'I know it's difficult but it will sink in soon enough. You – and he – may not think it now, but he's been very lucky. I'm sorry if this sounds blunt, but at least he's alive. That's not the case for everyone who gets wheeled in through these doors.'

'No, you're right. Thanks for all you've done for him.'

'Well, it's up to Captain Hunt from now on – and his loved ones, of course.'

'He only has Emma,' I say, sidestepping her comment.

She smiles at me again, more warmly now, but she doesn't know me. *I'm not his loved one*, I want to tell her. The last words between Alexander and me were cold, angry and bitter. A few days before Alexander went on this mission, we'd had a massive row that ended with me storming out of his house – with his blessing. Since then, I hadn't heard a word from him until the early hours of this morning when I found a letter he'd left for me apologizing – sort of – for what he'd said to me. And just hours after I'd got my head around *that* bombshell, the hospital called.

The nurse's face is a blur in front of me so I wipe my hand across my face, and am horrified to find my knuckles are wet with tears.

'Here you are.' A handful of Kleenex is thrust under my nose.

'Thanks.' My throat is clogged, my voice husky. The hangover and lack of sleep are taking their toll.

When I refocus, the nurse is watching me intently. 'Why don't you take a break, Lauren?'

'I will do soon, thanks.' I bite back my tears, ashamed of my reaction.

She touches my arm again. 'Good. I'll pop back in a little while.'

The door to the corridor closes with a soft click and I watch her chatting to a colleague through the window that allows the medical team to observe their patients. My knees are a little wobbly as I cross to the washbasin in the corner of the hospital room. The cold water stings my skin as I splash my face and when I glance in the mirror, I see that dark smudges ring my eyes and smears of mascara daub my cheeks. My God, I look almost as bad as Alexander.

Although the nurse told me to take a break, I can't seem to tear myself away. The late-morning sun slants through the blinds and casts bars of light and shadow across the sheet that covers him. If there's one consolation in the whole disaster of this weekend, it's that I was already in London when I got the call from the hospital – which reminds me, I have to call my college friend Immy as soon as I can. I still haven't told her where I am so when she gets back to the apartment we're sharing, she'll think I've either run off back to Washington or been abducted by aliens.

We'd been to a Boat Race party at a house on the Thames, hoping to have some fun and forget our troubled relationships. Immy ended up in bed with a Blues rower and I took a cab home after an encounter with Alexander's douche of a cousin, Rupert, and Alexander's poisonous ex, Valentina . . . but I refuse to think about either of them now.

I reach out and touch Alexander's hair, biting my lip at the feel of the matted blood on his scalp. 'So this is what you do, just to get my attention.'

I am just about to look away, wondering if the nurse is right and I ought to take a break, when I think I spot something. Was that his eyelid fluttering? I shake my head, thinking I'm really losing it now. But then I look back and his swollen eyelids are definitely open and those cool blue eyes are focused right on me. 'Alexander? Are you awake?'

It's possibly the most stupid question on the planet but I'm poleaxed by the way those eyes glared at me momentarily, as if nothing had ever happened.

'What the hell have you done to yourself?'

His eyes are closed now and there's no response to my whisper, just rhythmic breathing and the monotonous bleeping of the machines. Maybe I was hallucinating or seeing what I wanted to. I've hardly had any sleep and the booze from last night must still be affecting me.

'You really know how to drive a woman out of her mind, don't you?' I say, stroking the skin of his free hand again, around the patch securing the IV line.

'Uh-huh.'

What? His eyes may be closed but I'm sure his lips moved. I *heard* him and I'm not dreaming.

'Alexander . . . can you actually hear me or are you winding me up?'

'Like I said, he'll be in and out of it for a while.' The nurse's voice startles me. I hadn't even noticed her walk in but she's at the bottom of the bed, noting his obs again. I'm not so inclined to put his random comments down to the drugs, however. Nothing would surprise me about Alexander.

'Can I get you a cup of tea?' she asks, perhaps noting that I look like a zombie. She must have far better things to do than fetch drinks for me.

'No, but thanks so much for the offer. I might take a walk. I need some fresh air.'

'Good idea. Try and stay positive. We're as keen as you are to have Captain Hunt on the mend and probably driving you mad in no time.'

'How did you know he drives me mad?'

She rolls her eyes. 'Don't they always? Besides, it was all we could do to get Captain Hunt to lie down and behave while we examined him. He kept saying he had to get back to his men. He was delirious from the blood loss by then, but he was still quite a handful.'

'You wait until he wakes up,' I say, wildly encouraged by this statement while also apprehensive of what's in store when we do have to confront each other – and our problems – again.

The nurse gives a wry smile. 'Don't worry, I've seen it all. I can handle it.'

I wish I could say the same, I'm thinking, as I gather up my bag and follow her out of the room.

The moment the fresh air hits my lungs in the hospital grounds, I know I must have misheard Alexander's words. Outside, tulips crowd the neat borders and the cherry trees are thick with blossom. It's a bright spring morning; just a few damp spots in the shadows reveal any hint of the rain that poured down during the night. I sink my chin inside the neck of my funnel coat and shove my hands deep into my pockets.

What will I tell Emma when she gets here? She won't be long. I remember the letter Alexander sent me before he went off on his mission: *So if my corner of a foreign field ends up being some dusty hellhole, be a friend to Emma for me, would you?*

Oh, Emma. Clever, naive, vulnerable, even more maddening than her brother. The words in the letter are imprinted on my brain. I feel sick when I picture her reaction when she heard about this. She worships Alexander, when she's not arguing with him, and the news will have hit her hard.

Without warning, I feel a little light-headed so I find a bench in a patch of sunlight and sit down. At least my hands are steadier now, but I remember them trembling like leaves as I thrust a pile of notes at the cab driver when I arrived. He called after me, trying to offer me my change, but I was already jogging towards the hospital reception.

Despite the fact I vowed I'd never come running at Alexander's call again, I didn't hesitate when the hospital rang me. I didn't rush here because Alexander had asked for me before he went into surgery. I didn't come because he wanted to spare Emma from the shock of his injury until he was out of theatre. I came because I *had* to.

By the time I get up from the bench, I feel stronger and calmer, and the sun warms my face as I make a second circuit of the courtyard. Beyond the hedge, there are fields and a wood, where the first signs of green are clinging to the branches. The Easter vacation has started and I'd expected to be heading home to Washington soon. My mother was looking forward to a

9

belated birthday celebration with me, because I missed hers while I was away. And I'd already arranged a girls' weekend with my old Brown University friends and was looking forward to catching up with them and having fun after the stresses of last term of my master's in Art History. The exam term is coming up and it's going to be a toughie.

Now I'm wondering if I'll even be home in time. I don't know what state Alexander will be in when he's released, or if he'll want me to stay – or if *I'll* want to.

I think you can't stay away from me, Lauren, and I know damn well I can't stay away from you.

More of the words in his letter seem to float in front of my eyes. I shake my head, contemptuous of my own weakness. Any floating is sure to be a legacy of the obscene amount of Pimm's and wine I consumed yesterday.

I know you've hated me at times – perhaps most of the time – and especially now . . .

I can never forget those words because he's right; I *have* hated him at times, but not now. Now, I'm . . . scared of how vulnerable I feel, of how conflicted I feel. I could just walk right out of here and get the first plane back to Washington, and maybe that's what I *should* do.

I swear this: if I ever get the chance, I'm going to make good on all the things I've lain awake promising myself I'd do.

Remembering this threat, I don't whether to laugh or cry – or run. Right now, while I still have the chance, before everything starts again, before I'm sucked into his world and lured back into his bed.

The gates to the car park are only a few feet away; beyond that is the street. Above the birds, I can hear the rumble of traffic and, overhead, a plane's distant thrum. I stand up; it's that easy. *Just walk right through those gates, Lauren. Do it now.* The voice instructing me sounds like my mother's, like Scott's, like Daddy's.

'Miss Cusack?'

A new voice is speaking and it's the same one that I heard down the phone a few hours ago, that greeted me when I ran up to the reception desk a few hours ago. The ward sister hurries down the path towards me, her face anxious.

My heart rate rockets and suddenly I can't move.

'What's the matter?'

'Please try to stay calm, but I'm afraid we've had to take Captain Hunt back into theatre.'

Chapter Two

My stomach lurches. 'Back into surgery? I thought he was OK. What's happened now?'

'It looks as if we haven't managed to stop the internal bleeding; he's being taken into theatre again so the surgeons can try and fix it. Come inside and I'll tell you as much as I can.'

Outside Alexander's room, organized chaos reigns as the medical team wheel the bed through the doors in front of me. There are so many people in scrubs I can barely even see Alexander, and they all seem to be talking at once, overlapping each other. I catch phrases about 'BP dropping' and 'heart rate distress'. Then, in what seems like seconds, Alexander and the team are swallowed up by two doors at the end of the corridor and there is silence again.

I stand in the corridor, unable to move.

'Will they be able to stop the bleed?' I ask.

'We hope so, but he's already lost a lot of blood. It's possible we may have missed some internal injuries from the beating he took.'

The door to his room is still open; I can't avoid catching sight of the empty space where his bed was and the crimson pool spreading over the tiles. I put my hand over my mouth, feeling nauseous.

Sister Dixon closes the door firmly. 'Everything possible will be done to stabilize him, I promise you. He couldn't be in better hands, and he's young, fit and strong. Try not to worry too much.'

Before I even have time to process the implications of what she's saying, the entrance doors open and Emma dashes forward, followed by Helen. My heart sinks even further. What a moment for her to arrive.

'Lauren!'

Emma hugs me so hard I can barely breathe. She heaves in a huge sob and when she finally releases me from her death grip, she stares at me from a face that's almost as white as the hospital walls.

'How is he? What happened?' she cries, her voice high-pitched.

I exchange glances with Helen. I've been keeping enough Hunt secrets lately, but I don't want to distress Emma any more than I need to. Then again, I have to tell her the truth.

'Emma, please try not to worry . . .'

She glares at me. 'I hate it when people say, "Don't worry," because it usually means the exact opposite!'

'Your brother has just been taken into theatre again . . .' Sister Dixon cuts in, gently but firmly.

'*Again?* Why?' Emma's eyes are huge.

I leave the nurse to fill her in on the latest news. 'Oh God, please, you have to save him.'

'The surgeons are working on him now; they'll do everything they can, Miss Hunt, I promise.'

'I want to see him!' Emma's voice rises further in pitch and her eyes widen even more. Oh shit, clearly we're not doing a great job of reassuring her.

Sister Dixon, however, is a rock of calm. 'He's only just gone into theatre so I'm afraid you can't see him, but as soon as we have the situation stable and he's in recovery, you can visit him.'

Helen puts her arm around Emma. 'Try not to upset yourself. Alexander wouldn't want you to worry like this.'

'*Worry?* He almost fucking died! He might still!'

'Why don't you come into the relatives' room?' Sister Dixon ushers us towards a side door but Emma starts crying, and I don't blame her.

The decor in the relatives' room is probably meant to be calm and soothing, but I find the pale-green walls, retirement-home-style easy chairs and fake lily arrangement – not to mention a poster about counselling – have the opposite effect on me.

Helen joins us while Sister Dixon tells us a little more about Alexander's problems and what's being done to fix them. I guess I'm relieved that someone can explain his condition more coherently than I would, although I'm not sure any of us feel reassured afterwards. It will be a couple of hours before we know if the latest surgery has located the source of the blood loss and stopped it.

After our chat, the nurse shows Emma to the bathroom so she can wash her face, leaving me with Helen. Though she treats me with a degree of formality I've found hard to get used to, I also know she's a kind, warm woman who genuinely cares for the Hunt family.

'Do you want me to get you a cup of tea?' Helen asks with a concerned expression that makes me wonder just how wrung out I look.

'No thanks, I've had some already, but I can get you one.'

She shakes her head. 'Oh, I can't let you do that, Miss Cusack.'

'Helen, if you carry on calling me Miss Cusack, I'm going to have to have Alexander call a staff meeting when he returns to Falconbury and order everyone to call me Lauren,' I joke.

She gives a rueful smile and I notice how tired she looks. 'Old habits die hard but, actually, I'd love to see that happen.' She sighs. 'I'd love to see him come home at all.'

'I know.' I try to smile because I feel sorry for her. Running Falconbury can't be a picnic, especially with Alexander away so often and needing so much support from her and her husband, Robert, when he is there.

'I'd really like it if you could call me Lauren and I'm going to fetch you a cup of tea, whether you like it or not.'

Biting back her refusal, Helen finally nods. 'Thanks.'

In truth, I'm grateful for something – anything – to occupy my thoughts, even for a few seconds, so I walk over to the machine. 'Which is it to be? Dishwater or paint stripper?'

'Paint stripper, please.'

I feed coins into the slot and eventually a nozzle spurts rusty liquid into a plastic cup, which I hand to Helen.

'Thanks . . . Lauren.'

'You may not thank me when you try it . . . but I ought to thank *you*, for dropping everything and bringing Emma here. She must have been in an awful state, but I couldn't tell you any more than I knew at the time. I know Alexander will appreciate it.'

'She was very shocked and upset – we do have to confront we all were – but you can understand that. Poor Emma, she's been a troubled soul lately. Her father's death was a huge blow and it's been difficult for Alexander to support her the way he'd want to. We'd hoped he'd take a sabbatical from his regiment while he did his master's at Oxford, but Robert and I both guessed he was still on active service, rather than attending training camps. He hides his feelings, but we know him too well by now to be fooled.'

This statement is said with a world-weary resignation that is probably the closest I've ever come to hearing Helen give any hint of her real feelings about working for the Hunts.

'Since General Hunt died, he *was* meant to be on leave but I think he may have volunteered for this latest mission.'

Helen sips her tea and tries to hide her grimace. 'I would have thought he and Emma had more than enough to cope with as it is. With his work, dealing with his father's estate, and his master's degree, he's under enormous pressure . . .'

From the way her voice tails off and the fact she's resorted to the disgusting tea again, I guess she thinks she's already said too much about life above stairs at Falconbury at the moment.

'I'm aware of the pressure he's under,' I say, remembering the times when I've been on the receiving end of the fallout. No matter how many times I've reminded myself that I came to Oxford to focus on my own master's, to soak up the atmosphere and just have fun away from my parents' expectations, no matter how many times I've vowed to break away from the drama of Alexander's world, I've only been sucked further into it. Now, with him lying there, in genuine danger, and with Emma to care for, I feel overwhelmed with responsibility.

Yet there have been good times, wonderful times when we've shared each other's beds, lost ourselves in the sex, the hot, wonderful, insane sex . . . yet if it was just sex that kept us coming back to each other, surely I wouldn't be here now?

'You know, I'm happy to stay as long as you need me.' Helen's voice breaks into my thoughts.

'That's really kind of you, but I'll be OK and I'm sure you have a lot to do at the house. I'll call you when there's any news or if I need any help.'

She sips more of her tea with an ill-disguised shudder. 'Do you want me to call the de Courceys? They're Alexander's next of kin after Emma.'

'I'm not sure. I don't know them that well, only Rupert, but . . .' I don't know what to say next because while I know Helen means well, the de Courceys are the last people I need to contend with. I've only seen Rupert's parents briefly at a ball and at General Hunt's funeral. Frankly, it's all-out war between Rupert and me. He has done everything he could to cause trouble between me and Alexander.

'You might find them a huge support. I think you'd like Mrs de Courcey – that's General Hunt's sister,' says Helen. I notice she doesn't include Mr de Courcey in her statement. 'She and Lady Hunt were very good friends.'

'I don't think I spoke to her at the funeral.'

'No, but if you want me to call her, I will. You can't be expected to deal with this on your own.'

'I guess not,' I say softly. 'They have a right to know their nephew's been injured, so maybe you should call them.'

Helen deposits the half-full cup on a table and picks up her handbag. 'I'll go outside and do that now, but please can you let me know the instant that you have any news?'

'Of course I will. Thanks again.'

With a brisk kiss, Helen is gone, leaving me staring at the door to Alexander's room, feeling like a truck just ran over me.

A few minutes later, Emma emerges from the bathroom. I hadn't thought her face could grow any paler but she looks like a little grey ghost, almost transparent.

'How are you?'

She toes the floor tiles. 'How do you think? I almost vommed.'

She sniffs. I hand over a Kleenex as a tear trickles down her cheek. I've been doing a lot of Kleenex-handing for Emma lately.

'I'm sure he'll be OK,' I say, aware of how pathetic that sounds.

Emma barges on. 'I don't even know why he's here. I thought he was on some kind of training exercise, but you say it was a mission. Did he tell you where he was?'

'Not *where*. He would never tell me that sort of detail, but he did hint it wasn't an exercise. Beyond that, I know as much as you.'

Which isn't *quite* true. Alexander did hint that what he was doing was dangerous and unofficial but I'm not going to share that with Emma. She has enough on her plate as it is.

She sniffs. 'I *so* wish I could turn back the clock.'

'What do you mean?' I ask.

'I wish I could wipe out all that business with Henry Favell. Going off with him behind Alexander's back, causing trouble between you and Alexander and making him so worried about me. I wish none of that stuff had happened.'

'You can tell Alexander yourself when he gets better,' I say firmly, unwilling to rake up the business with Henry Favell now and stress Emma out even more than she already is. Over the past two terms, Emma has been having an on-off fling with Favell, who's ten years older and a grade-A shit. She told me about their relationship and begged me to keep it a secret from Alexander. Hoping the affair would fizzle out, and against my better judgement, I kept her confidence, but now I regret it deeply. Of course, when Alexander found out, everything exploded between us.

'You should know that if anyone's going to get through something like this, Alexander will,' I say, hugging her again. 'Before you know where you are, he'll probably be outraged and furious that anything has dared stop him from doing what he wants to. When he comes round properly, I guess we'll have trouble stopping him from getting out of bed and discharging himself.'

Emma doesn't smile but she gives a quiet snort so I know my silly comment hasn't made things worse. How I *would* love to see him march out of here, ignoring the advice of the doctors, blazing mad and demanding the keys to his Range Rover. In reality I can't see him driving it for a long time, or riding his horse – maybe he won't even be able to go back to active service. Even though he's said he'll have to leave the army one day, for Emma's sake and to run the estate, I know he'd hate to be forced out like this.

'If he gets through this,' she says, her voice wobbling, 'at least he'll be safe for a while.'

'Yes, he will.'

'You know, after what happened a few years ago, and Daddy dying, I've been worried sick about him getting killed and I'll never believe what he says again. The last time he was shot, Daddy tried to convince me Alex had been hurt in a live firing accident on the army range, but I knew it wasn't true.'

'I'm sure they didn't want to worry you.'

She snorts. 'Like, yeah, but I know the bullshit they come up with to hide what they're really up to. I'm not stupid.'

'Hey, I know what you mean, but I don't think it would help either of us to know the details.'

She sits in a chair and purses her lips. 'I *knew* something like this would happen. I can't lose him; I love him, no matter how much we fight and how angry he makes me.'

As she sets her chin determinedly in true Hunt style, I want to throw my arms around her, but I just give her an encouraging smile.

She curls her bottom lip over the top one, seeming very awkward. 'Lauren, I know you and Alex split up because of me. It was my fault, wasn't it?'

'I won't lie; when Alexander found out I'd been keeping your relationship with Henry a secret, he did kind of hit the roof. What did he tell you?'

She bites her lip sheepishly. 'I thought as much. He just muttered something about "fucking things up" at me after you left, then he told me he didn't want to talk about you any more. He acted a bit weird to be honest, sort of trying too hard to be super nice to me. That scared me more than him being angry and shouting. It's not like him, so I knew he was *really* upset.'

This sounds so much like Alexander that I have to smile; and it is strangely encouraging, though I can't put my finger on why.

'Lauren . . . do you love Alex?'

I am shocked that she would ask me this and I immediately dodge the question. 'I . . . can't answer a question like that now.' But I grin and squeeze her hand.

'Mmm,' she muses, while watching me like a hawk might a mouse. 'I bet you're either too scared or too smart to get that deeply involved with him. I can understand that falling in love with my brother would be a bad idea for all kinds of reasons.'

There she goes again, half child, half wise woman, an over-exaggerated look of innocence on her pretty elfin face. My head starts to throb; the Advil I took in the night wore off some time ago.

'Right now I just want Alexander to wake up and get better.' I stand up, desperate to do something, anything. 'Shall we go and get a cup of coffee? I don't know about you, but this place is giving me the creeps.'

Opposite me, Emma fiddles with a sugar packet, and I notice a pile of others, empty and twisted into shapes. I've no idea what's happened to the contents. The scent of cold coffee fills my nose. I glance at my watch. It's been almost three hours since he was taken into theatre.

'Do you think we should go to the nurse's station and try and find out what's going on?' Emma asks.

I want to but I'm almost too afraid to find out, though I daren't admit it. For Emma's sake, I try to sound positive. 'It's been a while so, yes, come on then.'

We're barely out of the cafe when Sister Dixon walks towards us, her expression brisk and businesslike.

'How is he?' Emma cries.

'Good news. They think they've stopped the bleed, so fingers crossed for now.' Emma lets out a little groan of relief while I seem to be unable to walk for a moment. 'He's already asked for you both. You should be able to see him shortly.'

Emma exhales loudly. 'Thank fuck. Oh, sorry!'

Sister Dixon smiles. 'Please don't worry. I've heard a lot worse. I have to warn you that he's still a little groggy because of the meds, but I think it will help him if he sees you. Please don't stay too long, though, because he's very tired, and don't expect too much of him. He's a little disorientated and you may find him . . . not quite himself.'

'Oh, if you mean he's being a royal pain in the arse, that's normal,' Emma says breezily. Life is simple for her now; all that matters is that her brother seems to be out of danger.

My main feeling is massive relief but it's tinged with apprehension. After all, our last words were bitter and harsh, and I've no idea what his reaction will be when he sees me.

It's a little while before we are allowed into Alexander's room. He's propped further up the pillows, one hand resting on the bedclothes, the other arm heavily strapped. Even though I'd prepared myself for the sight of his bruised and swollen face, I still wince inwardly, but for Emma's sake, I put on a brave face.

The nurse makes a quick adjustment to one of the machines and then leaves with a mouthed 'Ten minutes, max' to me. We tread softly, talking in whispers, because his eyes are closed and he seems to be asleep. Then, as we stand by the side of his bed, I see him trying to open his eyes, trying to focus on us.

Emma reaches out a hand and strokes the bruised, swollen skin on his face tenderly. It seems to help him open his eyes and now he really does seem to be looking at us both. For a few seconds, I don't think Alexander is certain who we are but then he croaks: 'What kept you?'

Chapter Three

Any flippant reply sticks in my throat at the sheer relief of hearing him speak again. Damn it, I hadn't expected to feel this full of relief and anger and I don't know what. I can't help but smile.

'What the hell have you done to yourself, Alex?' Emma demands, like he just fell out of a tree or something.

I can barely make out his low reply, squeezed out through swollen lips, but I think it's: 'You should see the other guys.'

Emma sits down on a chair next to the bed and his fingers tighten around her hand. I stand behind her, unsure of my role, of what to say.

'Thanks for coming,' he says to me, in a voice that sounds as raw as he looks.

'I'd like to say it's a pleasure, but that would be lying,' I say.

He tries a smile; but I suspect it hurts so he gives a grunt instead. Now I've got over the relief of seeing him awake, I feel slightly sick again as I force myself to confront the mess his face is in. But mentally I punch the air, because the old Alexander is definitely there, as combative as ever.

Emma whispers. 'I love you.'

Another grunt from Alexander that sounds like: 'You too.'

'Alex, please say you'll never do this again . . .'

He closes his eyes. 'Not now, Emma.'

'Swear that when you get out of here you'll really think properly think about leaving the army.'

I cringe inwardly but to my surprise he mutters, 'I'll think about it.'

'*Promise.*'

'Emma, I can't make decisions like that now.' He squashes down a groan of pain.

Emma puts her hand over her mouth. 'Look at the state you're in. You've been shot once, and now you've been stabbed and beaten and God knows what else and you still want to go back there. I can't cope with this.' She jumps up. 'I'll come back and see you later.'

She hurries out, clearly fighting back tears, leaving me alone with Alexander. Now he seems to be out of danger, should I get out of his life again too?

Instead I say: 'That went well . . .'

He collapses back on to the pillows, perspiration beading his forehead. 'Shit, I never say anything right.'

'It's a tough time for Emma as well as you. She'll calm down when she's had time to get over the shock. You're all she has left, and it must have been terrifying when Helen called her with the news. None of us really knew exactly how bad things were.'

Those ice-blue eyes stare at me, weighing me up. Oh yes, Alexander Hunt is most definitely there. 'I'm glad you came – I wasn't sure you would. It's good you were here for Emma.'

'I like Emma a lot, despite everything that's happened. And you asked for me.'

'And that's the only reason you're here?'

I shrug. 'Of course I came. You knew I would.'

He watches me thoughtfully. I wonder if he's seen a mirror yet. I want to cry at the state of his face, but it gives me hope to see him so feisty.

'Kiss me,' he says.

'What?' This is the last thing I expected and I shake my head. 'I'm not sure I should.'

'Why not?'

'The nurses will be mad at me . . .' And, I remind myself, we are not supposed to be together any more.

'Shut up and kiss me.' His voice is stronger now, still croaky but more insistent. He lifts up his good arm and waves it vaguely in the direction of his mouth, the line in the back of his hand trailing.

'I'm not sure you deserve it, or that you're well enough for it.'

'I'm sure I don't but you're going to do it anyway. Aren't you?'

His eyes flash with impatience and every misgiving rushes back, yet somehow I can't stop myself doing as

27

he asks, lowering my lips to his bruised ones, afraid to make contact with his swollen skin. This close, I can feel the warmth of his breath on my face, and the sheer proximity of his lean, hard, battered body close to mine makes me shiver.

Closing my eyes, I touch my lips to his with the lightest of pressure. I'm waiting for him to wince or cry, but his response is firmer than I expected and the kiss goes on. The world retreats, the insistent beep of the heart monitor melts into nothing and there is only him and me again. We could be back on the dance floor at a ball, or in the cloister at Wyckham . . .

Finally, I break contact, open my eyes and find him looking at me intensely.

'Lauren, I meant the things in the letter.' His voice rasps and I know it's hurting him to speak. I also know I'm not ready to face up to the implication of his words yet; the shock of the past day and night – of the past few weeks – still hasn't sunk in.

'Shhh. The nurse said you ought not to get too tired, so stop babbling on and for once in your life rest when you're told to, Captain Hunt.'

'I only follow orders I believe in.'

'Was that how you ended up like this, then?'

'Bollocks. Listen to me.' He grasps my fingers, his grip as strong as ever, and his eyes burn with a stubborn fire. 'When I'm out of here, I'll make good on my promises.'

'That's the drugs talking,' I answer lightly.

His voice is urgent now. 'I mean what I said; I'm not going to waste any more time.'

'If you remember, you were happy to see the back of me.'

'That was before!' he says, exasperated.

'What's happened to you doesn't change things between us.'

'Then for fuck's sake, Lauren, why are you here?' He tries to reach for me and his face contorts in a grimace. 'This bloody arm.'

'Alexander, be *careful*.' I stop him from toppling sideways out of bed. My face is inches from his bloodied one. I bite down a wince of sympathy and the urge to kiss him against my better judgement.

'Things are going to be different,' he whispers. 'Just give me a chance.' He tries to sit up again and hisses through his teeth. I spot the anxious and disapproving face of the nurse at the window but Alexander grips my hand again.

'For God's sake, lie down and keep still for a while. Look, the nurse has seen us now! Do you want to get me thrown out?'

'I thought you wanted an excuse to leave,' he taunts.

'I'd rather it was my own decision, rather than being escorted from the building.'

'I don't care. Christ, you make me so mad, but I want you in my bed. That's what's going to make me better. I want to be inside you right now.'

The nurse is distracted by the ward sister and despite every misgiving, and the fact he's a seriously injured man lying in a hospital bed, I can't deny the effect his words are having on me, let alone that look in his eye, which I can never resist. What kind of person does that make me? Giving into my feelings and desires, and going back to his bed, would only be a temporary cure and the real issues between us would soon surface again, like his secretive, volatile nature, the lack of trust between us, and the fact that in a few months we both have to make major decisions about our futures which will probably put us thousands of miles apart. I plan on getting a job in a gallery or museum after my master's, while Alexander will have to rejoin his unit and could be posted anywhere. *If* he fully recovers, that is.

The door opens and the nurse bustles in. She marches over and throws me a brisk smile.

'Time's up, I'm afraid. We don't want Captain Hunt getting worn out, do we?'

'No, not yet,' I say with a meaningful glance at Alexander, now lying quietly in his bed, the picture of the model patient. He returns my gaze with a fleeting tilt of his mouth that may be resignation or a challenge and before I can say another word I'm being firmly but politely ushered from the room.

Outside, there are thuds and rattles up the corridor, where Emma is abusing a vending machine. 'Crappy thing!' she mutters, banging the side.

'Sorry,' I say to the nurse, who shrugs.

'Don't worry; it's a very stressful time for you. Captain Hunt is probably going to sleep for the rest of the day and there's not much point in you staying. If you don't mind me saying, you and Emma both look exhausted. I suggest you go home and get some rest. I promise we'll call if there's any news but by the look of him, you can relax a little.'

Hearing this makes my shoulders actually slump in relief. 'I hope so, and you're probably right about us being tired, but I'll have to fix up where we're going to stay while Alexander recovers, and speak to Emma's school.'

'If there's anything we can do to help, just ask.'

'Thanks, but I'm sure we'll be fine. Can we come back this evening?'

'I think you should wait until tomorrow. The more rest he can get the better, if you can keep away that long.'

'I'll see what Emma says.'

As the nurse returns to her duties, I hurry to the vending machine to save Emma from a criminal damage charge.

I push the refund button three times in rapid succession and her change clatters into the slot.

'Bugger. Why didn't it work for me?' she mutters.

'Because you gave it a slap?' Her pout is full-on but I shake my head and reclaim the coins. 'It's the same machine as the one at the university tennis centre. It's got the same quirks.'

I feed the money back into the slot and a can of Coke rolls into the tray with a thud.

Emma collects it, a sheepish look creeping over her face. 'Thanks . . . Um, I'm sorry for rushing out like that but he is so stubborn, he drives me mad.'

'It's OK. I know what you mean but I should relax for now because I think he'll be on sick leave for quite a while. Even then, he might not be fit enough to return to duty, especially combat duty, for ages. At least you know he's going to be kept out of trouble for a long time. Be happy with that for now?'

She appears to mull this over briefly, then says, 'I suppose so.'

Emma pulls the ring from the can and the Coke hisses and fizzles.

I distract her by telling her we need to find somewhere to stay, and won't be coming back to see Alexander until the morning.

She sighs. 'OK, if that's really what the nurses think is best. But where will we go? It's too far to trawl back and forth from Falconbury or the house in Oxford.'

'I've been thinking about that. Maybe we should book a hotel near the hospital . . . Or perhaps Immy would let us stay in her apartment for a day or two, but after that don't you think you might be better off going back to school?'

'We break up for Easter today. It was the end-of-term sixth form party last night and Brandon was going to call for me later today anyway. I hope Alex is well enough to come home soon because I don't want to be on my own at Falconbury with just Robert and Helen. He won't want me to stay with Allegra after the last time, that's for sure.'

'You can understand that.'

'I still think he overreacted. The thing is, even if Alex did let me stay at Allegra's, her mother probably wouldn't have me. She hit the roof when she found out Allegra had told Alex I'd stayed with her while I went to a hotel with Henry.'

'Fingers crossed they let Alex out, and you could have a friend to stay. He won't mind that, will he?' I say, hoping Alexander will have far too much on his mind when he gets home to worry about any visiting friend of Emma's being a bad influence.

'I suppose so.' Suddenly Emma's face brightens. 'And you'll be at home with us anyway, so he's bound to be a good mood.'

This statement floors me temporarily. 'I . . . um . . . I'm not sure if that will happen, Em. Things weren't that great between us the last time we were together.'

'That was before he was hurt. He called you first, didn't he, so he must want you to get back with him. And you came, so that must mean you feel the same.'

'Emma, it's not quite as simple as that . . .'

'Bollocks. And you know it.'

I almost laugh out loud at Emma's breezy confidence. 'Emma, I have no idea what's going to happen. I'm here now and we'll just have to see. I am supposed to be heading home to Washington.'

Emma looks horrified. 'You can't just walk away from us.'

'I said "supposed to", Emma, I don't *want* to walk away. If you and Alex need me, then I might see if I can stay a bit longer, but it's not going to be that simple.'

She watches me over the rim of the can, poker faced, while she waits for me to make the next move.

'Hey, we're getting way ahead of ourselves here. First, Alexander needs to get better, and second, we need a place to stay for a couple of days. I'll give Immy a call and see what she can do.'

Emma hugs me, all smiles. 'Great. I knew you'd sort everything out, Lauren.'

Sure I can. I can sort anything out in Emma's eyes. But even if it gets me into deeper shit than ever, I figure have no choice for the time being. So, after an update on Alexander's progress – now 'stable' and 'comfortable' – and a glance through his room window to see that he's asleep again, and a lot of reassurance from the nurses, Emma and I manage to drag ourselves away and take a cab back to central London.

To my relief, Immy has finally returned my call. She had her phone turned off until she got back to the apartment after spending the night – what was left of it – with her rower at a hotel near Jocasta's house.

The first thing I had to deal with was a succession of 'Oh my Gods' and shocked gasps while I relayed the story of Alexander's injuries. However, I also love her to bits because, without me even asking, she offered to let me stay on at the apartment for as long as I want while Alexander recovers.

I felt awkward about asking if Emma could stay too, but Immy didn't seem to mind; she has known Alexander and his family for a few years – if not that well, then enough to want to give them support. The apartment actually belongs to her parents but she's assured me that they won't mind in the least.

The cab crawls into central London. Emma is texting frantically while I wonder when and how to tell my parents I may be in the UK for a while longer. They were happy enough for me to delay my return because I wanted to study, and really, they know they can't interfere with my decisions any more – but they miss me and, yes, I miss them. If they knew about Alexander, I think they'd put up much more of a fuss though. If I stay in London and then at Falconbury, I'll have been here for a chunk of the Easter vac and won't have long at home, but my parents will be so upset if I don't see them at all.

'Hello-oo, Earth to Lauren.' Emma grins at me. 'You were on another planet.'

'It's happening a lot lately. Hey, I think this is Immy's street.'

The driver slows down and finally stops outside Immy's apartment block. While I'm paying him, the front door opens and Immy runs down the steps to the kerb.

'Hello! I've been waiting for you. You poor things, you must be knackered!' Immy hugs me.

'Just a little,' I say.

'Hi, Emma. How are you?'

Immy hugs Emma too, and she doesn't seem to mind. 'OK, though I almost barfed in the cab.'

'Poor you. Come on up and I'll make you a drink. I've got most things.'

Immy takes Emma's bag and we follow her upstairs, Emma giving the apartment the once-over. It's a bohemian place, with original modern art on the walls, what my mother would call an 'eclectic' mix of furniture, and Chinese rugs covering the floorboards. I think it will appeal to Emma's arty side. She seems pleased to be here and I can tell Immy's trying to be super helpful.

'Shall I show you to your room, and then I'll make us all a drink?'

'Thanks.'

Immy opens a door off the hallway. 'Will you be OK in here? It's only a box room really, but there's a put-up bed and I thought you'd rather have your own room. I know it's not Falconbury . . .'

'It's great,' says Emma, walking inside. 'I only have a small bedroom at school and I'm so happy you can have us to stay. It wouldn't be nearly as much fun in some stuffy hotel Are you sure your parents won't mind?'

'Not at all. They said you can stay as long as you like. My mother was at school with yours, you know.'

'Oh, I didn't know that. Do you think she might have some stories about Mummy?'

It strikes me that Emma was only a little girl when Lady Hunt died so she must be desperate to hear other people's memories of her.

'I'll ask her.' Immy smiles, her face softening. 'Why not leave your bag in here. Have you got everything you need? I can lend you some pyjamas and a toothbrush if you like. We keep spares in the cupboard or we can nip out to the Waitrose on the corner. They have most things.'

'Helen made me throw a few things into a bag, but I haven't got enough stuff for a week,' says Emma.

'Do you think Alexander will be in hospital that long?' says Immy, betraying the first faint signs of alarm that she may be playing host to Emma for longer than she'd planned.

'I think they need to make sure he's out of danger and start a course of treatment and physio, according to the doctor.'

'Of course. Well, look, if you're here for long, we could go shopping for new things,' she says to Emma.

'Cool. I was going to have Brandon fetch my stuff from Falconbury but buying new would be a lot nicer than having Helen rifle through my knicker drawer, much as I love her.'

So, the prospect of shopping has cheered Emma up and I don't blame her; we could all use a little light relief.

'You two must be starving. Is pizza OK? I can order some in or we can get Chinese, Thai or Indian?'

'Any of those,' says Emma. While Immy makes us a coffee, and Emma admires the artwork, apparently delighted to be here despite the circumstances, I'm just wishing I could feel the same.

A few days later, I'm back at the hospital. Immy has tactfully taken Emma shopping in the West End to give me some private time with Alexander. While his face is still swollen and bruised, I'm relieved to find him awake. I grab a sneaky look through his window to see him flicking though the TV channels with his good arm, a scowl of disgust on his face. When I enter the room, he drops the remote on the covers and rolls his eyes.

'Do people really watch this crap?'

'Glad to see you're feeling better.' I grin.

He grunts, then manages a smile. 'Are you about to make me feel worse?'

'I don't know.' I take a chair by his bed. 'So, if it's not a stupid question, how are you today? You look more like your old self.'

'I'm not sure that's a good thing. I've seen myself in the mirror and now they've cut down my ration of happy juice, I do feel like I've been run over by a tank.'

He winces as he pushes himself gingerly up the pillows.

'You have some spectacular bruises . . .' What I'm really focused on, though, is that he has spectacular pecs – he's sitting up bare-chested, partly because the hospital room is warm but mainly as it's difficult to get a gown on him because his arm is so heavily bandaged.

He glances down at the mottled pattern on his chest with some pride. 'Are you impressed?'

'You should know by now that nothing about you impresses me,' I say coolly.

'Mmm, and yet you're paying a lot of attention to my body.'

'It's horrified fascination,' I say at least partly truthfully and rest my fingertips on an especially colourful cloud-shaped bruise. 'How did you get these?'

'I really can't remember much about it.'

I glance up into his face. 'Bullshit.'

'It's the only bullshit you're going to get.'

I press lightly in the centre of the bruise but he doesn't even flinch. Did I want him to? I'm not sure.

He takes my hand from his chest but keeps hold of it. 'I tell you what, give me a kiss and I may tell you a little more.'

Leaning forward, he pulls me towards him.

'I'll hurt you,' I whisper, half out of my chair already.

'I don't give a toss.'

With his good hand, he pulls me closer, until I'm standing, leaning over him. 'Come here.'

'I shouldn't. The nurses . . .'

'In the nicest possible way, screw the nurses. Come closer. I'd make you, if it wasn't for my bloody arm.'

A few days ago, I thought I'd never be this close to him again. I'd steeled myself not to feel like this: fizzing with desire for him, aching for the feel of his body against mine.

I put my arms around his waist, terrified of hurting his damaged shoulder and hearing him cry out in pain, but the only sound he makes is a sigh when he kisses me, like he's been starved of food for a million years. His lips are dry and the stubble on his chin rasps my skin but this kiss is amazing; I never want it to end. I push my tongue inside his mouth, desperate to be deep inside him and taste every part of him. I pull him closer to me.

'Ow!' He winces and I pull back.

'God, I'm sorry!'

His grimace of pain turns into a sort of smile. 'It's OK. This arm is a pain in the arse.'

'I knew we shouldn't have done that. I forgot about the wound.' I'm standing up now, away from the bed.

He snatches my hand in his. 'Sit down and shut up. I don't want to be treated like glass.'

'You should be careful, just for a little while at least.'

'I can be careful when I'm dead, and I won't let something like this stop me from doing what I want.

Now come back here or I'll call the nurse and tell her you've been treating me with unnecessary cruelty.'

'What? You . . . You're the one who . . .'

He curls his finger. 'Come here, Ms Cusack, before I scream for help.'

I laugh. 'I'd like to see that.'

He opens his mouth wide as if to shout.

I fold my arms. 'Do I look scared?'

'Help, Lauren won't give me what I need.' His voice ramps up a notch. 'She's abusing a war hero!'

'Alexander! Shhhh.'

'Not until you kiss me again,' he taunts, making me want to hit him and leap on him. I glance at the window, half expecting to see a face peering in at us with a disapproving frown.

'Well?'

I put my finger on his lips. 'Only if you behave.'

He opens his lips and tilts his head forward a little, drawing my finger into his mouth. I keep it there as he circles my fingertip with his tongue. His lips are hot and tight around my finger as he sucks it in deeper. He closes his eyes and I close mine, blocking out reality, just enjoying the sensation of his tongue making gentle circles around my finger.

I sigh in delight as he runs his tongue from base to tip, licking my finger as if it's a Popsicle. The pressure of his mouth around my flesh forces me to press my thighs together to try and assuage the ache between them. After a few delicate flicks of his tongue, he opens his mouth, releases me and lowers my hand to the sheet. What he's doing appears innocent yet is every bit as erotic as if I were lying naked with him above me.

My finger glistens with moisture in the sunlight.

'That's how it feels,' he says, his voice low and gravelly, 'to be inside you. So tight, so wet. I want that right now.'

'The nurses might have something to say about that.' I'm still coming down from the sensation and, quite frankly, struggling to breathe.

'Possibly, but if they weren't here, do you know what I'd make you do?'

Even the question sends a bolt of lust right through me. 'No, but I've a feeling you're going to tell me.'

'And I've a feeling you're desperate to know, aren't you?'

The way he has me squirming in front of him, I can hardly deny it.

'*Aren't* you, Lauren?'

'Yes!'

'If I thought no one would walk in, I'd make you take off that top right now and show me your amazing breasts.' He gives me a smile so hot it could strip paint at a hundred yards. 'And I know you're not wearing a bra today because I can tell.'

On cue, my nipples stand to attention under the cotton of my top.

He tuts. 'Bad girl, Ms Cusack.'

'I thought you deserved a treat after what you've been through. Now I'm not so sure.'

'I do deserve a treat, I've had a traumatic time. Do you want to know what I'd make you do next?'

It's on the tip of my tongue to say 'no' and walk out but I'm enjoying the teasing way too much. 'Get it off your chest if you really need to,' I say, while my body thrums with desire.

'I'd lie here and watch while you shimmied out of that mini skirt and stood in front of me in your thigh-highs.'

'How do you know I'm wearing thigh-highs today? You can't possibly tell for certain from there.'

'Because you always wear them with that mini and you know how much I love them.'

'That was *before*.' I can't resist reminding him – and myself – that the reasons for our break-up remain unresolved, no matter what has happened since.

'And this is now and you're here. Don't try and change the subject. You are wearing thigh-highs, aren't you, Lauren?

'Yes, damn you, of course I am.'

He sighs in satisfaction. 'I knew it. So, after you'd taken your skirt down, I'd watch while you pulled down your rather lovely Victoria's Secret knickers right in front of my face.' He grins. 'Very, *very* slowly.'

I'm almost panting. I'm definitely trembling. 'I'm in La Perla today . . .' I murmur, nudging my bottom a little further on to the bed until it's butting against his thigh.

'Knickers wet, are they?' he says, his eyes burning into me. 'I hope so, because I'd love to lie back and savour the sight of you with them around your ankles and imagine how wet and ripe for me you are.'

Now I really can hardly breathe. All I can do is keep my eyes on his, and eventually I manage to whisper, 'You are a disgrace to your uniform . . .'

'And you're as sexy and ready for me as ever.'

I glance down to find my hand pressed against the front of my skirt and pull it away.

He tuts again and says, 'Nice to see you feel the same way as I do. Go on, look what you've done to me.' He rests his hand over the bulge in the sheet around his thighs.

'What? I daren't.'

'There's no one watching. Touch me.'

After a quick check of the window to make certain no one's watching, I slide my hand under the cover and down the front of the boxer shorts he's wearing. He's hard and hot and it feels amazing to have his firm, silky flesh under my fingers again.

He closes his eyes as I cup him in my hand.

'Alexander, we can't do this in here.'

He opens his eyes. 'You have to. I've dreamed about this for almost two weeks.'

I stifle a giggle that's a combination of amusement, lust and nerves.

'This is therapy. Don't stop now you've started.'

His pleading voice is so sexy that I can't resist. '*Please*,' I add.

'*Please*, Ms Cusack, I'm desperate.'

'That's better.' I circle him with my fingers and slide them up and down. He arches his pelvis and moans. 'That is so good. I'd forgotten how amazing you are. Oh fuck . . .'

I'm not sure if it's a sixth sense or my hyperawareness of any sound or just good luck, but I snatch my hand out of his shorts and from under the bedclothes just as the door starts to open.

By the time the nurse backs into the room, pulling a drugs trolley, I'm fumbling in my handbag and Alexander is lying back on the pillow looking like the sky has fallen in on him.

The nurse swivels the trolley round and tosses us a smile. 'Everything all right? I've come to give Captain Hunt his medication.'

I stand up, my fingers burning, and I know I must look as guilty as sin. 'Yes, fine. I was about to leave.'

'There's no need. You can stay if you like.'

My face is on fire.

'No, it's fine. I need to get back to Emma. I'll come back tomorrow.'

She smiles at Alexander. 'So Captain Hunt, how are we feeling today?'

He sighs. 'I was feeling much better but now I'm a little deflated, to be honest. Maybe the shock of the stabbing is beginning to hit me.'

45

Behind the nurse's back, I mouth: 'You are unbeliev-able,' before scurrying to the safety of the hospital corridor. For all the embarrassment of nearly being caught in a compromising position with Alexander, I feel massive relief that he's back to his wicked madden-ing ways. Now all I have to do is sort out the mess between us – if I decide I even want to.

Chapter Four

A few days later, Alexander's smile has evaporated as Brandon drives the two of us back to Falconbury House. I'm surprised that he's been let out so soon, but he's made excellent progress, according to his doctors, and I also suspect he's badgered them into releasing him at the earliest possible opportunity.

I also know that the military have called in to debrief him further. In fact, I saw them walking out of his room when I arrived. He didn't seem unduly bothered by their visit, but you can never tell with Alexander. The doctors have told him he won't be able to use his arm as he'd like to for quite some time, but if he keeps up an intensive physio programme, he should eventually make a full recovery. But he won't be back on active service for some time. It could be a slow and frustrating process for him.

Alexander's left arm is still strapped up and supported with a black sling, although he's managed to get a shirt on and has a jacket draped around his shoulders. He has a treatment plan from the physio to carry out at home and will also have to attend sessions at a military rehab centre, as well as follow-up appointments over the next few weeks at the hospital.

On a normal day, Alexander is hardly chatty, and he's becoming more morose the nearer we get to Falconbury House. By the time we reach the entrance to the park, he's as silent as the stone pillars that mark the gateway. Every time I risk a glance at him, his face is turned out towards the window. I'm not sure what's occupying his mind more, concern about his responsibilities at Falconbury or worries about when – and if – he will ever return to active service. I know what's been occupying mine, ofcourse: the unresolved issues that led to our row last term; will they come to a head again now he's out of danger?

The last time I was here was for his father's funeral, on a bleak January day. The trees were bare spiky branches then; now they are cloaked in fresh green leaves. Clusters of yellow primroses are bursting out at the edge of the drive that leads to the house and deer graze in the open parkland at the edge of the woods. Finally the mansion itself comes into view. I also remember the other times I've been here before: happy fun times when we've ridden and walked the estate together, had glorious sex . . . and the times when we've been at loggerheads. Today, the bright spring sun renders the neo-Gothic facade a little less imposing, as do the hyacinths blooming in the stone troughs that flank the steps to the porch.

'I haven't seen those before. They look so pretty,' I say in an effort to lighten the atmosphere.

'What?' He drags his attention away from the car window. 'Sorry, I didn't hear you.'

'I said the flowers look beautiful. Your gardeners have been busy.'

Brandon stops the car in front of the steps.

'Oh, yes. They must have come out in the past couple of weeks. I don't remember them from when I left but I had other things on my mind.'

Normally, either Brandon opens my door first or Alexander insists on doing it if I'm not quick, but Brandon obviously thinks his boss needs the help today. He does, but *ouch*, despite the ultra polite 'thank you', anyone would think Brandon had given him a poke in the eye.

'Do you want me to get the bags, sir?' Brandon asks.

'I think it would be a great idea. Thanks so much, Brandon,' I cut in before Alexander can even try to refuse his offer, as I know he would.

Brandon brightens visibly. 'Of course, Miss Cusack.' Then he's off, popping the trunk and hauling out our bags.

With his arm in the sling, Alexander's obviously struggling to clamber out and I know he won't accept help. I take my time unbuckling my own seat belt and make a meal of checking I have my handbag so that by the time I'm out of the car, Alexander has managed to unpop his belt buckle and shuffle out without banging his head. I actually had to buckle the seat belt up for him before we left the hospital, which earned me an icy thanks. I guess he's already realized that fastening his seat belt is just one of a dozen things he's going to need help with until he can use his arm again.

'I could have managed the bags,' he mutters.

'Bullshit,' I say pleasantly. 'Make life difficult for yourself if you want to, but don't make the staff's work any tougher. They already have to put up with you as it is.'

He glares down at me but makes no further objections.

'Let me give you a hand,' I call to Brandon as he returns from the front door for another set of bags. However, I'm cut off by Robert almost tripping down the steps in his haste to help.

'How are you, sir? It's good to have you back.'

'Thanks, Robert.' Alexander does manage a genuine smile for his butler. 'Has everything been all right while I've been away?'

'Perfectly, sir. There are a few letters for you, but I've left them on the desk in your study. If you need assistance in opening them, or with anything else, please call me.'

'Thanks, I will.'

Our voices are drowned out by barking that echoes around the forecourt. A ball of black fur shoots out of the front door, leaps off the steps and launches itself at Alexander, almost knocking him sideways. Barking ecstatically, Alexander's Labrador, Benny, nudges his thighs, sniffs his legs, licks his free hand and for once ignores every command to 'settle down'. Finally, Benny drops on to the gravel, rolls over and presents his belly for attention.

'Ridiculous dog.' Alexander's tone is stern, but as he rubs the dog's stomach, I see a glimmer of pleasure on his face – mixed with relief. No matter what Alexander says about the burden of being responsible for Falconbury since his father's death, part of him must be genuinely happy to be home.

'That'll do,' he says gruffly as Benny snickers with ecstasy. 'Up you get, boy.'

He straightens up and Benny turns to me, licking my hand and panting.

I rub his ears. 'Good boy, we've missed you.'

The trunk of the car thuds down and Brandon gets behind the wheel again to drive round to the garages behind the house. 'Better go and get this over with,' says Alexander quietly. I know he is dreading the fuss that will ensue when he meets the rest of staff.

I take his free hand. 'Come on, step up to the plate and if you're a good boy and behave, I may give you a treat later.'

He shakes his head at me. 'I'm not Benny.'

'No, and that's a shame. He does as he's told. Come on.'

Emma is already at the house when we arrive, having been collected by Brandon earlier today, and has her friend and one-time partner-in-crime Allegra staying over for company. As we walk into the hallway, she trots downstairs, while Allegra hovers awkwardly. They're both wearing jodhpurs and riding boots.

'Alex!'

Emma flings her arms around Alexander, who just about manages not to flinch in pain as she gives him a bear hug. She steps back. 'Oh God, have I hurt you?'

'Not much.' He grins, or possibly grimaces.

She puts her hand over her mouth. 'Ouch. Sorry. Well, at least your face looks slightly less like Frankenstein's.'

'I think you mean his monster's,' Alexander replies tartly.

'Him too, but it's great to have you home. You won't believe me but I've missed you.'

'You're right, I don't believe you.'

Emma laughs. 'That's more like the infuriating brother I know and love.' She suddenly looks sheepish. 'Thanks for inviting Allegra to keep me company.'

'Did I? Hello, Allegra,' he says meaningfully.

Allegra acted as alibi for Emma last term, during her secret meetings with Henry Favell. Despite Alexander's greeting, she seems completely in awe of him.

'Hi,' she mutters.

'Allegra and I were just going out for a ride,' Emma says, as Allegra attempts to shrink into the background. 'Welcome home, Alex.'

'Enjoy yourselves,' I say.

'Be careful,' Alexander warns.

Emma rolls her eyes at him. 'Of course we will! See you both later. Don't do anything I wouldn't do.'

As she and Allegra scurry off down the corridor that leads to the stables, Alexander mutters. 'That leaves us plenty of scope, then.'

Before I can reply, Helen walks briskly up to us. 'Your room's ready when you are, sir. Yours too, Lauren.'

Alexander kisses her on the cheek. 'Thanks, Helen, you've been brilliant.'

'Do you want dinner served in the dining room or in the sitting room this evening? Emma and her friend have decided to have a takeaway so it's only the two of you.'

'The sitting room will be fine,' says Alexander, who hates the formality of the dining room since his father died and would far rather eat off a tray. Not that he may be able to manage that at the moment.

'I'll serve at seven, if that's OK. Shall I have some tea sent to the library in the meantime?' Helen asks.

'Can you give us a little while, please?'

'Of course.'

Upstairs, I push open the heavy oak door to Alexander's room and the moment we're through it he says, 'Lauren? What have you done to Helen to persuade her to use your first name?'

I sit on the bed. 'Oh, I don't know . . . Asked nicely?'

'That can't be enough.'

'It's just not my style to be treated like I'm lady of the manor, and especially not when Helen has done so much to help me when you were in hospital. Before you ask, I won't expect her to do the same with you. That would be too difficult for her.'

He shakes his head at me. 'Perhaps it's time a few things were changed around here. I've been too busy dealing with the aftermath of Dad's death and the estate to even think about the future, but it looks like I'm going to have to now.'

I pick at the quilt. 'Maybe we should sort out a few things from the past first.'

'You're probably right, but there's something I need even more. That we both need.'

I look at him; *really* look at him for the first time since he got out of his hospital bed and arrived back home. With his arm in the black sling and the jacket draped around his shoulders, he has a sombre, formal air that ought to inspire my pity but, frankly, is conjuring up altogether different sensations in me. His hair is tousled because he can't comb it properly and his insistence on shaving himself has left traces of stubble on his jaw and the odd nick. He looks tired, leaner and on edge but somehow more gorgeous than ever.

'Come here,' he says, pulling me to him. 'I really don't think I can wait any longer. It's not good for my health to be in a room with you and not have my wicked way with you.'

I can't help grinning, and rest my hands lightly on his

waist. 'Hmm, that's all very well, but are you sure you're fit enough? It hasn't been long since your surgery.'

'You'll just have to be careful with me, won't you?' he teases, stroking the arch in my back sexily, weakening my resolve.

'Sure,' I say, not letting on how much I want him too, 'but it won't be easy, you having one arm out of action.'

His eyes smoulder with desire. 'You love a challenge, don't you? Now, I suggest that you start removing our clothes, before I do it myself and do some damage. I need to rest after the journey.'

'Rest?'

'Of course. I need to lie down.'

'Oh, really?'

He flames me with a look and even though it's tempting to walk away just to see his face, I can't help myself. 'I seem to remember,' I say, toying with a button on his shirt, 'that the last time we were alone together you couldn't wait to see the back of me . . .'

I pause, midway, to pop open the middle button of his shirt.

His expression softens. 'I know and I'm sorry. I was upset and hurt and worried about Emma.'

'Hmm,' I sigh and open the button, and the one above, exposing the bruised skin, where the bruises are yellowing now.

Pulling apart the white cotton, I expose his abs and chest. I *really* cannot help myself at this point, sinking to my knees and steadying myself by grasping his fabulous butt. Then, as softly as I can, I press my lips to his stomach and the muscles of his abs ripple in response. His erection bulges through his trousers.

When I look up, his eyes are intent on me. 'I'd forgotten how good this feels. When I was banged up in that hole with no idea if we'd ever get out alive, the thought of this was what kept me going.'

Even as his words have an intoxicating effect on me, a tiny part of my mind still urges caution. I've had my fingers burned many times with Alexander, and I'm going to have to be very, very careful. But for now I'm focusing on the impressive bulge in front of my eyes, because his physical response is easier to deal with. I pop the top fly button on his jeans. 'You do know this is going to be tricky . . .' I murmur.

'I know. I suppose we'll just have to be creative.'

'I guess so . . .' As I say the words, I'm already on my feet and unfastening the next button on his jeans. Instead of the stretchy cotton of a pair of black boxers, my hand encounters bare skin. I flip the other buttons and raise my eyebrows. 'I see you decided to go commando, Captain Hunt.'

His face is the picture of innocence. 'It was simpler than putting on boxers.'

'Oh, really? What did the nurse say about that when she helped you get dressed?'

'She thought it was a practical solution and said I have to manage however I can for a while. I expect she's seen it all before. Anyway,' he breathes, his eyes never leaving mine as he guides my hand deeper inside his jeans, 'it's time you reacquainted yourself with what you've been missing.'

'Perhaps,' I agree. I no longer have any control over my actions and as I cup him in my hand, he inhales sharply, closing his eyes in ecstasy.

'We won't be interrupted this time,' I murmur.

'Thank God. I almost passed out with frustration when you left me the other day.'

'A little self-discipline won't kill you.'

'Want to bet? Ah . . .' His sigh of delight when I tug his jeans down ramps up my own desire to a new level. His bottom is so muscular and solid under my kneading fingers, I feel shaky with lust.

'You'd better sit down, Captain Hunt.'

He obeys instantly and sits on the edge of bed with his jeans around his thighs. I kneel at his feet and whip off his shoes. I hesitate briefly, when I slip off his dark silk socks and see the bruised and blistered feet. They are a testament to the action he's seen recently, and the sight and implication of it both horrifies me and turns me on.

I stand up again, transferring my attention to higher up his body.

Wow.

'I can see you've missed me,' I say. 'Hold that thought and lie there.'

Swiftly, I pull my top over my head and take off my jeans so that I'm left in only my underwear.

'New?' His hungry gaze seems to curl sensuously around my body, making goosebumps pop out on my exposed skin. Agent Provocateur is not my usual brand and this black set was an impulse purchase that's way racier than the rest of my lingerie.

'Yes, new – you like? I decided to treat myself after I'd finished the first draft of my essay. I've been working while you've been idling away in your bed, you know,' I tease.

'Top marks. Do I get to see you take it off?'

Reaching behind me, I unhook the back of the bra and let it slither down my arms and on to the floor. As the cool air hits my bared breasts, my nipples pucker. Three weeks of Alexander abstinence suddenly seems like an age.

Alexander stares at me with an intensity that scares me. 'You will be the death of me one day, Lauren.'

His words and his expression hit me like a sucker punch. 'No one ever died of lust,' I say lightly.

'Are you sure?'

Judging by his erection, I have to admit he may explode soon, but I'm having way too much fun and I'm going to make him suffer before I put him out of his misery. Slowly, I slide the lacy thong over my hips and down my thighs.

He shifts his pelvis, unable to keep still. 'I can't stand much more of this, Lauren.'

'Patience, Captain Hunt.'

'I'm out of patience.' His voice softens. '*Please.*'

I climb on to the bed next to him and straddle him.

'I think I may be in heaven,' he murmurs.

I lean forward and whisper, 'I very much doubt heaven would let you in right now . . .'

The hair on his outer thighs tickles the soft skin of my inner thighs and my muscles have to stretch wide to accommodate him. He reaches up with his good arm and rests it on my waist. Slick with arousal, I ease myself on to him and he lifts his hips to push deeper inside me. Sinking on to him, becoming part of him, feels so good, so natural that I scare myself.

I flatten my palms either side of my thighs and brace myself as he thumbs me with the lightest of touches, shooting tremors of pleasure right through my core. I love the tension, the tautening of his muscles and mine, the melding of our bodies.

He massages me with feather-light strokes, until I'm tangling the bedcover in my fingers and rocking back and forth on him. I didn't think he could grow any bigger or harder but he's stretched me a little more until I'm speared deliciously on his full length. He raises his pelvis higher off the bed and deeper into me, while he circles my swollen, tender nub with his finger until the first waves of sensation start to pulse through my body.

Wriggling and writhing, I want to draw him even deeper into me while my orgasm rockets through me. His fingers dig into my bottom and when I open my eyes, his are shut and his face is contorted with the pleasurable agony of his climax before he pulses inside me. I lean back and let another wave of sensation ripple through me, and another, and again . . . I never want this to end. I want things to stay like this for ever, in this perfect moment of pure uncomplicated pleasure.

A while later, I'm lying by Alexander's side, still naked, with him still minus his trousers.

Idly, I walk my fingers along his chest. 'You OK?'

'Sore. I thought I was OK while I was, shall we say, distracted. But I'm paying the price now.' He pauses. 'Maybe the only solution is to do it again.'

I splutter, thinking he's joking until I see his face. I shiver with anticipation. 'Do you think you could?'

By the look of him, and the way I'm pushing myself against his thigh, I realize that if I lie here any longer then the answer would be 'yes'. But I see a tiredness behind his eyes and his colour is not good, so instead I reluctantly remove my hand from his chest and wriggle into a sitting position.

He stays where he is, watching me. 'You know what, Lauren? I'm going to need a lot of TLC now I'm home. An awful lot.'

I raise an eyebrow. 'Really? I thought you wanted to be independent and dreaded anyone making a fuss.'

'I can make an exception if this is what TLC means.'

'I think that you can have too much of a good thing.'

'Bollocks. Come back to bed.'

'No. I need to take a bath and get dressed. And, believe it or not, you do need to rest. Do you want a hand to get up?'

'I don't know. Let me try.'

With a grunt, he uses his good arm to push himself up and manages to twist off the bed and stand.

I stifle a giggle at the sight of him, with his arm in a sling and his shirt hanging over his butt.

'What's amusing?'

'I'm wondering what Robert would make of the sight of Lord Falconbury in such disarray.'

He rolls his eyes. 'I think he'd say, "Good for his lordship." Now, if you're not going to oblige me again, I also need a shower . . .' His gaze lingers on me. 'Or a bath. How do you feel about saving water?'

I shake my head. 'We can't both get in the tub with your arm like that. Didn't the nurses tell you to keep the dressing dry until they change it next week?'

He pulls a face. 'True, but I have a solution.'

Warm water laps around my breasts as Alexander watches me take a bath. He's placed the padded stool from the dressing table next to the claw-footed tub in his en-suite. He's now sitting next to me, still in his shirt tails but with a bath sheet draped over his lap. The Creed bath oil I poured into the tub has a sensual woody fragrance that scents the steam rising from the water. Alexander's greedy gaze never leaves me while I rub the foamy sponge over my breasts and chest and lift my legs out of the water to wash them.

As soon as I get out of the bath, I expect him to hand me the bath sheet but he keeps still.

'Come here.'

'I'm soaking wet.'

'I hope so.' Once I'm within reach, he leans forward in his seat and presses his face to my wet stomach. With one hand he pulls me to him and splays it over one cheek of my bottom, his fingers sliding over my wet skin.

I tangle my hands in his hair and whisper, 'Your turn, Captain Hunt, but you're going to have to take off your shirt. Want any help?'

'Not really, but if it means you stay naked for longer, I'll take any assistance I can get.'

After I've let some of the water out of the tub, I help him slide the shirt off until he's naked too. With one hand on the rolled edge to steady himself, he climbs into the tub.

With a little assistance and a few curses, he manages to sit down and even though the water is shallow, some of it splashes over the rim and pools on the black and white tiles.

'Hey there, be careful.'

'This is bloody awkward,' he mutters, holding his injured arm higher above the water.

I pick up the damp sponge from the side of bath, squirt shower gel on to the centre and squeeze until it's creamy with lather. Foamy suds drip on to his bare chest as I dab the sponge on his bruised pecs.

'How sore are your ribs?' I ask, skating the sponge over his skin.

'Not too bad with the cocktail of painkillers I'm on, and, of course, the distraction of my naked nurse.'

Ignoring this remark, I pat the purple and yellow marks on his chest as gently as I can. 'These are very colourful, like an abstract painting. A little Modigliani-esque. Whoever made them must have been an artist.'

'They certainly took great pleasure in creating them,' he says curtly.

'I can believe it.' Still brandishing my sponge, I switch position to the rear of the tub. 'Lean forward a little.'

I apply the sponge to his shoulders and neck, drizzling the fragrant foam down his back.

'Would you like me to wash your hair for you?'

'Yes, why not?'

He's meekness itself, and I have to admit I love taking charge. He relaxes against the back of the tub while I massage his citrusy shampoo into his scalp and work up a lather.

'You'd better close your eyes. Tilt forward.'

I pick up an old-fashioned metal jug from the vanity unit, fill it with tepid water and pour the contents over his head. He shakes, spraying me with droplets.

Water chases down his shoulder blades, obscuring his bruises momentarily under rivulets of foam. Once again I wonder what the hell happened to him. Will I ever find out? Do I even want to know?

He shakes his head again, to rid his face of water droplets.

'You look like Benny after he's been in the stream.'

He laughs. 'Do I?'

'Uh-huh.'

His wet hair glistens in the sunlight streaming through the window and beads of water glisten on his forehead, cheeks and chest.

Crossing to the side of the tub again, I dip the sponge back in the water and rub it over his abs. It's a big tub but he still has to bend his legs to fit inside, and when I touch his stomach, he tenses. I'm not sure if it's pain or because the sponge is only inches from his vital parts. I push the sponge beneath the water and gently rub it between his thighs, feeling his erection grow. He looks at me and raises his eyebrows. 'Did you know your breasts jiggle when you bend over me?'

'Tsk. That's highly inappropriate, Captain Hunt.'

'And you bathing every inch of me, completely nude, isn't?'

'Be quiet or I won't finish the job, and you wouldn't like that, would you?'

Kneeling by the tub, I turn my attention to his thighs, rubbing the muscular planes with lather from the sponge, working my way from his groin, over his knees and down his shinbones to his feet.

'I've never been so clean,' he murmurs when I've washed both legs thoroughly.

'I haven't finished.'

Lathering my hands with the shower gel, I dip my fingers between his thighs and cup him in my hand.

He collapses back against the tub, eyes closed. 'Oh, fuck.'

'What's the matter? Does it hurt?'

'Only if you stop.'

I wash him thoroughly until he says hoarsely, 'It's no good. I have to get out.' I get up from my knees to help him but it's still a struggle for him to get out of the tub. Finally, he's back on terra firma, looking like some classical warrior fresh from battle. My God, if he knew what I was thinking, he'd laugh.

I don't care; I want him and give no resistance when, still dripping wet, he advances on me and presses me against him. Water runs down his face on to mine as he claims my mouth in a hot wet kiss before taking my hand and leading me into the bedroom.

We stand by the bed as he drops kisses on my bare shoulders and neck. Not *quite* knowing what's in store for me, I shiver with excitement as he curves his free hand around my bottom, urging me forward to the sofa in front of the window. His skin is still damp and his hair wet and tousled. He smells divine, of sex and spicy bath foam.

Wordlessly he moves behind me, stroking my stomach with the lightest and most delicious of touches before pushing me gently towards the sofa. I start to lean forward over it, hearing the sharp intake of breath as I do so. 'Lauren . . . Jesus, what are you doing to me,' he whispers, his voice ragged.

God, his voice, just the way he says that last line deserves a triple-X-rating. I face the window and tilt my hips forward, sliding my palms along the sofa cushion until I'm bent right over. The velvet roll-edge is soft against my stomach and I hear Alexander moving. I think he's on his knees behind me, kissing me.

My face burns up. It's so *intimate* and bordering on kinky but also wildly sexy.

After a few more kisses that have me pressing myself shamelessly against the sofa arm, he draws a line with his finger between my legs, from front to back. It's so unexpected, so . . . *delicious* that my stomach clenches with shock and lust. I crush myself against the sofa and dig my fingers into the velvet cushion.

When he follows up by pushing a finger gently inside me, I cry out, yet he's relentless, teasing me, stroking and touching me until I claw the sofa in desperation.

'The view I have is amazing. You have a truly magnificent bottom,' he says.

'I'm not – uh – a work of art and I'm, um – also going to – ah – come any moment. *Please*, Alexander, just come on!'

'Oh, if you insist.' He puts a hand on my hip to steady us both and then my toes are almost lifted off the floor as he guides himself inside me. Even though I'm wet and ready, the fit is tight, but wonderful. His thighs are hard against my bottom and I want him even deeper so I lift myself a little, fingers steepling against the sofa as he drives in and out of me. Each thrust increases the friction on my sensitized nub, trapped between his thighs and the velvet sofa, spreading sensation through me . . . His thrusts become wilder, my orgasm builds until I'm grinding myself against the couch, desperate to release the tension, the burning, raw tension, until finally my climax overtakes me.

Chapter Five

I walk out of the bathroom some time later to find Alexander trying to pull on his socks with one hand. To give him credit, he did manage to get his boxers on, but it's hard not to laugh at the sight of him cursing while he tries to work the sock over his foot. In fact, I stop trying not to laugh.

'It's not funny.' He shoots me one of his glares, making me want to laugh even more.

'Want a hand with those socks?'

'No, I can manage.'

I watch him struggle, knowing I need to leave him to it.

'How much longer do you have to wear the sling?'

'I'll have to see what they say at my next appointment but I hope I can get rid of it soon. It's driving me mad and I want to be able to start running and riding again. And,' he says, teasing a damp strand of hair out of my eyes, 'getting back to normal in every other way.'

The look he gives me makes me want to forget all about what I should be doing downstairs and pull all our clothes off again.

'It's so frustrating, not being able to do exactly what I want to you.' He reaches out with his good hand and gently strokes my hip, all the while never taking his eyes from mine.

'I think we've done pretty well,' I manage, trying to pull myself together, aware of the girls waiting for me downstairs and the knowledge that despite what Alexander may want, what he needs is rest. I pull on my shoes and prepare to head downstairs, saying briskly, 'Let's hope they agree to the sling coming off soon.'

'Even if they do, I'm still going to be quite helpless for a while,' he teases. 'I don't think I'll be able to allow you to go home to your parents,' he continues, more serious now.

'I see.' I rest my fingers on his chest, enjoying his teasing but remembering that I do have some decisions to make. He sees my frown.

'What's the matter?'

Where do you want me to start? I think but I give a casual shrug. 'Nothing . . . but you're right, I do need to call my parents and tell them when – if – I'm going home. It's almost three weeks into the vacation already and I haven't spoken to them since before the weekend. They think I'm still at Immy's.'

He drops his hand from my hip. 'You haven't told them about me yet? I can understand that, and of course I don't want to keep you away from them.' He gets up, turns his back and walks towards the window, where the drapes are still drawn across from earlier. He opens them and stands looking out over the estate.

I have no idea what to say; I have no idea what *he's* about to say.

'I have no right to do this . . .' he mutters to the window. I can't see his face and I guess that's intentional, because he's obviously finding it difficult to let on that he needs any human being apart from, perhaps, Emma. 'I've no right to keep you from your family and ruin your plans, but if you did decide to stay here at Falconbury, I wouldn't mind.'

'Wouldn't *mind*?'

He turns back to face me, stiff and awkward. 'I'm not going to force you, Lauren.'

'Or beg?'

He steps forward and I see a wry twitch of his lips. 'Would it help if I *did* beg?'

I see that making this all a jokey game is easier for him. 'Try me.'

'What? On my knees?'

I have an urge to laugh out loud at the battle raging behind those proud, arrogant eyes. He thinks I'm joking – he hopes I am – but he's not *quite* sure.

He still hesitates. 'You really want me to get down in front of you?'

'Uh-huh.'

Shaking his head, he advances towards me, takes a step and drops to one knee, then both.

'Please, Lauren,' he wheedles, 'will you spend the rest of the vacation with me?'

I give an exaggerated sigh. 'That sounds like sarcasm to me.'

'For fuck's sake.'

'Don't ruin it, Alexander.'

He assumes a chastened expression. 'My apologies. Please stay, Lauren.'

'You don't sound very convinced. Or convincing.'

His eyes burn into me but he reins in any backchat. 'Dear Lauren, I will die of sexual frustration and sheer boredom if you leave me here on my own at Falconbury. It would give me the greatest pleasure imaginable if you would consent to stay and favour me with your company and your insanely sexy body . . .'

'Better,' I mutter, fizzing with amusement and delight behind my 'yeah, whatever' facade.

'Even if you will also probably drive me mad with your teasing and outrageous demands.'

'What outrageous demands? I *never* make outrageous demands.'

His mouth quirks in a wicked smile. 'So why is an injured man, who is in constant pain, I might add, being forced to beg a woman to stay with him? I call that outrageous.'

'Because you, Alexander, have no choice.'

'So that's a "yes"?'

I heave another theatrical sigh and place my finger on my chin as if I'm considering the situation. 'I'll think about it,' I say, then seeing his crestfallen face, I add,

'I do want to stay, actually, but I have my parents to consider. I was supposed to be going home. Just let me get a few things sorted before I make any promises.'

'I suppose that's the best I can hope for.' He gets up, remarkably swiftly for a man in constant pain, and using his good arm pulls me tightly against his damp chest.

'Thank you, and I really do want you to stay, so I hope you can,' he whispers, this time without a trace of irony and with an intensity that shocks me. Then he kisses me, a long, deep and tender kiss that makes me tingle from scalp to toes. Something inside me fizzes and pops like I have just won the lottery and yet I can't quite stop the niggle at the back of my mind that tells me this wasn't the way I'd planned things at all.

Chapter Six

'Hi, Mom.'

There's a pause on the end of the line before my mother replies.

'Hi, honey. Are you OK? Only we haven't heard from you for a week now and we wanted to know when you'd booked the flight.'

Even though I was prepared for this conversation to be tricky, I feel even guiltier than I'd anticipated. I really do want to see my family and friends in Washington and now I've got to break the news that I'm probably going to stay here all vacation. But the worst part will be telling my mother the reason. So far, they have no idea that Alexander Hunt exists – or that I've been seeing anyone at all.

'I'm sorry I haven't called you. I'm fine – *totally* fine – but I don't think I'm going to make it home this vacation.'

'Oh.' There's a pause. 'Are you behind with your studies? We understand if you need to stay longer and catch up or do some research.'

'It's not exactly that, although I do need to spend a lot of time preparing for summer exams and finishing my essays . . .'

'Lauren, are you sick?'

'No, I'm totally fine. I feel great but . . . there's a friend of mine who's had an accident.'

'Is it Immy? Poor girl! Is she going to be OK? What happened?'

I fiddle with a strand of hair. 'No, not Immy. It's a, uh, a kind of male friend.'

The picture that instantly springs to mind is of my mother standing stock still, giving me the gimlet-eyed stare.

'A *kind of* male friend?' she says, in her uber-casual way. Boy, am I in trouble. 'He must be a special kind of male friend for you to need to stay all vacation with him.' Is it my imagination or has her voice turned a degree or two cooler?

Even from four thousand miles away, this conversation is excruciating, and my um-ing and ah-ing must only be making my mother even more suspicious.

I take a breath. 'I guess he is special. I've been close to him for a while and he's just had a serious accident – really serious. I was going to fly back this weekend but I've lost so much time since he's been hurt, I don't see how I can fit in a trip home. Plus, he kind of needs me, I think.'

'I see.' Those two little words are ripe with meaning: intrigue, curiosity, concern. Whatever her suspicions were, I've probably confirmed them now.

'We knew there must be someone, honey. Over the Christmas holidays, you weren't yourself. Your father

74

and I were worried and Grandma Cusack was convinced it was man trouble. I do hope this man *isn't* giving you any trouble. You seemed very quiet when you were last home.'

'I promise I'm not in any trouble, Mom, but I think I should stay. I'm very sorry not to be able to see you and I swear I'll be back the moment Trinity Term ends.'

'But Lauren, what happened to this boyfriend? Who is he? You say this man has had an accident serious enough to warrant your staying in England all vacation. You know I'm not a pushy mother, but at least do me the favour of telling me a little more about him. Your father will definitely want to know who's keeping his little girl away for so long.'

I can hardly blame them for asking and they deserve at least part of an explanation. 'He's a grad student on one of the other master's courses. His name is Alexander and we've, um, gradually grown close since the start of the year. He nearly lost his arm in a military exercise that went wrong last weekend. He's recovering, but I've spent all this last week with him and lost loads of time that I could have spent studying and I just want to stay here. Mom, I knew you'd be disappointed but like you say, I do need to get on with my work and it's so much easier to research here with the libraries and museums at hand.'

The pause that follows is so pregnant it's about to give birth to twins.

'Well, I suppose if you feel that strongly about the situation, Daddy and I will just have to accept your decision,' my mother says at last. I feel awful for letting them down, but it's a relief to have things out in the open.

After I told Alexander about the phone call – or at least a very brief part of it – we went to bed early because, while he didn't want to admit it, he was exhausted. I had to virtually drag him up to bed and he was asleep the moment his head hit the pillow. Now, the clock shows it's almost three a.m. He's sitting on the edge of the bed shoving his hand through his hair as if he could tear it from his scalp. The sheen of sweat on his forehead and chest gleams in the lamplight.

'It happened again, didn't it?' I say quietly, referring to the nightmare I've just witnessed. I've seen his violent dreams several times since I met him and each time I'm shocked by their intensity. Once, during one of his nightmares, after his father's funeral, he'd gripped my wrist so hard the bruises lingered for days.

'Uh-huh … Tell me I didn't hurt you this time.' There's a desperate edge to his voice that I could almost describe as panic.

'No, I'm fine.' In truth, he did thrash about, but the moment I woke up I got out of bed and kept clear. 'What about you?' I ask.

'I'm OK,' he says gruffly, but he couldn't hide the twist of pain as he pushed himself up from the lying position earlier. The way he was thrashing about can't have done his injured arm any good.

'Are you sure? You still have stitches in.'

'Screw these bloody dreams.'

'It's hardly surprising you had another after all that's happened . . .'

'What happened on the op has nothing to do with it.'

'OK, whatever you say.' My sympathy is tempered by annoyance at his brusqueness but I try to be patient, and I think he knows he's upset me.

'Come here.' He pulls me to him and his thighs are satisfyingly hard under me. 'I'm sorry, Lauren. I agree that recent . . . ha . . . events . . . probably haven't helped, and I'm still on a cocktail of drugs, but those nightmares started a long time ago. You know that.'

I grin at him and let him kiss me. 'Yes.'

For some reason, I find myself thinking about the moment I discovered the letter he sent me before he went on the mission, tucked into a zipper pocket of my overnight bag.

'I still haven't worked out how you got the note to me, by the way.'

He looks up, surprised. 'Brandon delivered it.'

'But . . . it was inside my overnight bag. You mean he broke into Immy's apartment just to put it there?'

'He was in and out without anyone noticing,' he says, with some pride.

I shake my head. 'I cannot believe you – or he – did that.'

'I suppose I should apologize but I'm not sorry. I don't just employ Brandon for his driving skills; that would be a waste. He served with my father in the Gulf War.'

'So he's some kind of ninja? What you asked him to do qualifies as breaking and entering.'

Alexander smiles. 'Actually, there was no breaking, only the entering. As I say, neither you nor Immy even noticed he'd been there.'

'I cannot believe your nerve!' I say, outraged but not really surprised.

I start to get up, but even with one arm he's strong enough to keep me down.

'Do you have any idea how great it feels to have you naked in my lap? You keep squirming your bottom against me.'

'Stop trying to change the subject. The letter was good. I'm glad you sent it.'

He strokes my spine, leaving a trail of tingly goosebumps on my back. 'I wrote some things in there I've never told anyone else.'

Aware I'm treading on eggshells, I make my reply careful. 'I'm very sorry for what you went through at school. I can see, now, why you were so dead against Emma seeing Henry.'

We kiss again, a little more deeply. 'I'm still sorry that I didn't tell you she was sleeping with him,' I say.'

'You thought I'd hit the roof. You were right, I would

have done, and I know you were in an impossible situation but Emma is all I have left, in terms of close family anyway. I'd do anything to protect her.'

Unexpectedly, he kisses my nipple, making me bear down on him. I feel his erection pushing against me, making me wet.

'When I wrote that letter, and especially after I wrote it,' he says, while dropping kisses on my breast, 'there have been more than a few times' – kiss – 'when I didn't think I would ever' – kiss – 'do this again' – kiss. I tilt my head backwards and close my eyes, loving the gentle pressure of his warm mouth on my breasts.

'Me too.'

'I mean I really didn't think I would do this,' he says. 'Or sleep in this room again. Or see Emma or Benny – or you – ever again.'

'Hey, I'm glad you have your priorities right.'

Kneeling right beside him, I bend low and close my mouth around him, loving the taste of him. His groan of ecstasy as I suck on him drives me half crazy. My scalp tingles as he tangles his fingers in my hair, gently pushing me a little further down on to him. It only takes a little pressure from my mouth to make him whimper in pleasure again. I love bringing Alexander to his knees like this; it makes me feel powerful and in control. I lick him and then blow softly on the moist skin. He arches his pelvis upwards as I tighten my lips around him again.

'No, wait . . .'

I lift my head to look at him and his eyes burn into me. 'Why?'

'Because . . . I want to be inside you. I want you to *feel* me coming.'

I stand up and gently push him further back on the bed, then move to straddle him, my eyes never straying from his gaze. I ease myself on to him – it's a little awkward as I'm trying so hard to avoid hurting his arm, but oh Lord, is it worth it when I feel him inside me. He struggles to move and thrust up inside me but I stop him gently, push him back on to the bed and wallow in the waves of pleasure as I continue to move over him. It's frantic, fast sex, and I relish the control I have over Alexander.

Finally, we're both lying flat on our backs, sheened in perspiration, and by the look of Alexander, he's done in. His eyes are closed and I wonder if he's fallen asleep; which would be no bad thing after the nightmare he's just had. He was ordered to rest. I'm not sure his doctor would count what we just did as rest, although it must count as recuperation. Then I feel a hand creep over mine.

'You know, when I was stuck in that hole of a place, not knowing if I'd ever get out again, I promised myself I'd have sex at least three times a day if I saw you again,' he says.

'I hope this isn't an extreme form of emotional blackmail.'

We look at each other. He may be exhausted and

sore but there's a wicked glint back in his eyes. 'I don't care if it is. What the past few months have taught me – losing my father and my recent adventures – is that we can't know what the future has in store for us.'

'I don't need to have lost my parents or been half killed to know that,' I say quietly.

'No . . . Of course not . . .'

There's a pause, a moment when he seems to be considering what to say next and, just like on our final night in Rome, I have the feeling he's about to ask me a question that I won't have an answer to.

'I know it was wrong to expect you not to go back to Washington but I'm glad you decided to stay.'

'Purely for therapeutic purposes, of course.'

'Of course. I know you're only here for the sake of my health.'

'I was worried you might relapse if I left,' I tease. Inside, I feel shaky with excitement, apprehension . . . a fizzy cocktail of emotions that's both lethal and irresistible.

His brief smile melts away. 'The next few months are bound to be interesting, you know. I have no idea what's going to happen.' He rests his hand on my bare stomach.

'Maybe that's why I'm really here, because I don't know what'll happen either. If I'd wanted safe and predictable, I'd have got the hell away from you the moment you turned your back on me in the cloisters at the start of term.'

'Really? I seem to remember you throwing yourself at me.'

'I tripped and fell on top of you. It was an accident.'

'Yet you *did* call after me, even when I was walking away.'

'The biggest mistake I've ever made.'

He walks his fingers, almost idly, between my thighs. 'And you keep on making it. Will you keep on making it, Lauren?'

'I don't know. Perhaps one day soon I'll come to my senses.'

'And until then?'

I get up until I'm sitting astride him, and lean down close to his face, ready to steal a kiss. 'I guess we'll just have to feel our way.'

I'm not given to skipping, but the way I jog downstairs the next morning comes pretty close. It's so much easier now that I don't have to act as if Alexander's nightmares are figments of my imagination. I think he accepts he has a form of PTSD and while it's never going to be something we chat about over the breakfast table, at least I don't have to pretend any more.

We both slept better after we'd got a few things aired and when we woke up this morning, we had some amazing if rather gymnastic sex. While Alexander does his physio, I've decided to go for a quick jog before breakfast. Although I asked him if he wanted any help,

I expected him to refuse. I'm sure the exercises will be painful and he can do without spectators.

Soon, I'm out of the door, walking down the steps and checking my watch while I crunch over the damp gravel. It rained overnight and now an early mist is burning off fast and the Falconbury estate looks like a freshly painted canvas in its spring hues. Breaking into a run, I make a beeline for the path that seems to skirt the deer park, hoping it leads in a loop back round to the house. If not, I'll turn back, because Alexander said he'd meet me for a late breakfast in an hour.

I also need to get some work done. Despite everything, I seem to have got myself into a position where I'm going to be juggling several balls at once this coming term. My exams, college life, helping Emma and being with Alexander. Mulling it all over, I find I've gone further than I thought and have to power-walk the last mile before finally reaching the house again. My jogging has never developed into a habit and over the last term my main source of exercise has come from cycling around Oxford, my dance classes and, of course, sex.

As soon as I reach the porte cochère, the front door opens and Robert steps out, his face a little anxious.

'Ah, Miss Cusack.'

'Hi, Robert. Is everything OK?'

'Yes. Helen thought you'd like to know we have visitors.'

My post-jog endorphins evaporate when I walk into the hallway to find Alexander with his cousin, and my arch-enemy, Rupert, his father and a petite and very well-preserved redhead who must be his mother, Letty.

Rupert and his father grunt a greeting almost in unison but Letty de Courcey steps forward, smiling warmly. 'Lauren, hello again.'

Recognition flickers, but I'm more aware of my sweaty palms and the ragtag mess I must look after my run. I shake her hand as briefly as possible but return the smile.

'Hello.'

'I'm Letty. We have met before but the circumstances weren't happy.'

'Oh, of course,' I say, vaguely recalling her at the funeral, although I'd hardly recognize her today in her skinny jeans and pale-blue sweater, with a pair of dark glasses pushed back on her auburn bob.

'How was the run?' Alexander asks, looking a little strained.

'Good, though I'm sorry I'm late. I took an unscheduled detour.'

Rupert smirks.

'It's a big estate,' says Mr de Courcey gruffly.

'And easy to get lost in,' Letty adds. 'I seem to recall a search party being sent out for you, Giles, when you took Rupert for a walk years ago.'

'I don't remember it.'

'My memory is better than yours and how could I forget? Rupert was still in nappies at the time and needed a complete change of clothes by the time you found your way home.'

Rupert groans. 'Mother!'

I am struggling not to snigger and even Alexander is smiling. 'Would you like to join us for some breakfast, Aunt Letty?' he asks.

'I had mine some time ago,' says Mr de Courcey tartly.

Ignoring her husband, Letty slips her arm through Alexander's. 'I'd love a cup of tea, but only if you drop the "aunt", please, Alexander. It makes me sound like I'm a hundred and one.'

He laughs. 'Whatever you want, Aunt.'

She glares at him but soon the smile is back on her pretty face. She seems much younger than her husband, though she must be in her late forties because Rupert is a few years older than me.

'What about you, Rupert?'

'I'll have a black coffee,' he mutters.

'I suppose I'll have some tea too, if it's going,' Giles grumbles. Alexander calls to Helen, who's been hovering on the sidelines. 'Helen, would you mind serving breakfast now, please? And bringing some extra tea and coffee? I'm sorry we're so late.'

'It's my fault,' I say. 'And I need to leave you again to change. I'll be as quick as I can but please start without me.'

I scoot off, ignoring a look from Rupert that's

somewhere between loathing and lust. While I take the fastest shower ever, and pull on jeans and a top, I try to decide how to react to the de Courceys' visit. Alexander doesn't know yet that it was Rupert who emailed the sex clip to me last term. I still cringe even now, when I recall the images of Alexander and Valentina having kinky sex, but I don't think telling Alexander about it now, in front of his aunt and uncle, is the best idea, even though I'd love to see Rupert's face.

I dash downstairs, my still damp hair restrained with a clip.

Alexander and the de Courceys are sitting around the table in the breakfast room, with tea cups in front of them. The breakfast plates, however, are still on the dresser so they have waited for me. Alexander stands when I enter the room.

'Sorry to have kept you waiting,' I say.

Letty smiles. 'Oh, don't give it a thought. I bet you're starving after your jog.'

Despite their earlier claims, Rupert and his father pile food on their plates. Like me, Letty selects a croissant from the tray.

While we're eating, I can't resist a dig at Rupert. 'So how are you, Rupes? How's your vacation going? I haven't seen you since the Boat Race party, when we had such an interesting chat – really, so enlightening.'

'I've been working,' he says, suddenly reluctant to meet my eyes. He *must* wonder if I've already told Alexander what he did. Then again, if I *had*, Rupert might not have got as far as the hallway, let alone the breakfast room.

'Rupert has a lot of catching up to do, if he's going to get his degree,' Letty says acidly.

Rupert almost chokes on his bacon but then mumbles, 'Thanks, Mother.'

'It's true. He seems to have spent most of his time in that dreadful drinking society or else raving all night in some club.'

'I promote club nights, Mother, I don't rave!'

'You know what I mean. You've been virtually nocturnal since you've been back home so I assume it's a habit you developed at Wyckham. You see more of my son than I do, Lauren, I'm sure. You'll have to let me know what he's been up to.'

Alexander smiles and Letty laughs. 'Perhaps we should go for tea some time while the boys are busy hunting.'

'Lauren won't want to do that and the season is almost over.' Rupert sounds horrified at the prospect of his mother and me cosying up over a slice of cake and a cup of Earl Grey.

'I think it sounds like a lot of fun, Mrs de Courcey,' I say brightly.

'Oh God, call me Letty. Mrs de Courcey makes me feel ancient!'

'OK, Letty.'

Alexander holds up his arm. 'I'm not allowed to ride until the medics sign me off but I'm hoping I'll be fit by the new season, if I get any leave that is.'

Letty pats his arm. 'Poor you. You've had some terrible luck this year, apart from meeting Lauren, of course.'

Rupert rolls his eyes and I cringe a little, though Alexander smiles politely.

When we've finished breakfast, which was far more fun that I'd expected thanks to Letty, Alexander disappears into the study with Mr de Courcey to discuss some papers relating to the probate of the estate. Rupert's father is an executor of General Hunt's estate but I'm not sure how much actual help he's being.

Rupert, clearly fed up that things haven't gone his way this morning, seizes the chance to escape and mutters something about going to make a call outside.

The door slams and Letty and I are left alone. 'Oh dear, perhaps I overdid the teasing, I say.'

She sighs. 'It won't do him any harm though. He was such a lovely child but I'm not sure the company he's been keeping at Wyckham has been entirely good for him, you and Alexander excepted, of course.'

Letty smiles but I suspect she may be hiding her real anxieties over Rupert. It can't be a happy thing to realize that your kids aren't the people you'd like them to be. I feel deeply sorry for her because I don't think even she can know quite how mean-spirited her son has turned out to be.

'I hope you don't mind me saying this, but you're a very beautiful girl. I think Rupert may have a crush on you.'

'A crush? I don't think so! I also look a terrible mess. I'm sorry you met me when I'd just got back from a run.'

'Rubbish. You look natural and lovely and as for Rupert, I know him better than anyone – and I can also see that Alexander is mad about you.'

My cheeks are heating up. 'I really don't know about that.'

'It's obvious to us all.'

She steers me to the window, where Rupert is striding up and down the courtyard with his mobile clamped to his ear. 'Mmm. Have it your way, but I do know that Rupert hasn't got a cat in hell's chance where you're concerned. I love my son, no matter what he gets up to, but he needs a kick up the arse for his own sake.' She sighs again. 'I can't say he'll find life hard after he leaves Oxford because he'll just walk into the family firm, but as for relationships, I don't want to see him badly hurt, alone or heartbroken.'

'I can promise you that I will not be the one to break his heart.'

She smiles, but she is definitely nobody's fool and her eyes bore into me like an interrogator's.

'I hope you're not planning on doing it to my nephew.'

I laugh lightly. 'Alexander doesn't allow his heart to be broken.'

'You'd be surprised. If he falls, he falls hard. Very hard.'

I stiffen. 'If you mean Valentina, I know he was upset when they broke off their engagement.'

She blows out a sharp breath. 'Valentina? God knows why they got engaged, or rather I do know. Valentina wanted to get her hands on this place and his title and Alexander thought he was pleasing his father – and his dead mother too, poor boy. No, I didn't mean her, and I'm *very* glad it ended.

'You're young, Lauren, and I'm sure the world is your oyster as they say, in terms of men and careers, but behind that devil-may-care facade Alexander is a very deep and intense young man. Wound him and the hurt cuts deep.'

'I'm sure there won't be any wounding on my part,' I say, wondering if it would be such a great idea to have tea with Letty, after all.

'An honest answer. I appreciate that, but sooner or later you will be responsible for what happens. Sooner, I'm guessing, and then you will have to make a choice. I can't tell you what that is but make sure it's the right one.'

I'm getting uncomfortable now – I'm not ready for this. Most of Alexander's relatives seem terrified that I might one day end up as mistress of Falconbury; now Letty seems terrified that I won't. For once, I'm lost for words, and that takes some doing.

Letty is smiling. 'I've said too much; as you've noticed, I always do – but I stand by my opinion of Alexander, and *do* meet me for coffee one day. I'd love some female company.'

'I will,' I say, smiling. And I do mean it, but our girly

chat is cut short by the door opening and Alexander and his uncle walking into the room.

Letty collects her handbag. 'All done? Shall we leave these people to get on with their day?'

Rupert is waiting in the hallway as we say our goodbyes and Alexander kisses Letty. 'You're staying then,' Rupert mutters with a sneer.

'Of course,' I say with a huge grin, then Letty kisses me and sweeps her son out of the door. He still manages a glare at me before he gets in his father's BMW, which I return with a cheery wave.

If I wasn't sure about my decision to stay before, I am now.

Chapter Seven

'Hi, honey, how are you?'

It's with mixed emotions that I answer the phone to my mother a few days later. I've popped back to Oxford for the day to do some research in the Ashmolean, and she calls while I'm in the juice bar in the Covered Market, grabbing some lunch. It's only breakfast time in Washington, so I know she must be keen to speak to me.

'I'm fine, Mom.'

'And how is Alexander?'

'On the mend,' I say as lightly as I can.

'Where are you? It sounds very noisy.'

'In a cafe in the market.'

'In Oxford? Are you back in college?'

I touch the table for luck. 'Only for the day to do some research. I've been staying with Alexander at his family's home.'

There's a pause. 'His *family's* home? Do they mind? Can't they help him?'

'Well, he lost his mother when he was young and his father died in January and he has a young sister to take care of.'

My mother's voice has softened when she next

speaks. 'How awful for them both! Well, I'm sorry to hear that ... But remember, you have your own life, Lauren; you mustn't let yourself get sucked into other people's tragedies. But it sounds as if you have made your mind up and you're not going to listen to me.' She pauses for a beat or two and I think I'm over the worst, and then her tone changes. 'You know, this situation may turn out to be a blessing in disguise.'

I have to make a conscious effort to stop twirling my hair. 'What do you mean?'

'Your father desperately needs a break and London's only a few hours away, as you kept reminding us when you took up this place to study. I'm sure England looks wonderful at this time of year and I've been meaning to come over again. This is the perfect excuse.'

I push my salad bowl away, my appetite gone. I could slap myself. Why, oh why, did I not foresee this would happen?

I swallow – I have to handle this right. 'Um, that sounds a nice idea. But I'll be very busy with revision and work so I may not have much time to spend with you, and won't it be tricky to get flights and hotels at such short notice?'

Her voice takes on a determined tone. 'Nonsense, Lauren. We'll be sightseeing some of the time so we won't get under your feet. It will do you good to take a break and I'm sure you can spare a little time to see us. Now I come to think of it, this is serendipity. Your father needs a holiday and it means we can meet Alexander. I'll email you when I've booked flights.'

There is no stopping my mother in this mood so, like a gigantic wave, I let her words roll over me and carry me along. There is nothing I can do now. My parents are going to meet Alexander and know everything.

'Lauren? Are you still there, honey? Did you hear what I said? We can't wait to see you.'

'You too, Mom.'

'And Alexander, of course,' she adds, and with a final 'See you soon,' the line goes dead.

'Is there anything wrong with your meal?'

Back at Falconbury later that evening, I glance up from chasing a carrot baton around my dinner plate to find Alexander eyeing me thoughtfully from the other side of the small dining table in the sitting room.

'I'm OK.'

'Really? You're very quiet and you haven't eaten much. I'd have thought all our activities would have given you an appetite,' he grins. 'I know I'm ravenous.' He pops a forkful of fish into his mouth. He's managed to hack pieces off his fillet of sole, which was served with bite-sized forestière potatoes and sliced vegetables. Good old Helen, she obviously consulted the cook on what to serve a one-handed man to spare him the indignity of having to have his food cut up for him.

I rest my fork on my plate. 'Sorry.'

'Why are you sorry? If anything's worrying you, you can tell me.'

Can I? I'm not so sure about that. 'Well,' I sigh, deciding to get it over with, 'the thing is, I spoke to my mom earlier and it seems my parents are planning to visit, since I can't get home.'

Alexander swallows, then puts his fork down.

'I had to tell them about us.'

He regards me steadily. 'About us?' The remark hangs in the air between us. 'You mean the fact that we're shagging each other senseless.'

I smile. 'Well, anyway, they want to come over for a visit. To check you out, I suspect.'

He reaches for the wine bottle and manages to top up my glass without spilling any. 'You can hardly blame them. They must be disappointed you're not going home as planned.'

'I know, but . . .'

He smiles. 'But what? I'd be delighted to meet them. In fact, why don't you invite them to Falconbury?'

It's only with a monumental effort that I don't spill the wine halfway to getting it to my face. I can't believe he seems so cool with the idea that my parents are going to meet him – and I'm even more amazed that he's asked then to Falconbury.

Alexander is sleeping peacefully on his back with his wounded arm out of its sling and supported on a pillow by his side. I haven't been able to sleep and now

I'm lying next to him, thinking over what he said earlier.

Why don't I ask my parents to Falconbury? I guess I have no choice now he's issued the invitation but I can't imagine their reaction. I'm not sure whether they'll be impressed or horrified at the scale and grandeur of the place. They'll certainly think things have become 'serious' between us and yet we've barely even discussed being back together.

Once again, I've allowed myself to be dragged back into Alexander's life. I listen to him breathing peacefully, and see his long lashes fluttering against his cheekbones. Everything is so peaceful, so tranquil and calm. I rest my hand on his chest and feel the rhythmic rise and fall, and the glorious warmth of his body.

I turn over and sigh into my pillow. Maybe I'll ease my parents in gently at first, arrange to meet them on neutral territory in Oxford and introduce them to Alexander there, before launching Falconbury on them. I'll see how the land lies and if need be, maybe I can get away with them not seeing the place at all.

The following week, I'm enjoying the warmth of the sun on my arms as I walk out of the Sackler Library. Brandon dropped me in Oxford again, before driving Alexander to London to see his lawyers. I have so much to do here and I'm grateful for the chance to spend some time catching up with normality. The cherry blossom hangs in thick clusters from the trees and the golden stone of the colleges seems to glow as I walk along the Broad towards Wyckham. My phone rings and I grin at the name on the screen before remembering that I have some news he may not be happy to hear.

'Scott, hello!'

'Hi there. How's Washington?'

Oh fuck. 'Even warmer than here, probably, but I'm actually in Oxford right now; I just got out of the Sackler.'

There's a pause, then, 'I thought you were going home?'

'Sorry, I ought to have called. Things got complicated.'

'It doesn't matter. I decided to stay on for a while myself. In fact, I'm in Oxford too. It's suddenly hit home that I have a master's to complete and only a term to do it in,' he jokes, making me laugh as he always does.

'Well, if you will try and be a Boat Race hero . . .' I tease. 'And as you're studying Water Policy, it shouldn't take you more than five minutes to learn all you need to know.'

'Make that more like ten.' His deep laughter down the phone makes me smile. 'However, I do need to knuckle down because I ought to leave Oxford with more than blisters. Anyway, how are you?' he asks. 'I heard you and Alexander broke up . . .'

Arghh, this is going to be excruciating. 'Oh?' I stall for time.

'Jocasta told me at the party. I thought you might have told me – we're meant to be friends, aren't we?' he teases.

'And rain on your parade? No way; you were having a great time and you were with Lia. She seems . . . um, nice.' I remember how inexplicably jealous I had felt when Scott waltzed in with Lia, a gorgeous rowing medic. I remember the feeling now with a jolt of surprise – Scott is my friend, and yes, I think he might have a soft spot for me, but why did I feel so jealous? Does that make me a bad person?

'So are you staying with Immy? When are you going back to Washington?' he asks before I have time to tell him the rest of the story.

There's no point waiting any longer so I plunge straight in. 'I'm staying with Alexander actually. We, er, didn't stay broken up for long, I guess.'

'What? Oh . . . wow.' He bursts out laughing. 'This story has more twists than a switchback ride. OK, so fill me in. Where exactly are you now?'

'Walking towards Wyckham. You?'

'In the middle of town. How do you fancy lunch? Better still, a picnic?'

'Sounds lovely. I have no food though.'

'I'll take care of that. Meet you by High Bridge in thirty minutes?'

I end the call, feeling much better. I'm looking forward to seeing Scott. The last couple of weeks have been so crazy and so much has happened that I haven't had a chance to really think, and seeing a good friend who always lifts my mood is just what I need.

After calling in at Wyckham to check my pigeonhole and popping into a wine merchant for a bottle of Prosecco, I scurry eagerly past the Pitt Rivers Museum to the Parks. The breeze ripples through the reeds at the edge of the river and moorhens pootle around in the shallows. I'm a little chilly in my skinny jeans and Joseph top but thankfully I grabbed a cashmere cardigan on my way out. Finding a spot in the shade of a willow, I sit down on the grass to wait for Scott. Punts glide past; laughter and shrieks combine with the quacking of drakes harrying reluctant ducks. Oxford lives up to every idyllic cliché at this time of year, on the surface at least.

Scott greets me with a kiss on the cheek and a grin. 'Hi, beautiful, how are you?'

I give him a hug and grin back. 'I'm good, all the better for seeing you actually. The last few weeks have been frantic.'

'I aim to please,' he says, holding up a bag filled with delicious food and a rug to sit on, which he spreads on the grass.

'Wow,' I whistle, looking at all the treats he's brought and suddenly feeling very hungry. 'You're a regular Martha Stewart.'

He grins. 'You have no idea.' He proceeds to unpack chips and dips, some Brie, black grapes, mini baguettes and a pyramid of profiteroles, and couple of bottles of Peroni.

I hand over my bottle. 'This is my contribution. I haven't really celebrated your awesome victory yet and I presume you're not teetotal any more.'

He unwraps the tissue from the bottle. 'No way. This is great, thanks for the thought.' He smiles. 'However, even though I'm not training these days, I could still eat a horse. Shall we get started?'

Scott bats away a gnat before taking a Swiss Army knife from his pocket and sawing a hunk off a baguette.

I pop a grape into my mouth while Scott slathers Brie on his bread. 'So, what is all this drama with Alex? Are you OK? It sounds like you've had a pretty tough time with him.'

'I don't really know where it's going myself,' I say lightly. 'We had a big fight and I thought everything was off but the morning after the party, Alexander had a really serious accident. He asked for me, so I went, and I've kind of not left.' I look up sheepishly.

Scott frowns. 'Jesus. Is he all right?'

'Things were a little hairy for a while but the surgeons fixed him up and he's on the mend now.'

'My God, how did it happen?'

'I don't know. It all kicked off while he was on a mission.'

'I'm sorry he's been injured,' he says, then adds, 'genuinely.' He swallows a grape. 'And what about *you*?'

I don't know quite how to answer this, all I know is I can't keep away from the flame, no matter how many times I get burned. I can't really explain or justify it, it is just the way things are at the moment.

I take a deep breath. 'Well, I had no choice initially, I had to go to him when he was hurt, and then, I don't know . . .' I tail off. 'We're both feeling our way, Scott. I guess that's all we can do.'

'Well, that's an honest answer,' he murmurs, giving my arm a friendly squeeze. 'Look, whatever happens, just remember I'm here, always, you know, if you need a shoulder. We're buddies, you and me.'

'Buddies?' I laugh.

He looks at me, his eyes teasing. 'Do you want us to be more than buddies?'

I blush, as the memory of a kiss in the street, with Alexander looking on, comes back to me. We exist in this limbo land, Scott and I, somewhere between very good friends and would-be lovers. But I ignore the facetious question and give him a playful shove.

'Hey, thanks, I appreciate the support. Really. But now tell me, what about Lia? Anything to share with me about her?' I ask lightly, my tone gently teasing.

'Hmm, not really. She's fine, we're good,' he says, giving nothing away.

'I love being able to talk to you . . .' I say.

'Good.' He smiles and squeezes my hand. His hand is shovel-sized and calloused from the oars, yet the pressure he exerts on my fingers is of the lightest kind. 'Can't you talk to Alexander?'

I shrug, unable to give an honest answer, which is 'no'. I'll always be tiptoeing around Alexander, and the contrast with Scott has never been more stark than now. Scott represents a life I could choose: of steady, uncomplicated fun, of laughter and good times. I'm attracted to him: who wouldn't be to a six-foot-six hunk of blond gorgeousness with a great sense of humour to boot? Scott would never get himself into a knife fight, or be filmed in a sex video, or leave me curled up on my bed in misery or walking the streets of Oxford with tears streaming down my face.

As if he can read my mind, he says in a mournful voice: 'You know, life isn't fair. I go through hell to make the Boat Race squad, I thrash myself to win the race for Oxford, and it still isn't enough. You want me to parachute into some hellhole and get myself half killed to impress you?' He grins, grabbing another piece of baguette.

I can't help but laugh at this – he is outrageous – but while I am flattered by what he says, I don't grace him with an answer, swatting him away and suggesting he open the wine and stop yanking my chain.

He picks up the bottle. 'Sure,' he says easily. 'Let's drink to both our futures, whatever they may be.' He raises an eyebrow at me and I shake my head at him, laughing.

There's a pop as he twists out the cork and holds the bottle out to me. 'You first.'

'No, I think you earned that privilege.'

He drinks deep and then hands the bottle over. The Prosecco is cool, dry and deliciously fizzy against my tongue. I drink too much in one gulp and hiccup in a very unladylike fashion. Scott bursts out laughing and I do too. Perhaps it's simply the release of tension between us, but I realize that I've laughed too little when Alexander has been around.

The evening sun is slipping towards the horizon when my cab arrives at Falconbury the next day. I stayed in a college guest room last night and managed to get quite a bit of work done. All of the undergraduates have left for the vacation but there were a few master's and DPhil students around. In fact, I bumped into a couple of friends, Chun and Isla, this morning and we went for a late breakfast.

On my way out of college, I also bumped into my tutor, Professor Rafe, who asked me why I was still in Oxford and hadn't gone home to Washington. He's been trying to hit on me all year and warn me off Alexander, but he obviously knew about Alexander's accident – he is a member of the senior teaching staff and they had to be informed, naturally. I couldn't deny I'd been visiting Alexander but I lied and told him I'd been staying with Immy. Even so, he gave me a lecture about focusing on my revision and take-home exams and not being distracted.

In one way, he's right, of course: I *am* distracted by Alexander's drama – not to mention his body – but there is no way I'd ever admit that to Rafe. He may be my tutor but he's also a creep and I would never give him the satisfaction. I mull all of this over on the drive back to Falconbury, where Helen walks down the steps the moment my cab rolls up on the forecourt. From her anxious face, I can tell immediately that something is wrong.

'I ought to warn you we've got a visitor,' she says in a voice so quiet I can hardly hear.

'Who?'

She swallows, and I have a terrible feeling of foreboding. 'Well, Lauren, I'm afraid Valentina arrived last night.'

I was expecting something bad, but not quite this level of bad. 'What?' *Oh Jesus*, I think to myself, *this really might finish me off*.

Helen grimaces. 'I know, I'm sorry.'

I swallow hard and try to look slightly less like I'm on my way to the guillotine. 'Hey, it's nothing to be sorry about. It's not your fault. Where is she?'

'I think she's gone to the stables with Alexander.'

I tell myself to get a grip. 'OK, thanks for the warning. I appreciate it.'

'Do you want Robert to take your bags to your room so you can go straight to the stables?'

'Thanks, but no. I'll take them up myself. I could do with a few moments.'

Helen allows herself a brief smile. 'Good luck.'

OK Deep breaths, Lauren. You. knew *she'd turn up sooner*

or later . . . I sit on the edge of the bed and try to calm myself. Any fool might have guessed Valentina wasn't going to disappear so easily, and that she'd come running as soon as she heard about Alexander's accident. Maybe she knows I'm here too and wants to cause more trouble – Rupert might have told her.

I pace the room, unable to keep still. No amount of deep breaths will make me feel calm about this; I just know it will end in a massive row and mostly likely heartache for me. I close my eyes and remember the easy, relaxed time I just had with Scott. Am I really up for all this, I wonder to myself. Why am I so bothered by Valentina? She's just a vindictive witch, and Rupert an idiot who does whatever she asks.

It's no good, I decide. I can't leave Alexander to Valentina any longer. I touch up my make-up, like I'm putting on a suit of armour – then laugh at myself for doing it. After scooting downstairs so fast I'm out of breath, I force myself to saunter casually along the back corridor that leads through the boot room to the stables.

I stop a few feet from the boot room, the door of which is open a few inches.

'*Amore*, you must listen to me. Surely this latest disaster has convinced you that you must leave the army. When I heard you had been mortally wounded, I almost fainted.'

'It wasn't mortal, Valentina, or I'd be dead.'

I hold my hand over my mouth at Alexander's sarcastic reply. It must be nerves making me giggle.

'Yet look at you. You barely escaped with your life!' She tuts. 'I think you are being very stoical, but at least it will be a wake-up call for you, and now I am here to help you.'

Help? Stifling the urge to swear, I hover by the door.

'You see, you still need me, Alexander.'

There's a pause after this statement that goes on so long I have to open the door.

'*Arggh! Fuck!*'

'Shit, I'm sorry!'

Alexander's face is screwed up in pain where the door hit him on the shoulder. His Barbour jacket slides to the floor.

Valentina's glare is enough to strip the flesh from my bones.

'What do you think you are doing? Alexander is in agony.'

He clutches his lower arm with his hand and winces. 'I. Am. Not. In. Bloody. Agony.'

'Sorry, I didn't know you were behind the door!'

'You should be more careful, Lauren,' Valentina snaps, looking me up and down like I just crawled out of a swamp.

Ignoring Valentina, I pick up Alexander's Barbour but she snatches it from me and tries to drape it around his shoulders. 'Here, *tesoro*, you must not get cold.'

'I'm not an invalid,' he growls and, shrugging the coat aside, brushes past us and stalks off up the corridor.

She sweeps into the library after him. I follow too, my head held high.

Alexander is facing away from us, standing by the window, clutching his arm.

'I don't care what you say, *amore*. I am going to stay here until you are well again. Lauren will fail her exams if she stays, and she doesn't know how to take care of you anyway.'

Valentina walks up to him and touches his arm but he shakes it off.

'I'm not bloody helpless. There are plenty of people to help me here. Robert and Helen can lend a hand if I need it, and Lauren is here by choice; we don't need you too.'

And with that, Alexander stalks off. Pushing open the heavy door with one arm and a sore body gives him trouble but I wouldn't dare intervene.

I am left with Valentina, standing with her hands on her hips, her lips pursed in frustration. 'You see the agony he is in? He is a wreck. You are obviously not looking after him properly. I will stay no matter what he says!'

She sits down in Alexander's chair, and crosses one long leg over the other.

'The last thing he needs is a nursemaid, Valentina.'

She curls her lip in contempt. 'A nursemaid? I have no intention of being a nurse.' She shudders. 'I would hire someone for that, if I needed it. Obviously, our ideas of therapy are very different.'

A hot fury burns through me. I stare coolly at her and take my time to reply. 'Yes, of course, I've seen,' I say lightly. 'That sex clip left nothing to the imagination. Thank you for sharing it with me.'

She smirks. 'You are so puritanical, but I guessed you would not be giving Alexander what he needs, what he loves. I am his age, with more experience than you have in your little finger.' She waves her pinkie at me, tipped with a glossy talon. 'You know what you are up against now, little Lauren – a real woman – and you'll be gone before the end of the week now I'm here, you'll see.'

Her audacity takes my breath away. I don't want to get in a catfight but really, how much am I supposed to put up with? 'Oh really? A "real woman"? Not a desperate witch who can't leave her ex boyfriend alone?' I ask, with an arched eyebrow. It's a little below the belt, I admit, but you can be pushed too far.

She raises her eyebrows. 'Don't you think hurling insults in Alexander's home is a little inappropriate? At least you've shown your true colours, and your lack of class, if I may say so.'

'Well, your true colour is definitely green,' I snap back, utterly furious. 'Emerald to the core. Try any therapy you want on Alexander, and see what he thinks about it. I have my own life to lead and I've wasted enough breath on this ridiculous conversation.'

I try hard not to wrench the door open and let it slam but the sound of the wood hitting the frame echoes around the grand hallway of Falconbury and causes Robert to stare at me as I stomp up the stairs to my room.

I walk along the landing, where Helen is arranging tulips in a vase. As I pass, she shoots me a questioning look but I can only give her a hands-up WTF gesture. I think I can hear Alexander thumping around in his study but I carry on, back upstairs to our room. I won't be part of some undignified scrap over him.

If I thought the first dinner party I 'enjoyed' at Falconbury was awkward, tonight's knocks that occasion out of the park. We've gathered for supper in the dining room. I don't know why Alexander wants to eat here; maybe he wants to make a deliberate statement about keeping things formal or about Valentina being part of the past – perhaps it has nothing to do with him and Robert merely assumed that because we had guests, dinner should be served in here.

Whatever, the atmosphere is somewhere below glacial. We sit around the dining table, Valentina at one end, me at the other, with Alexander in between. Valentina is in a skintight dress with a plunging neckline and out of sheer determination not to be accused of trying to 'compete' and, I admit, to show how 'at home' I am here, I decided to go for a more casual look with new tightly fitting cargos from Anthropologie and a top that's simple but beautifully cut and always gets Alexander hot under the collar. Though the way Alexander has his eyes focused on his dinner, I don't think he'd notice if both of us were dressed as clowns. This is one occasion when I so wish Emma was here, 'accidentally' putting her foot in things in her own inimitable way, but she's away for the night at a charity fashion show.

Alexander manages to get through the soup and main course by communicating in monosyllables. You could cut the atmosphere with a knife. It hardly matters what he says because Valentina is too busy regaling us with stories about her vacations, her parents' new villa in Sardinia and the expansion of the gallery she owns in Positano. I have a sneaking suspicion that she's making so many hand gestures to show off her admittedly impressive cleavage.

As soon as dessert has been served, we all retreat to the sitting room – if you can call it a retreat, with the Cold War raging between us. Valentina can't resist a few remarks about missing General Hunt and how 'things aren't the same at Falconbury without him'. I don't know how Alexander can put up with her comments, they're so close to the bone.

When she gets up to try and push a cushion under Alexander's arm, I have murder on my mind. On the other hand, it *is* funny.

'What are you smiling at?' she asks, glaring at me as Alexander grunts an 'I'm fine' at her. 'You think it is amusing that Alexander is in pain?'

'I'm not in pain,' he growls, clearly wincing as she rearranges the cushion.

'There, you see, he's not in pain. Not from his injury anyway,' I shoot back, stung at last.

'That's because you don't know him well. Anyone as close to him as I am would know how he really feels.'

Suddenly, Alexander gets up. 'I am actually in the room. Shall I leave so you can carry on discussing me in private?'

'*Amore*, don't be silly. I'm only concerned for you!'

It's too late. Alexander stalks off, and the cushion falls to the carpet.

'You see what you have done now?' Valentina says with a glare of triumph.

Realizing it's useless to argue with her – and a little pissed at Alexander including me in his comment – I escape to the library and lock the door to give us both time to cool down. The last thing I want is to get into a row with him with Valentina in the house because I suspect that's exactly what she wants. Maybe Alexander really *is* tired – it hasn't been long since his op – or just brooding, because when I finally slip into bed beside him, he doesn't make any attempt to have sex, which is unusual. Irritated by the idea that this would please Valentina, I sit up and do some reading.

I opened my eyes this morning to find his side of the bed empty and a note on my pillow saying he's gone to walk Benny and will see me at breakfast. I don't know when he left the house but working on the assumption he'll be back sooner rather than later, I pull on skinny jeans and my top from last night and head downstairs.

The aroma of cooked bacon and sausages drifts down the hallway from the morning room, but before I can walk in, I hear raised voices. My Italian classes don't cover some of the vocabulary on Valentina's side but I can get the gist. Alexander, on the other hand, is making himself perfectly clear.

'I've said I appreciate you coming over to see how I am, but now I think it's time you left,' Alexander snaps.

Valentina switches to English. 'You are a fool! She is only after one thing, your money and your title.'

'Now you're being ridiculous. Lauren couldn't care less about that stuff. And I'm not listening to another word.'

Though I'm seething mad, I'll give Valentina one thing. She does a very elegant snort.

'I never thought you would be so naive, *tesoro*, but now I realize how deeply you have been taken in. She must be better in bed than I'd have given her credit for. She doesn't have the body of course,' she says dismissively, 'so she must have some tricks up her sleeve that have warped you.'

I almost laugh at this; she is utterly outrageous. Ignoring the temptation to burst in and throw a few insults her way, I decide to wait in the hallway as Alexander assumes his chilliest tone.

'Valentina, please don't force me into asking you to leave this house.'

'What?' she blusters. 'You can't throw me out! Your mother would turn in her grave and if the general were alive, he would weep to see how you treat me. You will regret it too – when things go wrong with your cheap little American, you'll come running back and by then maybe it'll be too late.'

Impatience tugs at the edge of his voice now. 'I don't care what my father would think and I won't discuss my mother with anyone. I'm sorry if your parents are offended, but it can't be helped. And as you told me yourself, you're very busy with the gallery expansion. I expect you'll want to get back this evening,' he says firmly, making it clear the conversation is over, as he makes his way to the door.

There's an audible gasp from Valentina and then more expletives. I suppose I ought to laugh or cheer, but the last thing I want to do is walk in on them and risk a full-scale war. It's like volcano versus iceberg and for now, I think I'll stay out of it.

Back up in the bedroom, the minutes stretch to thirty before I hear the door open. I bury my head back in my art book, not that I've taken in any of the contents.

'Lauren?'

I wait a few seconds before I glance up at Alexander. 'Oh, hello. Sorry I didn't make breakfast. I must have lost track of time.'

If he doesn't believe me, he doesn't show it, but he does look fed up. 'It's a good thing you didn't come down,' he sighs. 'I've asked Valentina to leave. Ideally right now, but I doubt she'll be able to get a flight from Heathrow until later this evening.'

I close the book. 'I thought she travelled everywhere by private jet?' I keep my tone light.

'Not on this occasion,' he says ruefully.

'I'm not going to lie. I'm relieved she's leaving but I'm sorry it's been awkward.'

His face is inscrutable as he crosses to the window, then all I get is a back view. 'I need to do my physio,' he says dully, sounding like the sky has just fallen in on him. When he turns around, I realize he genuinely does look worn out and I'm reminded that he's on a long road to recovery.

'Is the arm getting any better?' I ask tentatively, all too aware of his volatile mood.

'It's fine.' He walks over to me and sits by the bed. I think he's in far more pain than he lets on and the realization that it may be a long time before he's fit for duty is beginning to sink in.

'OK.' I pause. 'Well, unless you want help with the physio, which I'm guessing is a 'no' . . .' He confirms with a shake of his head. 'Then it's probably too late for breakfast now so I may as well go for a run and then grab some brunch.'

He brightens. 'Yes, why don't you take Benny out with you?' Delighted to see his dark mood lift even a little, I readily agree.

Soon, Benny is loping around me, sniffing round hedgerows, marking his territory and wearing out his tail muscles in his delight at being taken out for a run twice in one morning. I haven't gone that far because

I'm starving and really I just wanted to give Alexander some space.

This time, I do a quick circuit of the deer park and start walking back towards the stables for my cool down. I'm skirting the side of the house, turning the corner towards the boot room entrance, when a red-faced Talia dashes up to me.

'Have you seen Alexander?'

'He was in his bedroom but that was half an hour ago. Why? What's happened?'

'Bloody Valentina! She took Alexander's hunter out for a ride without asking and she says he's thrown her. You'd think she'd broken her ankle from the way she's shrieking.'

'Where is she?'

'Back at the stables, giving everyone hell in between screams.' Talia pulls a face. My heart sinks as I wonder if this will mean Valentina won't be leaving as soon as I'd hoped.

Chapter Eight

'Does she need an ambulance?' I ask, walking alongside Talia.

Talia snorts. 'Of course not. I'm not wasting their time; she can go off to A&E like everyone else.'

What sounds like a howl of agony comes from the direction of the stable yard. 'I guess I'd better go and find Alexander,' I say reluctantly. I'd really hoped to be able to leave him to get some rest.

Talia stomps off, while Benny, who seems delighted with this new excitement, races ahead into the hallway, his claws clattering on the tiles. After I find Alexander and fill him in, we hurry down to the stable yard and the sight that greets us is like something from a comic opera. Valentina is sitting on an old mounting block, holding her ankle and moaning at Talia, who is behaving with admirable restraint.

'Can I fetch you a pack of frozen peas? You should get some ice on that . . .'

Valentina rounds on her. 'Frozen *peas*! What the hell do you think I am? I don't need vegetables, I need expert medical help.' *I'd second that*, I think, but not of the kind she means. 'Oh, Alexander, thank God you are here. Your stupid hunter threw me.'

Alexander strides forward. 'Why were you on him in the first place? What were you doing to him?'

'Me doing to *him*? He is the most useless animal on the planet. I have no idea why he decided to throw me.'

'I thought you never fell, Valentina,' he retorts, then in a softer tone: 'Here, let me see this ankle.'

He kneels down and with his good hand probes the flesh around her ankle. I'm no doctor, but I can't see any swelling. Then again, she can't have fallen very long ago so maybe the bruising has yet to come out. I'm desperately trying to be charitable and failing by the second.

'Owww!' She screws up her eyes in pain.

'I'm sorry,' says Alexander soothingly, while continuing to check her foot and ankle with his good hand. I remember when I twisted mine outside his house and he did the same to me . . . I nearly went through the roof, in more ways than one.

Valentina watches him, wincing occasionally.

Carefully, Alexander replaces her foot on the concrete yard and stands up. 'I don't think it's broken.'

'What? How can you tell? I need an X-ray.'

'I doubt it but if you want to get checked out, Brandon will take you to A&E. Shall I call the contessa for you?'

She manages a brave smile. 'There's no need to trouble my mother but you must know I can't possibly go to A&E on my own.'

'I don't expect you to. I'm sure Helen will be happy to go with you.'

She purses her lips. 'You mean you won't come?'

He stiffens. 'If I thought it was necessary, of course I'd come, but I have a meeting with someone from the regiment later today.'

'And they are more important than me, of course!'

'That's not what I'm saying. Do you really want to sit for four hours in the local minor injuries unit only to have some doctor say you might have bruised your foot?'

'*Might* have?'

'A&E isn't the nicest of places, Valentina, and the hospitals are stretched to the limit as it is. I really think you'd be better at home.'

'You could call out your doctor,' she says sullenly.

'I suppose I could, if you really want me to.'

'You can't just leave me here like this!'

'Look,' he sighs. 'Let's help you to your room and get an ice pack on it, give you some paracetamol and then rest it for a while. Talia can give you some vet tape to strap it up.'

'*Vet* tape? I am not a polo pony!'

'It's the best thing for it,' I say, trying not laugh. 'I can vouch for that.' This is the same remedy Alexander offered me when I fell over outside his house in the autumn.

'Will you bandage it for me?' she wheedles, ignoring me completely.

Alexander holds up his sling. 'With one hand? I don't think I can, but I'll ask Helen to help you.'

Valentina curls a lip. 'Thanks for nothing,' she mutters, then seems to cheer up. 'Of course, I can't possibly leave until it's healed.'

'Of course . . .' I mutter.

She glares at me but Alexander says, resignedly, 'Let's see how it is after you've rested it. Of course you can't go if it's too bad, but you'll have Brandon to help you at the airport.'

'The airport? I will be black and blue by tomorrow,' she says, then directs her next comment straight at me. 'It will be days before I can even think of leaving Falconbury.'

I can't keep silent any longer. 'You might find you have remarkable powers of recovery.'

'My genes are excellent, but an injury like this will need a lot of rest,' she snaps back.

Talia stands by, tight-lipped. Suddenly Benny dashes forward and sniffs Valentina's foot.

'Get him off me,' she cries, batting at him.

'Here, Benny!' Alexander calls but it's obviously the most excitement Benny has seen for months. With a joyful bark, he lunges forward and licks Valentina's foot like it's a beef bone.

'Vile creature!'

Benny obviously doesn't speak Italian and takes her shriek as encouragement to cover her foot in drool. 'Get off me!' She snatches up her riding crop and catches Benny's rump with a sharp crack. Yelping in pain, he skitters backwards.

We are all frozen in shock.

'How dare you!' Talia lunges forward and wrenches the crop out of Valentina's hand. She grabs Benny's collar and pulls him protectively against her legs.

Valentina's 'O' of outrage changes into a sly smile. 'Did you hear how your groom spoke to me?' she says to Alexander.

'She was worried about Benny – we all were. You didn't need to go that far,' I cut in, furious.

Valentina regards me with contempt. 'I would expect you to defend her.' She addresses Alexander again. 'You heard that, *tesoro*?'

Alexander's face is like thunder. 'Yes, I heard.'

Benny slinks over to Alexander and eyes Valentina with a blend of hurt, fear and confusion that deserves a canine Oscar.

'I'm sorry, Alexander,' Talia's voice is quiet and small. It's not like her at all but she's obviously worried she's going to lose her job and despite what she had to put up with when the general was alive, I know she respects Alexander and adores the horses.

Valentina's eyes flash. 'You should apologize to me, not him.'

Talia folds her arms. 'You shouldn't have hurt Benny, and I know it's not the first time you've hit him,' she accuses.

'Talia was trying to protect my dog, and I don't blame her,' Alexander says coldly.

Valentina pouts and says, 'I was in pain, and I'm

sorry for lashing out but my foot is so sore. Come here, Benny, I did not mean to hurt you.' She holds out her hand. 'Here, boy.'

Benny shrinks back behind Alexander, a look of horrified innocence in his eyes.

'He won't come to you now,' snaps Talia.

Valentina merely smiles. 'I hope you're going to fire her for this, Alexander.'

Talia is as tough as they come but I can see she is worried.

'Valentina. Shut up,' says Alexander, looking thoughtful. 'Talia. Are you accusing Miss di Cavinato of mistreating my dog?'

She looks up, taken aback by the question. 'Well, yes, I am. I've seen her hit him and kick him. More than once.'

Valentina snorts. 'She's lying.'

'She's not.' I can't stay silent any longer. 'I also saw Valentina hit Benny with her riding crop on the day of the hunt.'

'She's making it up, *tesoro*; she and your groom have always been against me and they would say anything to make me look bad. It's her word against mine.'

Alexander turns to Talia, grim-faced. 'Talia, I think I've heard enough now. Some people might expect me to insist you apologize to Valentina,' he says. I am shocked to hear him talk like this and start to interrupt.

He shoots me a warning glare that makes me instantly

shut up. 'However, on this occasion, I'd fire you if you *did* say you're sorry.'

Talia's mouth is open in astonishment and I want to punch the air for joy.

He turns to Valentina and his tone is glacial. 'I've always known you loathe Benny, and I've tried to overlook it. Not everyone likes dogs, which is fair enough, but as for beating the animal, lying about it and then trying to have one of my most loyal and valuable members of staff fired – I can't forgive you for that, Valentina.'

She narrows her eyes. 'What are you saying? That you care more for your dog and your groom than me?'

'At this particular moment, that's a pretty accurate assessment.'

'But what about my ankle?' she shrieks.

'I'm sorry you've been hurt but I'm sure it's not as bad as you think. Talia, would you mind fetching Robert and Brandon so that they can help Valentina up to her room?'

'It would be a pleasure, your lordship.' Not bothering to hide her glee, Talia saunters off to the house to fetch help.

With Talia gone, Valentina clearly needs a new target and I'm in the firing line.

'How dare you treat me like this in front of her,' she cries, jabbing her finger in my direction. 'And how could you even think of throwing me out with my ankle like this!' she shouts at Alexander.

'Like I said, I'll have Brandon take you to the airport and make sure there's someone there to help you. In fact, I'll ask Helen if she'd mind calling Alitalia right now and book you a ticket on the first flight to Naples tomorrow morning, if you want to be back in Positano? First class, of course, and I'll charge it to my account.'

Forgetting her injury, Valentina jumps to her feet and stands with her hands on her hips in the yard. 'You will not treat me like this!'

'You seem to have made a rapid recovery,' I say calmly, raising my eyebrows at Alexander.

The look she gives him is pure venom, then she laughs at me. 'You shut up. I know what you are like. Playing the innocent victim, the nice little all-American girl, and all the while you are turning Alexander against me.'

'You've done a good job of that all on your own.'

'I know why he is treating me like this. You've told him about the sex clip, haven't you? Just to make me and Rupert look bad.'

Alexander frowns. 'What's this about the clip?'

She shoots me a death look. 'I knew she couldn't wait to tell you. I knew she would go running to you, bleating about it.'

'Actually, I haven't even mentioned it,' I say, still calm, waiting for the fireworks which will surely now come.

There is a long pause as Alexander looks from me to Valentina, and then we both watch as the colour gradually falls from her face.

'Lauren?' He turns to me.

Oh no, this isn't the way I wanted to tell him but I guess I'd better get it over with. 'It's true,' I mumble. 'That sex video . . . I found out at the Boat Race party that she was the one who sent it, with Rupert's help. I was going to tell you but the time never seemed right.'

There is another long pause, during which I wish there was a huge hole in the ground that could swallow me up and transport me straight back to my uncomplicated life back in Washington.

'I see,' he says quietly. I don't think he truly wanted to believe that his ex fiancée would do something that low.

Valentina sneers. 'Acting the saint suits you, Lauren. How can you stand it, Alexander?'

'I'm glad to see you feel better, Valentina,' he says icily. 'It seems like you can leave immediately after all. Robert and Brandon will be here in a moment if you still need a hand.'

He turns and strides off towards the house.

She trots after him, her injury apparently miraculously healed. 'Wait, *tesoro*! We can work this out.'

I go up to my room – I have to leave Alexander to sort this out and have, quite frankly, had enough of the pair of them. I get out my books and do my best to focus on what I realize I should be spending my time on anyway. For the first time, I really seriously question my decision not to go home and get away from all this.

From downstairs I hear shouting and doors slamming and I guess the staff are having a field day, probably selling tickets to watch the drama.

A few minutes later, I hear the thud of someone walking up the stairs.

The footsteps walk past the room and down the hallway, then pause. Seconds later, they start again and grow louder. They stop again outside my door and I stand up, expecting the door to fly open at any moment. My pulse picks up, ready for the fray, but there's only silence and then a hissed whisper.

'You little bitch. You think you have won but it's not over. No one does this to me and gets away with it. Wait and see; you'll regret the moment you ever got involved with Alexander.'

With a final expletive, and before I have a chance to open the door and return fire, she stomps off along the landing again, and there's a loud thud as she slams her door.

I roll my eyes, getting back to my studies, or trying to anyway.

Eventually, I give that up. I really can't concentrate so I try to find solace in my art, getting out my pencils and sketch pad. I flip through the drawings of Alexander I did when we were at Falconbury for the hunt ball. He found them and teased me about them, mainly because they were of him, not because of my skills, or lack of them. Looking at the sketches now with fresh eyes, I see they're not nearly as bad as I'd remembered although, as ever, I can see acres of room for improvement.

Analysing them is a sobering exercise and I decide to go for a safer subject than Alexander so I sketch a picture of Benny, tail wagging, rooting in the hedgerows. I find drawing a mixture of delight and frustration; at times I can get lost for hours in my work but there's always a point where I want to throw the sketchpad at the wall.

Before long, I've abandoned the dog and moved on, sketching the outline of a brooding Alexander, bare-chested and with his arm in a black sling. My fingers move faster, driven by the compulsion to capture his scowling fury with Valentina.

I've no idea how long I've been working but I become aware of raised voices outside the window and push my pad and pencil aside. Gravel crunches loudly and then a vehicle pulls up and stops at the front of the house. When I peer out of the window, I see Valentina tripping down the steps in her spiky boots – no sign of the ankle injury – while Robert packs her bags in the truck of the Bentley. Next to the car, Emma is handing notes to the driver of a cab just as Valentina waves away Robert's attempt to help her into the Bentley.

I think she's called to Valentina, who doesn't seem to have replied. Robert shuts the door and a few moments later the car pulls away, leaving Emma watching from the steps. Knowing this is way too good to miss, I run downstairs into the hall and find Emma shrugging off her rucksack.

'Hi there,' she says, scrunching up her face in bewilderment. 'Am I hallucinating or was that Valentina leaving just now? What have I missed?'

I give her a huge hug – I don't think I've ever been so glad to see her. 'Come in. I'll tell you later,' I mutter, helping her with her bags.

Later that evening, I'm sitting in the library with my laptop. Before dinner, Emma and I had a good catch-up and I filled her in on most of the day's goings on. By evening, peace finally seems to have broken out in the house. Emma is in her room, Skyping her friends. Alexander has kept to his study – working, presumably, though whether it's on his course or estate business, I don't know. Earlier on, some officer from his regiment turned up at the house, and he's been even more distracted ever since. I think the consequences of his injury and the effect it may have on his career, at least temporarily, have begun to hit home and it's no wonder he's been even quieter than usual.

The officer has long gone now and Alexander walks in to join me, carrying a bottle. 'Want a drink?' he asks, holding up some red wine. 'I thought we could both do with one.'

'Sounds good, but are you supposed to drink alcohol on your meds?' I say, only half teasing.

He gives me an 'Am I bothered?' glare. 'I'm not supposed to do a lot of things, but you'll have to open it, I'm afraid. There's a corkscrew and some glasses in the cabinet.'

After I've poured the wine, Alexander stands in front of the fireplace with his glass while I curl up on the leather chaise. Although it's April, it's cool enough for a fire, and the room is pink with the glow of the setting sun and flickering flames. I love the tang of woodsmoke; it reminds me of winters at home. It seems like a very long time since January, when we were last together as a family, and I'm shocked to feel a pang of homesickness. Maybe it's a good thing my parents are visiting after all. They're due to arrive in a couple of weeks' time, though I'm still waiting to hear about the flight details.

'Penny for them?' he asks as I sip my wine.

'Oh, I was only thinking of home. We have a fire in the sitting room sometimes. My dad loves to light one if he's not working or flying round the country, which is rare.'

'I'm sure he's a very busy man. But I'll get to meet him soon, won't I?'

'I guess so . . .'

'Hmm, you don't sound too keen.' He watches me thoughtfully from the fireplace. 'Lauren, I wish you'd told me about Valentina sending that video.'

'There never seemed a good time, honestly, and we were past all that. I didn't want to go over it again, and it seemed irrelevant after your accident. I thought it was better to move on and I had no idea that Valentina would show up here. Not this soon, anyway.'

'I'd already realized she must have had a hand in it – there was no way anyone but her could have filmed and shared the clip – but I must admit I'm shocked at Rupert's part in it.'

What can I say? He knows there's no love lost between Rupert and me. And yet Rupert is his cousin, and was – still is – his friend.

'Lauren?' he prompts. Come on, just how much was Rupert involved?' Clearly I'm not going to get away with not answering this part. 'Don't make me resort to interrogation techniques.' He's trying to look serious, but the twinkle in his eyes is darkly sexy.

As always, I am powerless when he is like this. I lift my chin up and send him a challenging look. 'I'm almost tempted to keep schtum, just to see you try some on me.'

He raises his eyebrows, laughing. 'They'd involve you having no clothes on.' He takes a step closer.

'Then I'm definitely not telling you,' I counter, my insides turning to liquid as I imagine the many things he might do to me with my clothes off.

His eyes are hooded now with desire, but he isn't quite ready yet to give in.

'Look, can't we move on?' I plead. 'I honestly don't know any more than I've told you. He and Valentina just decided it would be fun to taunt me when they thought you and I were history. That's it.'

He glances away.

'But why would Rupert do that? To me?' He stops. For all his jibes at me, all his obvious resentment and jealousy – and envy – of Alexander, Rupert is one of his closest relatives.

'I don't know,' I say, unwilling to speculate.

The smile is fleeting and he says, 'You know, I can't let this pass. I'll have to deal with Rupert.'

Deal with. I wouldn't like to be in Rupert's brogues. 'Alexander, leave it. You don't want to upset Letty and your uncle.'

His tone hardens. 'There's no need for them to know. I'll deal with him in my own way.' He pauses. 'I've also been thinking. Valentina talks a lot of rubbish but maybe she has a point in one respect. It was selfish of me to ask you to stay at Falconbury and keep you away from your family and friends.'

She said that to him? She's even more cunning than I imagined. 'You know, Captain Hunt, that doesn't sound like you at all. Are you suffering from a terrible bout of self-pity?' I tease, desperately wanting to lighten the situation.

He looks at me steadily and gives a little sigh. And then he laughs. 'Lauren, you never cease to surprise me, you know?'

I hold out my hand to him. 'Sit down, Captain Hunt. That's an order.'

There's a gleam in his eye as he obeys. 'I don't know about you, but I think we both deserve a smoother ride for a bit,' he says, looking at me in that way that only Alexander can – as if he can see and feel every inch of me, as if he will never get enough of me.

'I'm not sure that I want a smooth ride.' I hold his gaze. 'Not in one way anyway.' I watch as his thigh nudges mine and I feel my heart might literally stop beating with the need I feel to kiss him.

'In that case,' he smiles, using his good hand to turn me towards him before snaking it under my T-shirt, 'I can make it as rough as you like.'

'How about I make it rough for you? Do you think you could handle that?' I whisper.

He laughs. 'Of course I can. I can take anything you can throw at me. Go on. Surprise me, Lauren,' he says, his eyes alight with mischief.

'Oh really? Let's see, shall we?'

A short time later, we're upstairs and the bedroom door is firmly locked because Alexander is lying naked on the bed. One of his arms is already effectively out of action, and the other is now secured to his bedpost with his old school tie.

I'm standing by the bed, still with my clothes on, watching him.

'So, is this the best you can throw at me?' he says.

I gaze at the impressive sight between his legs. 'I haven't even started. You'll be begging for mercy by the time I've finished with you.' At that I start to take off my top and unhook my bra.

'I never beg.'

I smile but I can see he's bursting to touch me. The fingers of his tied hand twitch.

I wag my finger. 'No cheating. You can't touch me. Not till I say.'

'Not a problem.'

'Yeah, sure.' I unzip my mini and step out of it, taking a step closer to him.

He shakes his head. 'Thigh-highs, heels and those knickers. Christ, that's an underhand tactic.'

I arch an eyebrow innocently. 'All's fair in love and war.'

By the time I've climbed on to the bed to kneel between his legs, Alexander is unable to keep still and muttering curses under his breath. When I close my mouth around his penis, he moans shamelessly and the mattress creaks as he struggles against his bonds. He feels great, tastes deliciously wicked, and the power of making him writhe against me is wonderful.

'You'd better let me go or it'll all be over, Lauren, honestly.'

I carry on teasing him with my tongue, enjoying every delicious stroke.

'Untie me, Lauren, come on!'

I glance up momentarily and smile, then go back down on him.

He moans and bucks his pelvis. 'For God's sake. I don't think I can hold on. If you want me inside you, you seriously have to stop.' I pause and he looks at me, grinning wickedly. 'Otherwise, carry on, Ms Cusack.'

He says the last two words like he's my commanding officer and he's just given me an order. Although I'm bursting to be touched or to have him inside me, I restrain myself from freeing him and push myself to my knees. 'I don't think you've quite understood the game.'

'What game?'

'This.' I climb off the bed and stand by the side. Then, grabbing an ice cube from one of the drinks on the table, I slowly move it round my breasts, rubbing it over the nipples.

He sighs deeply and murmurs, 'You do know the US Constitution forbids cruel and unusual punishments . . .'

'I believe it's the Eighth Amendment. You consider this cruel and unusual?'

'Yes,' he groans. 'Do you want me to die of frustration?'

'Not die, just suffer quite a bit.' I move closer, dropping the ice cube and he leans forward to suck my nipples. Having his hot mouth on my breasts is almost more than I can bear, but after a few seconds, I back away out of reach again.

The bedpost rattles and thumps against the wall as he tries to jerk his hand free of the bond and I must admit there are red lines around his wrist. That knot *does* looks vicious.

'What have you done? I can't get out of this. Lauren, I need to get out. I can't wait any more.'

I almost give in and then I remember that he's trained in resisting interrogation techniques. I harden my heart.

'Sorry, not falling for that.' Standing by the bed, I turn around. With my back to him, I inch my thong slowly down over my thighs. I'm aware that he has a close-up view and that's the intention. As I stretch further over to give him an even better view of my backside, the curses and moans coming from the bed make me want to giggle. However, I'm so turned on myself, it takes everything I have not to climb on top of him right now. Finally, I step out of the thong, pick it up and turn around. I dangle it in front of his face, tickling his nose with the lacy hem.

'Lauren, really, you win. I think I might actually explode. Let me go, *please*.'

'Is that begging?'

Carefully, I arrange the thong like a war trophy across his stomach. The wispy lace looks great against the muscles of his abs and I wonder how much longer I can keep this up. It's definitely becoming a torment for me too. His lips twist in a defiant smile. 'I wouldn't exactly call it begging.'

'Have it your way, then.' I snatch up my thong and make as if to pull it back up my thighs as coolly as I can.

'OK! OK, you win. I'm *begging* you to untie me, screw me, anything, just put me out of my misery,' he moans and I can no longer hold myself back. I straddle him, holding eye contact as I slide myself over him as quickly and easily as I've ever done anything in my life.

I watch as his mouth opens in sheer ecstasy, and then I am lost myself as he circles his hips and thrusts up into me, crying out with the relief.

Then I start to touch myself again, and he loses it totally, squeezing his eyes shut and pumping into me. But I don't want to climax yet; this is too delicious, and I . . .

Wow!

Slowly, gradually, I come back down and into the real world, my hands braced behind me, still sitting on top of him.

He watches me, breathing heavily.

'Lauren, the moment I'm capable . . . you'd better watch out, because I can promise you my revenge will be very, *very* sweet.'

I ease myself off him, throbbing and tingling inside, out of breath, exhausted but elated. 'I'll look forward to it, but first I have no idea how I'm going to untie that knot.'

Chapter Nine

A week later, I'm sipping cocktails with Immy on the deck of a riverside bar in Henley-on-Thames. She doesn't live too far away so we've met up here for dinner.

'So, how's Alexander doing?' she asks as we watch the scullers glide past on the river, and the water sparkles in the early evening sun.

'Much better. He had the stitches taken out the week before last and he might be able to do away with the sling soon, if the physio gives him the all clear at his appointment tomorrow. I hope so – it's been driving him insane not being able to drive or ride or do the stuff he wants to.'

'Ouch.'

'Yes, but, you know, the past week or so has been a period of amazing calm. We've been on lots of walks around the estate, and it's been chilled; I've never really seen Alexander like that. We've had the odd smart trip out, a dinner at the Fat Duck in Bray, and a couple of lazy pub lunches, but other than that we've just been relaxing, and I've been working a bit. Not enough probably, but a bit.'

'Hmm. Not just relaxing I should imagine,' snorts

Immy. 'There's no way you two can go without sex for long. It must have been challenging though, with his arm out of action?' she says, her eyes twinkling.

My cheeks heat a little. 'Yes, well, you're right, it has demanded some creative solutions . . .'

She laughs. 'I can imagine. And has our Valentina materialized again since Alexander sent her packing?'

'Not heard anything, but there's always the potential for her do a *Fatal Attraction*,' I say with a smile, making light of things but hoping I don't hear from her again.

Immy swirls her cocktail with the swizzle stick. 'I guess Rupert's off Alexander's Christmas card list too?'

I shrug. 'I have no idea. Alexander's said nothing to me but I know he's seen Rupert. He went to some family thing at the de Courceys last week, which I managed to avoid because I went to a bachelor party for one of the girls from dance class. I'm not sure if he had a chance to say anything to Rupert then, or even if he wanted to.'

'Hmm. It must be tricky for him with Rupert being family.'

'Mmm,' I agree. 'Alexander won't want to upset his aunt and uncle now they're pretty much his closest relations. I really like Letty, by the way; she took Emma and me for tea at the Ritz last week.'

'Wow, did she? I'm impressed. And what does Rupert think of you being friendly with his mother? He really loves his mummy, you know,' she laughs.

'I gathered. Letty didn't talk too much about him,

with Emma around. I think she wanted us just to have a lovely time for a change, without any stress, but she did ask me if I thought Rupert was happy at Wyckham. Apparently, she thinks he's got in with a bad bunch since he joined his latest drinking club. I don't think she has any real idea of what he *does* get up to, poor woman.'

Immy rolls her eyes. 'If you do join a bunch called The Hellfire Society, it's kind of asking for trouble. What did you say to her?'

'I couldn't bring myself to tell her that I didn't give a fuck if Rupert was happy or not, after the trouble he's caused us, so I tried to skirt the issue. I'm getting good at that these days . . .' I toy with the stem of my glass. 'However, I'm not looking forward to college dinners much next term, that's for sure. The atmosphere could be a little awkward.'

'I'm not looking forward to this last term at all, and I can't believe it's coming around so fast. Only a week of the vac left.' Immy wrinkles her nose. 'But I've no choice, with Finals looming. I've started some revision and sort of finished my dissertation but I think it's going to be awful.' Immy takes solace in her cocktail.

'I've been working on my take-home essays because I have to hand them in at the start of next term. I don't want to give Professor Rafe the slightest excuse to have a go.'

'It'll be a bit of a come down to be back in college after Falconbury, won't it?' Immy asks, with mock innocence.

'Of course,' I laugh. 'Do you know, living at Falconbury is a little surreal and at first I thought it was a gloomy Gothic pile, but it does grow on you. I've been happier there than I thought I ever could be. What about you? Have you heard from the Blues rower again?'

She shrugs. 'Nope, it was a one-night stand and I don't mind too much. Like I told you, he was gorgeous but not much of a shag as it happens, although admittedly that might have been because he'd just won the Boat Race and had a magnum of Moet. He did text me a couple of times but I haven't tried to contact him . . .' In front of us, two scullers are lifting their boats out on to the slipway. Immy sips her drink, then says, 'Have you heard from the lovely Scott recently?'

'Not since we had a picnic in the Parks, but I think he's gone back to Washington for a while.'

'And Lia?'

'I assume that's still on, but I don't know how serious it is.'

'Oh well,' she sighs. 'Whatever's going on there, I still think he has a thing for you.'

I smile. 'Immy, you're very loyal, and I'm flattered, but I think we've had our moment. Wrong time, wrong place, I reckon.'

'Maybe,' she says, doubtfully. 'Well anyway, let's just hope we can all get through next term free of any drama, at least until after our exams.'

'Drama? I don't seem to be able to stay away from

that, but I'll do my best,' I promise. My stomach tightens a little as I think of Alexander.

'Are your parents still planning on coming over?' she asks.

'Yes, they've arranged to come at the start of term. My mother called yesterday to say she'd booked the flights so I've got a week to prepare myself.'

'So will they be visiting Falconbury?'

'Not if I can help it. I'd far rather deal with them in Oxford, on my own territory, than have them hit by the full Falconbury experience.'

'Probably best,' says Immy. She smirks and picks up the menu. 'Look, I was conned into going on a horrendously long bike ride with some girls from my old school today and now I could eat a horse. Let's order before I keel over.'

Even while we're scanning the menu, the knot won't unravel. This last term is short. Once our exams are over, it's the Wyckham Summer Ball, and then it'll be the end of term before I know it. Immy will leave; everyone will go their separate ways, including Alexander and me, most likely. I feel shocked at how awful this thought feels. With everything that's been going on, I haven't given any real thought to what I will do when term finishes.

Even if this term does turn out to be calm and uneventful, we both have to face the fact that our futures after Wyckham might separate us. Alexander has no idea what will happen – whether he'll be well enough to return to the military, or whether he'll have to devote more time to Falconbury. It's all so up in the air, and my immediate future is too.

I have to start thinking about my career – what am I going to do next? Where in the world am I going to do it? I probably should have already started making contacts and looking for a place in a museum or gallery . . . OK, I know I could use my parents' and friends' network to get my foot in the door somewhere, and that's what they'll be expecting me to do, but that's not me any more. Since I came to Oxford, I've changed. This feeling has snuck up on me during my time here but I know it's become more important to me now to make my own way in the world.

It's late by the time I arrive back at Falconbury in a cab. Immy's brother, George, who's just passed his driving test, gave her a lift home. I know she was dreading being driven by him and I smile to myself as I picture her face when he screeched to a halt outside the bistro, like he was in a cop series. Even as I get out my bag to pay the cab driver, her text beeps on my screen:

God help me, I need Valium.

Helen lets me in – Falconbury's not the kind of place where you have your own front door key – and tells me Alexander has gone to bed, looking 'washed out' after he'd done his physio, so I creep in beside him and soon I'm out cold too.

In the morning, I wake to see him sitting fully dressed next to me on the bed.

'Morning,' he says.

I rub sleep from my eyes. 'Hi, sorry I was late last night. I didn't want to wake you.'

'That's OK. I needed to get some sleep, according to Helen.'

'Does she blame me for wearing you out?' I tease.

He lifts the covers with his free hand and raises his eyebrows. 'If you insist on coming to bed looking like that, what do you expect?'

I glance down. 'I did have my cami and shorts on but it got a little warm in here.'

He sighs heavily, drops the cover reluctantly and stands up. 'If I don't leave now, I'll be late for my appointment. Hard as it is to tear myself away from that delectable body of yours.'

I flush, wishing too that he didn't have to go. 'Do you want me to come with you to the hospital?'

'Thanks, but no. Brandon's taking me in the Range Rover in case I get the all clear to drive home.'

I spend the morning studying in the garden, Benny snoozing at my feet, and when Alexander arrives home, his arm is still in the sling and he looks subdued. Benny hurtles forward and I trot up to him at a more sedate pace.

'Hello,' Alexander kisses me while Brandon takes the car to the garages.

'How did it go?'

'OK.'

'But you still have to rest the arm?'

He pulls a face. 'It seems like it.'

'That's too bad.'

Alexander seems thoughtful and quiet as we take a walk round the estate. I guess he must be frustrated at having to keep the arm in a sling but he's taking it stoically enough. He points out various improvements that are being made to the parkland and when we reach the house, Benny runs off to the stable yard to visit Talia.

In the boot room, I take off my Barbour and hang it on a peg before doing the same for Alexander who has his coat draped over one shoulder. While I'm sitting on the monk's bench to pull off my Hunters, I hear the key scrape in the outer lock.

'What are you doing?'

'Locking the door.' He turns the key in the inside door, effectively trapping us in the boot room. 'I need to finish off what we should have started this morning, and besides, I need cheering up . . .' His pupils darken with desire.

'Sure you do, but in here?' I laugh.

Even as I say it, a shiver of excitement ripples through me. The prospect of having sex somewhere we could be caught or overheard is intoxicating and I am incredibly turned on. I need no more encouragement and unbutton his jeans, pulling them down along with his boxers. 'Oh God.'

'Told you I needed this.' He slips his hand inside my jeans and underwear. 'You too.'

'Oh, sweet Jesus,' I moan, closing my eyes and leaning against him, utterly helpless. I hadn't realized how ready I was, and continue to be shocked every time at how amazing it feels to be touched by him, to have his fingers inside me.

Outside the back door, I hear Benny barking as if he can sense – hear – that we're in here. Alexander ignores him, turning me around and reaching under my top as I yank down my jeans and lace panties, stepping out of them neatly, nearly passing out as he continues to drive me crazy with those amazing fingers on my skin, my belly, my breasts. I brace my hands on the back of the monk's bench and press my bottom against him as he grasps my hips firmly.

With *both* hands, I register, with shock.

I twist around to see the sling hanging around his neck. He grins wickedly.

'You . . . oh God, Alexander,' I moan as he pushes up inside me, making me cry out. Oh Jesus, it feels so good it almost hurts. 'Your arm is fine,' I manage to stutter.

'Not fine, exactly, but it's on the mend,' he murmurs, in between kissing my neck, his hands everywhere again.

I cry out again. I want him deeper in me, so I push myself back on him, grinding against him and making it clear I need more. 'Shhh,' he laughs, 'someone will hear us.' Then he almost lifts me off my feet and tightens his grip on my hips.

The glass on the outer door must be steaming up, we're going at it so hard, but it's wonderful to just let go and not worry about hurting him. Actually, this probably *is* hurting him but neither of us seems to care as he drives in and out of me. My fingers cling to the wooden bench as his thrusts get faster. It's almost impossible not to make some noise, breathing hard and gasping with the effort and the sheer fucking wonderfulness of it. And the fact someone might hear – that's only making it more fun.

Alexander comes so hard the bench bangs the wall. I tighten my grip on the wood, letting my orgasm pulse through me. The moment I come to my senses – while my heart is thumping away and I'm still shaky with the aftermath – Alexander puts his arms around me, equally spent. It feels amazing to be held by him, by his two arms, and I breathe in the smell of him. *Who cares what we do at the end of term*, I think to myself. *I'm just going to enjoy the here and the now if it's as good as this.*

Then I hear voices on the other side of the door, outside the staff offices.

'Have you seen Lauren and Alexander lately?' It's Robert's voice. 'Brandon brought his lordship back from the hospital but said he disappeared off round to the stables with her.'

'Shit,' I mouth but Alexander goes, 'Shh,' then smiles.

'Well, I haven't seen Lauren since she took Benny out for a walk, so don't ask me.' Helen sounds impatient.

'He's probably giving her one in the woods some-where.' There's a chuckle. 'Again.'

'Robert! Shh!' But Helen doesn't sound that shocked, and then there's a pause, during which Alexander has to put his hand over my mouth to stop me from giggling.

'Well, we'll have to try and find them, no matter what they're up to, because I can't keep her parents waiting in the sitting room any longer.'

It takes a second or two for that bit of news to sink in, and then my stomach truly hits the floor. I look at Alexander, who seems as shocked as me. '*What?!*'

Alexander puts his hand over my mouth.

I remove it. 'My *parents?*' I mouth frantically.

He holds up his hands in a helpless gesture and, in the next moment, we're both frantically trying to get dressed.

'Did you invite them here?' I hiss in his ear while I shove my feet back into my Hunters.

'Of course not!' He looks as horrified at me and points at the back door. 'We'll go out this way and try not to look as if we've just shagged each other sense-less.' He grins, then sees my stricken face. 'Relax, Lauren! Come on, I can handle this.'

'But why didn't they tell me they were coming? They must have changed their flight. I'd have met them at the airport,' I gabble as we walk around to the front of the house.

'Hoping to give you a nice surprise, I should think,' says Alexander with amusement. He whistles. 'Benny! Here, boy!'

Hearing his master, the dog races up to us.

'If anyone asks, we've been for a walk in the woods,' he says.

'In the woods? Robert will definitely think you've been "giving me one", as he so elegantly puts it. Remind me again how I ended up having sex in the boot room?'

'You didn't take much persuasion,' he says archly.

'I know, but I didn't realize Mom and Daddy were going to turn up when we started this!'

He takes me by the shoulders. 'Look, I know you weren't expecting them to land on you like this but they have, and it isn't so bad, is it?'

'No, but I wanted time to . . . prepare them.'

'For the house or for me?'

'Both.'

He takes my hand and virtually drags me towards the house, still seeming amused by the whole situation. 'Well, it's too late now. They're going to have to face the full horror.'

So now I have around thirty seconds to compose myself and deal with the transit from post-orgasmic lover to demure and surprised daughter. Why has there been no warning?

As if he understands, Alexander squeezes my hand

as we walk through the door to find Helen on the phone. The relief in her face when she spots us is obvious.

'Oh, I'm so glad you're here. I've been trying both your mobiles but got no answer. Lauren, your parents are here.'

I try to look surprised. 'Oh my gosh. My parents? I wasn't expecting them!'

'I think they wanted to surprise you.' Helen looks as baffled as I feel. 'They're in the sitting room, having coffee.'

'Thanks,' Alexander replies. 'Sorry we've been unavailable. I didn't take my phone to the hospital.'

'I've been out for a walk,' I say, still struggling to process the fact they're actually here.

'Come on.' Alexander grips my hand tightly and we're off down the corridor. Even before we walk in, I think my parents must have heard us, because the moment we get inside, my father and mother are already on their feet.

'Lauren!'

'Hi, Mom.' My throat tightens with emotion. Oh God, I hope I'm not going to cry. It's been three months since I last saw them and the kick of happiness I experience reminds me that I have really missed them, despite all the excitement and drama here. They still represent normality and stability; my other life. My real life . . . It strikes me that I've lost my grip on what 'real' is while I've been away.

When I finally let my mother go, I manage a pretty convincing: 'Mom, this is such a surprise.'

'A nice one, I hope?' Mom looks elegant in her smart pants and jacket, her hair freshly highlighted.

'Of course . . . but I had no idea you were coming so soon – I thought you were coming next week.'

'We changed our minds and I'm glad. It is *so* wonderful to see you, honey.' My mother hugs me tightly and then Daddy puts his arm around me and murmurs, 'You've been missed.' His sweater is soft against my skin as he embraces me and the fact he's in his favourite 'vacation' outfit of chinos and a golfing sweater makes me smile. I love them both so much but they look so odd in this setting, like a modern sculpture amid the antique furniture.

'Is everything all right at home?'

My mother cuts in. 'It's a long story.'

I frown at her, intrigued by what this 'long story' might be, but my mom steamrollers on. 'Aren't you going to introduce us to your host first?'

'Oh, yes. Mom, Daddy – this is Alexander.'

Alexander steps forward, seeming completely at ease with the arrival of two strangers in his house without any warning or invitation.

He kisses my mom. 'As Lauren seems too overcome to mention it, I'm Blythe Cusack,' she says. The mischievous glint in her eye and her comment are very worrying. She is going to want to know *everything* about Alexander.

'I'm Bill.' Daddy smiles and gives Alexander the full political handshake.

'Very pleased to meet you both. Lauren's told me so much about you.'

I frown. 'Have I?'

'Uh-huh,' he says, bringing a wry smile to my father's lips, and a horrible suspicion the two of them may try to gang up on me.

My mother cuts in. 'Alexander, we must apologize for turning up at your beautiful home like this but we wanted to surprise Lauren. I hope you don't think we're being rude or pushy?'

'Not at all. Can you stay for dinner?'

'We wouldn't put you to the trouble,' Daddy says firmly.

'It's no trouble, I assure you.' Alexander is equally firm. Under other circumstances I'd be fascinated by their desperate need to outdo each other in politeness and establish position, but these are my parents – and Alexander – so I just feel disorientated.

'Well, we were going to have dinner at our hotel . . .' my father says, slightly doubtfully. 'We're booked into the Churchill. Do you know it?'

'Of course. Great choice but I won't hear of you staying at a hotel tonight. I'll have our house manager, Helen, make arrangements for you to stay in the guest suite.'

'Alexander, we can't inconvenience you like this,' says my mother.

'It's not an inconvenience, it would be a pleasure. Please excuse me; I'll be back shortly.'

With the smile he reserves for melting the hearts of elderly ladies, waiting staff and his dog, he is on his way out of the room. I'm not sure whether to be pleased or horrified at the invitation he's issued – or was it an order?

Either way, my mother plumps back down on the sofa, looking slightly shell-shocked, while Daddy waits until we're definitely alone to hold up his hands in a gesture of surrender and confusion.

'I guess we're staying here tonight then, Blythe.'

'It looks like it,' she agrees, smiling at me. 'Look, Lauren, maybe we shouldn't have sprung ourselves on you but we – wanted to surprise you.'

'You've certainly done that,' I splutter, realizing how really very pleased I am to see them.

My father takes my hand between his again. 'And how are you, honey?'

'Good . . . I'm good . . .' *Don't be too kind*, I think to myself, feeling suddenly a little emotional. His worried face reminds me of how much I am loved.

'Are you sure? We've been a little concerned about you,' he probes, and I avoid eye contact, knowing I might cry if I look at him.

'Why? I've been fine. When we spoke last week, you didn't say anything about changing your plans.'

My mother pipes up. 'Daddy had some business in London. He's been invited to the embassy by the ambassador and so we rescheduled our flights. We checked in to the hotel last night but we decided to come over and see you today.'

'How did you find Falconbury?'

My father laughs softly. 'Sweetheart, how many Falconbury Houses do you think there are in England? The cab driver had no problem getting here and besides' – he glances at my mother meaningfully – 'your mother had already Googled it and been on the Debrett's website.'

'We didn't realize Alexander came from quite such a smart family,' my mother teases. 'You kept that quiet.'

Here we go. It's started. 'It didn't seem relevant. It's not why I like him; that stuff means nothing to me.'

My parents exchange glances. 'Of course, but it would have been nice to have been told a bit more. Lauren, it has a *deer* park.'

'I know,' I acknowledge, remembering how in awe of the place I was when I first came here. 'The estate is run as a business, and they sell the venison. There are sheep too, and several farms . . .' I say, fighting a mix of irritation and guilt. I can't blame them for being shocked at Falconbury, especially as I only mentioned Alexander a few weeks ago. Perhaps it would have better to come clean a while ago but then I'd have had to share every moment of drama too and I just couldn't have stood for that. It's been painful enough, having to deal with the ups and downs of our relationship on my own, let alone having to cope with my family's worries and opinions.

'Lauren,' my father says, so gently that my skin prickles with foreboding, 'Alexander's wealth isn't what concerns us. Do you realize exactly what you've gotten yourself into here?'

I frown, unsure of exactly what he means. 'Now wait a minute, Daddy . . .'

Alexander walks back in, smiling warmly. 'There, it's all arranged.'

My mother glances at my father. 'Um . . . I don't think we have our bags.'

'That's no problem. I'll have Brandon fetch them from your hotel.'

My mother looks even more confused. 'Brandon?'

'My driver. Now, Helen will show you up to your rooms. Then we can have lunch and I can show you around the estate, if you'd like.'

Chapter Ten

While my mother and father are freshening up in the guest suite, Alexander and I get changed in his room. I open the drawer of the quaintly named 'tallboy' and pull out some fresh underwear, trying to take stock of what just happened.

'Have you recovered yet?' Alexander says with a wicked grin, emerging from the en suite, drying his chest with a towel.

'What the hell are you trying to do to me? Inviting my parents to stay over!'

He shrugs. 'It's only polite, and why are you so worried? How much had you told them about me?'

'Nothing. I only recently told them you existed at all!'

He throws the towel on the bed. 'They seem perfectly at home here. I'm sure that the American embassy and the White House are considerably grander and more intimidating than here.'

'You think? Besides, the President doesn't actually own the White House and I'm not staying there!'

Casually, he manages to pull on a fresh shirt. 'And this is the woman who went ballistic when I didn't invite her to Falconbury last year because she was worried *I* was ashamed of introducing her to *my* family.'

'That's different. I know now *why* you were so worried.'

He raises an eyebrow. 'I did warn you about my relations but yours seem perfectly reasonable.'

'It's my father's job to seem reasonable.'

He buttons up his shirt while talking to me. 'And he – and your mother – are very good at it. Look, your parents are here now and I'm going to be polite and friendly to them. They may as well get to see that this place is really not as strange as they may think, *if* they're thinking that at all. You underestimate them.'

'Do I?'

'I'm sure you do. Your father is a senator and you've told me your mother is a consummate hostess and diplomat combined. Let me have the chance to show them I'm perfectly normal and ordinary too.'

He smiles benignly, which in itself is worrying. Normal? Ordinary? Alexander? I don't trust him as far as I can throw him and since I can't even lift him off his feet, that's not saying much.

He tucks his shirt into his trousers. 'Perhaps,' he says, flaming me with a look, 'it might be helpful if you put some knickers on before we take them round the estate.'

I think I must be dreaming. Or hallucinating. Alexander is showing my parents his estate – or at least around the grounds next to the house. After lunch in the dining room, we've had a mini tour of Falconbury House, walked through the formal gardens, skirted the deer park and now he's leading the way to the stables.

I still have that strange sense of surreality, when you meet familiar people out of context. Having my parents here suddenly makes me take stock of my surroundings and of Alexander. Along with all the other students and Brits, I've become used to the way Alexander speaks, but with them here, his accent seems foreign and uber-English again – so aristocratic, for want of a better word. And the house – the sitting room is one of the cosiest rooms but there's still art on the walls, antique furniture, a grand painting above the fireplace and high ceilings with ornate plasterwork. I've grown used to it without even noticing, yet now it's like some stage set. OK, my parents are well-travelled, cultured people but they're not at a civic function or touring a stately home; it's my boyfriend's place.

Outside, the sun is out and the woods and hedgerows are thick with bluebells and wild garlic. It all seems idyllic. My mother has borrowed a pair of Emma's Hunters and looks the part of the country lady. Daddy certainly seems relaxed enough even though I know he can find it a challenge to get around unfamiliar places after he lost most of the sight in one eye in an attack a few years ago.

Even so, when we near the moat-like ha-ha that marks the edge of the park, I'm on the lookout for him but before I can even say anything, Alexander is by his side, pointing it out as a feature of the park.

'Is that a ha-ha?' my mother asks. 'There's one in an Austen novel, isn't there?'

Alexander shades his eyes with his hand. 'That's right. It was built in the eighteenth century to keep the sheep and cattle out of the garden without interrupting the view from the house.'

'So, how large is the estate in total?' she asks. I cringe inwardly. Does my mother have any idea that she sounds like an Austen character?

'Oh, I think the park is seven hundred acres, give or take, but there are some outlying farms too so maybe seven or eight thousand acres in total,' says Alexander.

My father gives a low whistle. 'Sounds like a major enterprise. How do you manage to run it all, with your studies as well?'

'I don't.' He smiles to try and take the sting out of the terseness of his reply. 'I have a very competent and understanding team of staff who take care of all the day-to-day running of the estate for now, and make a much better job of it than I ever could.'

'That's good to hear, but you must still have to make the big decisions about the estate since losing your father. We're very sorry for your loss, by the way.'

Normally, Alexander finds condolences embarrassing, but my father makes them in a simple but sincere way that I know Alexander won't object to.

'Thank you, and you're right, I have had to spend a lot of time away from Oxford over the past term and it's made things rather tricky at times, but I've had to get on with it.'

Rather tricky at times? I allow myself a little smile at his understatement.

'Lauren told us about your accident too . . .' my mother says gently.

Alexander holds up his arm. 'Oh, I'm on the mend now; in fact the doctor gave me the all-clear to take off the sling this morning, which Lauren was delighted about. No more helping me cut up my food and tie my shoelaces, eh, Lauren?'

'Lauren ties up your *shoelaces*?' My mother seems astonished.

'Not now, Mom.'

My parents exchange a 'she's changed' look.

'So, how exactly did you get injured, Alexander? Was it in the line of duty? Do you mind my asking?' My father tosses this remark into the mix as we stroll back towards the stables. My mother has linked her arm with mine and we're walking a few feet behind them, catching up on some news from home, but I can hear every word and my ears prick up. *In the line of duty?* I know I told them he'd been hurt, but not how.

I can see Alexander is uncomfortable, and he does his best to steer the conversation elsewhere. 'It's nothing. Just a scratch,' he says dismissively.

Daddy stops by a gate. 'If you don't mind me being frank, I'm guessing you're making light of it. I know my daughter and she doesn't make a fuss over nothing.

Quite the opposite in fact, and I'm pretty certain she wouldn't have stayed here if it was only a scratch.'

Alexander stops too, and we catch them up so we're all together now. The atmosphere has subtly changed and I have a sense of impending doom.

'I'm afraid I can't tell you the details of what happened, and I'm sure you understand that, but yes, I was injured on active service. Let's just say I got into a sticky situation and I ended up having my arm slashed and taking a bit of a beating. Not my ideal way to spend a few days but thanks to the medics, as you can see, I'm in one piece.'

My mother's arm tightens around mine. 'My God, it sounds awful. I'm so glad you're home safe and well.'

He smiles. 'Thank you. Me too.' Then Alexander says politely but definitely coolly, 'Now, would you like to see the stables? Do you ride, Mrs Cusack?'

'Occasionally and not well, and please call me Blythe.'

'Oh, I'm sure you ride very well if you're anything like Lauren. She's a fine horsewoman. She can stay in the saddle for hours.'

A fine horsewoman? In the saddle for hours? I've no time to be amused by Alexander's innuendo, because I'm still wondering how my parents know he was wounded in action. As we walk into the stables, I suddenly realize: my mother must have been Googling him to death, and so she not only may know something about at least part of his army career and his family history but probably his inside leg measurement and favourite colour too.

I allow myself a smile at my own jumpiness while Alexander introduces my parents to Harvey, the safe horse I use for hacking round the estate. I guess Alexander will be able to come with me as his arm recovers, if we get the chance to spend any time at Falconbury during term. Suddenly, I realize that term starts in a few days and it's only eight weeks long; then it's exams, and it's all over.

'Lauren?'

'Mmm?'

When I shake myself back into the present, everyone is looking at me. 'Alexander was telling us about the hunts they hold on the estate, honey . . .'

'Was he?' I tell myself to stop brooding. The next eight weeks are going to be filled with study, and hopefully some fun. It's pointless to waste a second thinking beyond the next day or week. Besides, I have the next twenty-four hours to get through first, with my parents clearly keen to give me the third degree on Alexander.

With a pat for Harvey, we return to the stable yard, where Talia is just bringing back Alexander's hunter after his exercise. After a quick word with her, he rejoins us.

'Shall we go back into the house for some tea? I'll ask Helen to serve it in the library because I'm sure you'd like to talk to Lauren and I need to do my physio.'

Alexander goes off to his room, and I escort my

parents back up to the guest suite. It's the same one I used to occupy while General Hunt was alive. OMG, my parents are staying under the same roof!

'What a beautiful suite this is, Lauren.' Mom seems genuinely impressed when we walk in and I don't blame her. The room is furnished with antiques and overlooks the parkland at the front of the house. 'So where's your room?' My mother's tone sounds innocent but there is nothing innocent about it.

'I'm sharing with Alexander,' I say firmly.

'I see.'

Daddy takes her arm and steers her over to the window that overlooks the deer park. 'Blythe, have you seen this view? It really is something special.'

I'm almost twenty-two; they know I slept with Todd, so why does my mom assume that things would be any different with Alexander? I guess I've sprung him on them so they've had less time to get used to the idea.

I point out a few landmarks in the distance, the church spire in the village and a folly on the hill to the west, while my mother 'oohs' and 'ahs'.

'It was very good of Alexander to ask us to stay. I can see he's a man who likes to have his own way though,' Daddy says, turning away from the window and back to me. My antennae twitch. 'Lauren, tell me to butt out if you like, and I guess you probably will, but do you know what you're doing, getting so embroiled with Alexander?'

'I'd never tell you or Mom to butt out.' I feel a little

shaky with irritation and because I hate having a confrontation with my parents when they've only just arrived.

'We're not trying to interfere but this . . .' My mother waves her hand in the general direction of the whole room.

'What?' I snap. 'You'd rather I go out with someone back home? A lawyer maybe? Someone you hand-pick for me?' I am surprised by my anger.

'Don't be silly, you know us better than that.' My father's tone hardens a little. 'And we know Todd wasn't right for you, but your mother and I are concerned about this whole situation.'

'What situation? The fact I'm with an English aristocrat who just happens to want to serve his country?' I can't believe I'm defending Alexander so fiercely. Is it because my choices are being called into question? 'There's no need to try and protect me from him. I'm not little Laurie now, and I haven't been for a very long time. Alexander is . . . He is what he is.'

'Lauren . . .' Daddy softens a little but my mother cuts in.

'When your father got the invitation from the ambassador, we decided to come over sooner than we'd first planned. Then his office received an email from a friend of yours. His assistant saw it referred to you and it seemed personal, so she flagged it up for Daddy.'

It takes me a few seconds to reply because my brain

is scrambled by this news. 'An email about *me*? From who? What friend?'

'From Imogen. Isn't she the girl you hang out with here?'

'Yes, but ... Immy sent you an email? That's impossible.'

'Your father has a copy of it. She said she'd spent a long time before deciding to send the email but she thought we should know that you might be in trouble. She said that you were living with Alexander and that he'd almost been killed on an illegal special forces op, and that we should know that he's emotionally damaged, he has issues from his mother dying and some kind of post-traumatic stress disorder that makes him prone to violent outbursts . . .'

'What?' I laugh even though I think this is the least funny situation on the planet. 'That's a pile of bullshit and there is *no way* Immy would have sent you an email like that. She wouldn't dream of it!' All the same, I am rather shocked. What on earth is going on?

My father is silent, but I can tell he's holding himself back by sheer will.

My mother stands up and touches me on the arm. 'Someone who knows you has. We're not stupid, and your father gets a lot of crank letters and emails, but this Imogen seems to know your circumstances very well. She said she was very worried about you and thought we should know the kind of man you were involved with.'

Light dawns and I feel slightly sick – and mad as hell. 'Are you sure she signed it Imogen?'

'Of course I am,' Daddy says.

'Then I know who the email was from and it wasn't Immy. Valentina must have sent it. She's a crazy bitch.' I shake off Mom's soothing hand.

'Lauren!' My mother sounds genuinely shocked at my language.

'This isn't like you, honey.' Daddy now sounds sad and that makes me even madder.

'I don't give a stuff. Valentina is a malicious monster of a woman and you shouldn't take any notice of what she says or writes.'

'Look, I don't know anything about this Imogen, or Valentina. We took it with a pinch of salt, honey, that's why we didn't say anything until we were face to face, but are you surprised we're worried?' says my father. 'Who is this Valentina anyway, and why would she do something so mean as to send that message and sign it from a friend?'

'Because she's deranged and she's Alexander's ex fiancée.'

My mother's mouth falls open. 'Alexander was engaged to this woman?'

'Until last summer he was, and now she's jealous and can't let him go.'

'Why did they split up? Did she end the engagement?'

'No, he broke it off.'

164

Their faces. Horrified comes close on my mom's side, and Daddy, who's seen just about everything in his time, looks pale and shocked. I can read what they're thinking and yes, it sounds bad. Alexander dumped his fiancée, who is so traumatized and hurt she resorts to a malicious hate campaign against me – but it *really* isn't like that. I have to let them know the truth.

'It really isn't like that,' I say out loud. 'Valentina's barking.'

'Barking?' They frown.

'Barking mad. Nuts. So nuts, it's almost funny,' I say with a forced smile, trying to make light of things. 'Hey, you mustn't take any notice of what she says. She's an old family friend of the Hunts and she was only interested in Alexander's wealth and title anyway. I know what I'm doing.'

'So is *any* of what this woman says true?' Daddy's voice is quiet and I can see he's worried and upset. 'Alexander *was* wounded in the line of duty.'

'He told you that,' I say quietly. 'He is a soldier, Daddy. What do you expect?'

'And is he in the special forces or has she made that up?'

'Yes, he is. I'm not exactly sure because obviously he can't and won't tell me, but I think it's some reconnaissance or support unit connected to the British SAS.'

'Oh my God.' My mother steadies herself with a hand on the table, which I'm not sure isn't for dramatic effect.

'He's not even supposed to be on operational service while he's doing his degree, but a colleague was injured and Alexander volunteered to take his place. Of course I don't *like* him going on these missions, but it's his life. He loves the army and there's nothing I can do about it.'

'No, I guess you can't.' Daddy says. 'And I understand he's serving his country, but this Imogen –'

'It was *not* Immy!'

'This Valentina claims that Alexander is . . . unstable, for want of a better word . . . and that he has some form of PTSD and lashes out.'

'For fuck's sake, that's not his fault!'

They both stare at me, and I could kick myself for having confirmed the content of the email.

'Lauren!'

'I'm sorry, Mom. I'm sorry and I can see you're worried about me, but Valentina has made the whole thing seem far worse than it is. I'm so happy to see you and I've missed you more than I can say, but if you've come here to save me from Alexander, then you've wasted your time.'

The last time I had a confrontation like this with my parents was when I told him that I was going to Oxford to do my master's. I guess they were worried I'd get into some kind of trouble, and now they probably think they were justified.

Daddy comes over to me and rests his hands lightly on my shoulders. He kisses my forehead and looks me straight in the eye. 'Honey, don't bite my head off because I love you – we both do, and we don't want to see you get hurt again – but I have to say my piece. Can I?'

I tense up but nod silently, almost in tears now.

'We can see that Alexander is a good-looking guy, he's wealthy and an aristocrat, but he's also older than you . . .'

'Daddy!'

'Please, let me finish. I know you're not shallow enough to let all that impress you but you're alone here in this strange world. He's also a soldier, a hero, and we can see how you might feel you owe him something and have to stay, but please, be careful . . . You're very young. You have your whole life ahead of you, your career, your life back in Washington.'

Careful? Too late for that. I push my father away. 'How can you say this? How can you underestimate me like this? Didn't you hear what I said about being here at Falconbury of my own accord, about making my own decisions and being independent? I love you, Daddy, and Mom, but this is *exactly* why I wanted to move to Oxford.'

'Lauren, we don't want to stop you enjoying yourself. Please, listen to your father.'

'I have done. I *really* have, but you can't protect me from everything; and I don't want to be protected. I want to put my hand into the fire – over and over if I need to. If I get burned, then I've made that decision myself, and I'll take the consequences, no matter how painful. Isn't that what being your own person is all about? Did Grandma and Grandpa cheer when Daddy insisted on going into politics? You know they were terrified that he'd be abused and rejected, and wouldn't be able to take the shit and the backbiting. Do you think that crazy guy would have attacked you, Daddy, if you'd been just anyone? I don't think so and I know this: if Daddy can handle the Great American Public, I think I can cope with Alexander Hunt!'

There's a silence, my pulse spikes and then my mother says, 'OK. We hear you.'

Do they? 'I know what I'm doing. Trust me.'

'It's not you we have to trust,' says Daddy.

Realizing this argument is going nowhere, I summon up all my powers of self-control and give my father a brief hug before saying firmly, 'I'm going down to the library to have some tea. I'll see you down there when you're ready.'

After tea, I give my parents a tour of the Falconbury art collection while Alexander does some work. I think he's also been on the phone to his regiment, but I'm not going to highlight that to my parents. As we admire the paintings in the ballroom and sitting room, I wouldn't say the atmosphere was relaxed, but peace has at least broken out temporarily.

I think both Mom and Daddy are surprised at how far my appreciation and knowledge of art has developed since I arrived at Oxford. My mother slips her arm through mine at one point, when we stop to look at a Gainsborough portrait of one of the earlier marchionesses of Falconbury.

'That's Alexander's father,' I say, stopping in front of a painting of a young General Hunt in his Guards uniform.

'The likeness is pretty striking,' my father says.

'You can see the resemblance, but Alexander is far better looking and not quite so austere.' My mother turns to me. 'What kind of man was General Hunt? Does the painting do him justice?'

I glance up at the stern, proud profile watching over the ballroom. 'Obviously that was painted twenty years ago, but yes, it captures his character.'

'Was he as intimidating as he looks?'

I smile. 'I'm afraid so.'

'Oh dear! Even so, Alexander and his sister must have been devastated by his loss.'

'They were. Emma seemed closer to him than Alexander, although I don't think he was ever very touchy-feely with either of them, especially after Lady Hunt was killed.'

'I read about the accident in an article online. How terrible for her husband and children.'

'I heard they were lucky to survive,' my father joins in.

Thank God they don't know the full story, that

General Hunt blamed Alexander for his wife's death and punished him for it by withdrawing his affection . . .

'I'm surprised Alexander and Emma haven't ended up in therapy,' my mother says with a sigh, still gazing up at the portrait.

'They don't do that sort of thing as much over here,' I say, almost amused. 'And they especially don't do it in the Hunt family. Shall we move on? It will be time to get ready for dinner soon.'

Dinner is served in the dining room. My parents aren't overawed by the occasion, of course, but there's a definite edge and it's with some relief that we retreat into the less formal surroundings of the sitting room for coffee.

Coffee cup in hand, my mother stands next to me at the open French windows , admiring the garden. The clouds have just parted and the moon casts a silvery sheen on the formal beds and lawns.

'It's a beautiful place,' she says.

'Alexander told me Lady Hunt had the garden redesigned when she married the general. She used to love working in it, and painting here too.'

'What a tragedy she died so young.' She snatches a quick glance at Alexander, who is showing my father a landscape of the park as it was in the eighteenth century.

'Yes, I can't imagine it.'

I hear the clink of cup on saucer behind me. Daddy faces Alexander and I have goosebumps.

'So, Alexander, do you want me to have some people look into this Valentina? I understand it was her, not Imogen, who sent that malicious email?'

I have to stop this. I start to move towards my father.

'Lauren!' My mother lays her hand on my arm.

Alexander frowns. 'I'm sorry?'

Daddy looks at me hard. 'It seems that Lauren hasn't told you. My office received an email purporting to be from a friend of Lauren's. It was signed from Imogen but Lauren tells me it probably came from a friend of yours. Valentina?'

Carefully, Alexander replaces his cup and saucer on the mantelpiece. 'She hasn't mentioned it, no. What did it say?' His voice is dangerously quiet.

'Nothing flattering, I'm afraid, if you don't mind my frankness, and while I'm sure it's a pile of hogwash, you can understand why we were a little concerned.'

'It was bullshit,' I say. 'You know what she's like.'

'But she was your fiancée?' Daddy says.

I know my father in this mood, and he won't back down. He and Alexander have a lot in common there.

Alexander presses his lips together, then replies, coolly, 'Yes, she was. Valentina and I have known each other since childhood.'

'Alexander and I can fight our own battles, Daddy.'

'Are you sure? The woman sounds like she has the

potential to cause a lot of trouble for you, not to mention Alexander.'

'We're fine,' I say, pulling away from my mother.

'Lauren's right,' says Alexander. 'If it was Valentina who sent the email, the best thing to do is ignore her.' He smiles. 'I can appreciate your concern, as Lauren's parents, but Valentina thrives on attention and drama, as I found out to my cost when we were engaged. The best course of action is to pretend you haven't even received that email – *did* you respond?'

My father shakes his head. 'No, we weren't a hundred per cent sure it wasn't a sick hoax, and we didn't want to phone Lauren in case it was a crank – God knows, there are enough of those around – but since we were coming over anyway, we decided to find out your take on it.'

'So you never see this Valentina now?' my mother asks.

'She came over quite recently to see how Alexander was after his accident,' I say.

Alexander cuts in before they can comment. 'My mother and hers were very close and my parents were her godparents so she was naturally concerned about my welfare. Now, please, don't concern yourself with her any more. I'm certain it would be a waste of time for your office to pursue what is a domestic matter any further.' He smiles. 'Would you like more coffee? What are your plans while you're over here, apart from making sure Lauren hasn't got into too much trouble?'

*

'*Naturally concerned about your welfare?*' I repeat Alexander's words later when we're sitting up in bed together.

'Isn't everyone?' he asks.

'I'm sorry that my father thought he should mention that email,' I say, feeling guilty and embarrassed that my parents may even half believe the crap in it.

'Forget it. I have.' He undoes the ribbons of my cami top. 'Like I said, Valentina hates being ignored, and that's exactly what we – and your parents – should do. Now,' he says, his voice loaded with meaning, 'let me try to think of something that will take your mind off all this.'

He pulls my cami down and cups my breasts in his hands. 'You see, two hands are *so* much better than one.'

He takes my right breast into his mouth greedily and circles his tongue around my areola, lapping at the nipple.

Closing my eyes, I allow my head to drift back, and brace my palms against the mattress.

He takes his mouth away momentarily, leaving my breast warm and tingling, and kisses me. 'Good?'

'You know it is.'

His reply is to tackle my other breast, sucking my nipple firmly, then blowing on the wet bud. The contrast of sensations, hot and cold, wet and dry, has me squirming shamelessly.

We lie down facing each other. One hand rests on my bare bottom while with the other he strokes every intimate inch of me until I can't bear it any more.

'Alexander!' I cry out, desperate to feel him inside me. He smiles, enjoying his power, and rolls over on top of me, missionary style.

'I'm not sure you should be doing this,' I say, seeing the thinly veiled wince as he positions himself on his elbows.

'I'm not sure how long I can do it for, so we'd better be quick.' Then without any warning, he slides right into me. It feels amazing. It always feels amazing with Alexander, almost like it's the first time every time. His weight over me, the look on his face as he pushes himself inside me, it's still irresistible.

'I never thought I'd miss missionary so much,' he says, his voice hoarse with lust.

'Me neither. Ohhh . . .'

The pressure of him inside me, against my G-spot, is enough to make me clutch at him, digging my nails in as I build shockingly quickly to the inevitable. The glorious throb deep inside me tells me Alexander's there too, and then he collapses with a groan that may be due as much to pain as pleasure.

Soon, we're lying side by side again, him facing me, looking like a cat that got the cream.

'Better?' he asks.

'Much better,' I say, with a smile.

'Good,' he breathes. 'I know this evening was tough.' He gives a wry smile. 'I think your parents may be worried I've led you astray.'

I give a wry smile too. I'm sure that I haven't heard

the last of their concerns, but I make light of them now. 'They definitely think that. Hey, *I* think you've led me astray.'

'I do hope so . . . but I don't think that your descent into sexual depravity is quite what they have in mind. I think your father's concerned about you getting out of your depth.'

I prop myself up on one elbow and laugh off his comment. 'I know exactly what I'm doing.'

He pauses before he replies, watching me intently. 'Do you? I'm glad one of us does . . .'

When he kisses me, deeply, his tongue darting into my mouth, I already regret my words. As for knowing what I'm doing with Alexander, or not feeling out of my depth, nothing could be further from the truth.

Chapter Eleven

Trinity Term

'Well, this is, um ... *cosy*, honey. Shall I open a window?'

I'm not sure whether to laugh or cry at my mother's reaction when I unlock the door to my room at Wyckham a few days later.

She unlatches the casement and takes a gulp of air. 'There, that's better!'

I decide on laughter because the smell of cleaning fluids and general stuffiness hasn't come as such a shock to me, having moved in here twice now after the vacations. I'm also determined to avoid any more lectures about Alexander and to keep things friendly and happy between us. They haven't said anything specific since our row, but there's an underlying current of tension.

My parents left Falconbury the morning after their visit and have been staying in Oxford since, using it as a base for touring. They also went to the event at the US Embassy and now I've arranged to meet them and show them around Wyckham before term starts officially tomorrow. Alexander has gone to Emma's school to see how she is and take her out for lunch.

My father is a thoughtful man and thinks before he speaks, but he seems even quieter than usual.

He joins my mother at the window. 'The view is quite something from here, Lauren. Are those statues above the Great Hall?' Despite his vision problems, he can make out quite a lot.

Encouraged by the genuine interest in his voice, I walk over and put my arms around my parents' shoulders. I *have* missed them a lot since New Year; and this is a visit I should have been looking forward to, not dreading because I was worrying about what they'd think about Alexander. I resolve to make it a happy one from now on.

'They're the college founders. Mrs Wyckham was a wealthy widow and she used her inheritance when her husband died to endow this college,' I say.

My mother blows out a breath. 'Wow. She looks quite a formidable woman.'

'And then some, apparently. She was a strict Puritan and she founded the college to educate the sons of poor clergy. No women were allowed, except for a laundress and she was "to be of such age and condition as to be above suspicion".'

'That seems to have changed,' my father observes, turning to me with a wry smile.

'It is a little spartan . . .' My mother surveys my room again. Compared to Falconbury, it *is* spartan, with its sloping ceilings, bare walls and 'thrift shop' style furniture.

'It's got all the essentials I need. There's a washbasin in that cupboard and almost enough room for all my luggage.'

'Where's the bathroom, honey?'

'There's a loo on this landing but the showers are in the basement.'

'Three floors down?' My mother's face is aghast and my father bursts out laughing.

'I never thought I'd see the day when my daughter was happy to go down three flights of stairs to a communal bathroom.' He shakes his head but I can see he's very amused.

'I didn't say I was happy about it, but I cope, same as all the other students.' I smile, and also keep to myself the fact that for many nights of the past two terms I've shared Alexander's room at his house in Oxford. 'That's about all there is to see in here. Most of my stuff is in the trunk room along the landing. Shall we take a look around the rest of the college?'

Outside, my parents seem impressed by the rest of college and it does look stunning this morning, with the sun shining down on the dark honey stone from a sky so blue you'd think it had been Photoshopped. The Hall is always a winner with visitors, and even I feel the impact of its formal splendour today. Even though my parents have been to embassies and palaces, Wyckham's combination of tranquillity and grandeur can't fail to make an impression.

'I can see why you love it here.' My mother puts her

arm around my back as we wander through the cloisters. I can't help but remember that this was the place I first met Alexander, or rather where I almost fell on top of him.

'Where's Alexander's room?' my father asks.

'He has a house about half a mile away on the way to the Parks.'

'A student house?'

'No, it's one of the properties owned by his family.' They make no comment but the brief silence says everything. 'Would you like to see the gardens?'

As we stroll through Wyckham's gardens, you'd think the old place had pulled out all the stops especially for my parents. The trees are thick with pink cherry blossom and rhododendrons are bursting out in delicate purple and cerise. The lawns are manicured to perfection and students lounge on the grass, reading and chatting. It's an idyllic scene and one, I realize, that I'm going to find very hard to leave behind. Again, I get the fluttering in my stomach when I remember that I have barely eight weeks left. The thought of saying my goodbyes to my coursemates and friends from my dance class, let alone Immy, brings a lump to my throat. And I don't even want to think about Alexander.

'There's a man waving to you.' My mother tugs at my arm and when I glance over to the archway that leads from the quad to the gardens, my spirits take a nosedive.

'It's Professor Rafe, my tutor.'

'He's coming over. How nice of him!'

'Isn't it?' I mutter, as Rafe strides over the lawn towards us.

The moment he reaches me, he gives my parents a charming smile and greets me warmly. Realizing I can't avoid what's coming I manage to turn my grimace into a smile of my own.

'Professor Rafe, can I introduce my parents, Bill and Blythe Cusack?'

'Mrs Cusack, Senator Cusack. How lovely to meet you.'

'Bill and Blythe will be just fine,' my father says solemnly. I can see he's amused by Rafe's 'Englishness'. If only he knew the truth . . .

'You know, you two could be sisters,' Rafe says. My skin crawls and for a horrible moment I think he might actually kiss her hand, but fortunately he seems to decide against it.

My mother rolls her eyes but I can tell she doesn't hate the compliment, however cheesy. 'Oh, not at all. I'm so glad we've met you. You know, when you emailed Lauren to say you were so impressed by her application for her master's, she never stopped talking about it. I've never seen her as happy as when she heard she'd been accepted.'

'Mom!' I'm dying of embarrassment, not just at my mother's bragging on my behalf, but at the memory of a time when I was seriously in awe of Rafe. I'm still thrilled to have been accepted and impressed by his academic prowess, but since then, his manipulative, creepy ways and attempts to hit on me have plunged him to rock bottom in my estimation.

'Yes, we are delighted to have her here at Wyckham.' I'm still cringeing when he turns to me. 'So, Lauren, I'm delighted to see you back, ready for the fray. This is the most important term, but I don't have to remind you of how critical the next few weeks are, do I, and how vital it is not to be distracted?' He directs a piercing look at me. I hold my breath, dreading that he might start warning me not to spend time with Alexander.

'No, Professor, you don't have to remind me.'

'Of course I don't. Lauren's one of our most conscientious students,' he says and my mother fails to hide her delight. I'm not sure what Daddy thinks; his diplomatic smile could be genuine pleasure at hearing me praised – or merely diplomatic.

Rafe carries on. 'Now, Blythe, Bill, you must tell me what you think of Wyckham. Has Lauren given you the grand tour yet?'

'Yes. It's very impressive,' says my father, while slanting me a look. Does he suspect that Rafe has been hinting about Alexander being a distraction? Even if he does, it's none of my parents' business how I run my life here, but . . . how I wish they weren't so uptight about Alexander.

My mother beams. 'I had no idea the gardens were so beautiful and I love the Great Hall. The main part of the college is Jacobean, isn't it?'

'Oh yes, it was built by Puritan founders. Has Lauren told you about some of our more famous alumni?' Rafe asks.

'Not yet,' I mutter.

'Oh, I must fill you in, Blythe. Would you like to see the Fellows' Garden? Visitors aren't allowed in but I can take you on a private tour, if you'd like.'

No, no, *no*! I want to scream but of course my mother is already telling Rafe she'd be delighted and when Daddy glances at me in a contented way that I rarely see from him, I know I've lost the battle. All I can hope for, while I trudge after them, is that they never bump into Rafe again. Telling them he's actually a lecherous creep would only make them worry about me even more and have my father threatening to phone the Dean or punch Rafe's lights out. They've already heard enough drama in the past few days to make them want to whisk me back to Washington on the first plane out, without me adding to their concerns.

Finally, we're back at the gateway which leads into the main gardens, and the chapel clock chimes half past the hour.

'Will you join us for lunch, Professor Rafe?'

Just in time, I squash down a squeal at my mother's invitation.

'That's extremely kind of you but sadly I have to go and meet some prospective students and try to convince them I'm not as terrifying as my reputation.'

My mother tsks. 'Oh, I'm sure no one could be terrified of you, Professor!'

'I hope not. Lauren isn't scared of me, are you?'

I throw him my widest smile, while wanting to push him in the compost heap. 'Not at all.'

'Good to meet you, Professor.' My father holds out his hand and shakes Rafe's. 'Thanks for taking care of Lauren.'

What am I, twelve? 'I don't need taking care of, Daddy,' I say coolly.

'She certainly doesn't.' So Rafe's acting like he's on my side now? I don't need his help either, but I do want to be out of here so I make an exaggerated show of checking my Cartier. 'We mustn't be late for lunch. Brown's gets very busy at the start of term and we need to be there early to get a table.'

With a brief kiss on the cheek for my mother, Rafe is gone and my favourite sight of the morning is of his back disappearing through the arch to the Front Quad.

'Well, that was interesting,' Daddy says while my mother inspects a statue of one of the college's previous wardens and I give a silent sigh of relief. 'Your professor has some unusual political views.'

'And here's me thinking you were confining your conversations to the flora.'

Daddy raises his eyebrows questioningly.

'Professor Rafe has given me the benefit of his political views before,' I explain.

'I guess it's good to be challenged,' says Daddy carefully.

'As long as the person is well informed? I'm here to study art, not politics. That's Alexander's area,' I say.

'So I heard. He has some robust views too.'

'That's why he's doing his master's here, Daddy, to develop his opinions.'

'True, and while I don't agree with some of them, he strikes me as much better informed than your professor.'

'Which is why Rafe is a History of Art academic, not the Politics tutor.'

My father laughs softly. I'm not sure exactly what he thinks of Rafe but knowing Daddy, he won't be taken in quite as easily as my mother by Rafe's charming facade.

'You've always had opinions of your own, Lauren, and they've definitely become more robust since you came over here.'

My skin prickles with tension but I'm determined to stand my ground. I also see something I rarely see in my father's expression: doubt, uncertainty. It must be hard for him to have to let me go.

'I *am* my father's daughter,' I say gently and kiss him briefly on the cheek. 'It's my duty to have robust opinions, even if you and Mom don't like them.'

'Even so, it's still my duty to stop you from getting hurt and it always will be.' He looks at me and I weigh up whether to continue the debate but we're both saved by my mother, for once, who hurries over the lawn.

'Shall we go? I'd hate to miss lunch. Your tutor seems charming, if a little eccentric; handsome too, in a geeky way. Do some of his students have a crush on him?'

'I don't!'

'Not even an intellectual one? You seemed very keen at the start of the course.' My mother assumes her innocent face.

'He's very smart but he's my tutor. I appreciate his knowledge and insight into art.'

She links her arm with mine. 'I'm sure you do.'

Lunch at Brown's was a great idea. I love the buzz and vibe, even today when the place is heaving with nervous students and anxious parents trying to pretend they're cool with leaving their sons and daughters again for their exam term. I remember when mine left me at Brown University, which now feels like a very long time ago. The contrast with the day I arrived at Wyckham and the confident way I lead my parents through the streets and alleys of the city makes me realize how much I've found my way around Oxford, both geographically and metaphorically, despite the dramas of the past two terms.

I only wish I knew my next move as clearly.

We take a mini tour of the Sheldonian Theatre after lunch, and as we gaze over the 'dreaming spires' and meadows beyond from the cupola, the whole of Oxford is spread out before me. Once again, the reality that I have one term left to enjoy it all is brought home to me. I have one term left to get a really good master's degree and soak up the experience. One term to spend with Immy and my friends, one term to spend in Alexander's bed and life. One term before everything is flung up in the air again. Right now, the future is as unknown to me as the world beyond that horizon.

A few days later, my parents have left to spend some time in London and the whirlwind of term has started in earnest. Alexander is back at the Oxford house trying to catch up on his studies and I've stayed in college to give us both a chance to concentrate on work but after spending so long staring at books and the computer screen, I really need to get out with Immy. As well as revising for exams in the Theories and Methods of the History of Art at the end of term, I have two essays to prepare for my option paper and a dissertation on my special topic – unfortunately with guidance from Professor Rafe, which means I'll have far too much contact with him for my liking.

We left it so late to get to the Turf they were about to call last orders but it's a fine, if chilly, night and they still have the heaters on in the courtyard, where a brandy slips down nicely.

'You do know we might not ever do this again.' Immy glances up at the tower of New College, lowering blackly against the inky sky.

'Oh, don't say that!'

'It's true, though. Every time we visit a pub or cafe, it will probably be the last time.'

'It isn't like you to be so down,' I say. 'How's work going?'

She curls a lip. 'Even though we've only been here a few days, I've already lost the will to live and I'm stressing about Finals. I'm not good with exams, but my father has read the riot act to me. I'm also missing sex. I know Skandar turned out to be a grade-A shit, but he was a wonderful shag. I had lunch with Freddie the other day and I almost thought of asking him for a quickie but he's going out with a Theologian from St Hilda's.'

Freddie is one of Immy's many exes and a sweet guy, but if she's thinking of rekindling that particular flame, she must be desperate. 'Best let sleeping dogs lie,' I soothe. 'Although I know what you mean about time running short and about being stressed. I keep telling myself that whatever academic pressures I'm under, it must be worse for Alexander, so I need to knuckle down. We've agreed to try and spend more time on our studies and less time with our clothes off. It's very distracting!'

187

Immy snorts. 'Like that will happen!'

'I have to try.'

She sips her brandy and says, super casual, 'How is he?'

'His arm's still very sore and he gets frustrated when he can't do what he wants with it.'

She wiggles her little finger. 'You too, I should imagine.'

'Immy!' I say in mock outrage. 'I have to admit though, the injury has had one upside. We've done some interesting improvisation . . .'

She laughs. 'But he's on the mend?'

I consider my answer for a second or two. Physically, yes. I'm not sure about other ways. 'He seems to be.'

'Have *you* made any plans yet? Are you going back to the States?'

'I don't know. I think my parents would like me to.'

She sighs. 'I'll miss you. *Promise* you'll keep in touch.'

I sip my drink before replying, knowing if Immy gets maudlin on me, I might start blubbing in the pub garden. 'Of course!' I smile. 'Hey, I bet when we're fifty, we'll all be sitting at the Wyckham Gaudy, talking about the good old days.'

She sticks out her tongue. 'Fifty? God, that's a horrific thought! We'll be all wrinkly and decrepit and sensible.'

'I hope not! Though we'll probably have kids by

then, maybe even grandkids.' Suddenly I picture myself in tweeds and a headscarf, riding behind Alexander across the estate at Falconbury . . .

'Never. I intend to stay young, free and single from now on,' Immy declares. 'What about Alexander?' she asks.

'I expect he'll look just like his father,' I say, the image of Falconbury etched on my mind.

'I didn't mean in thirty years' time. I meant what's going to happen to you two at the end of term?'

I shrug and take a long gulp of my drink.

'It's going to hurt, you know,' she says, refusing to let me off the hook. I'm not sure I like the tough love but she's right. 'Assuming of course that you do go back,' she adds.

'I have no idea what I'm going to do,' I sigh. 'I just can't think about it right now. So, what about *your* plans? Have you decided to stay on or get a job?'

'Me? Stay on here! They can't wait to get rid of me. No, I've had enough studying to last me for the rest of my life and I'm not sure I'm employable either. I'm thinking of going travelling for a year, maybe, while I decide, but I have to get through my Finals first.'

'So you're not going to be distracted by anything or anyone?' I say jokily.

'If the gorgeous Scott is taken, then no. I think I ought to pay a little attention to my work, just for a change.'

'All work and no play . . .' I say.

Immy winks. 'Well, maybe I'll squeeze in a little time for some fun. It's May Morning tomorrow, you know. I'll call for you at three-thirty.'

I've already been awake for five hours when my mother's name flashes up on the screen of my phone the next morning. Immy and I got up while it was still dark and went down to Magdalen Bridge with a bunch of friends, to hear a choir sing a madrigal from the top of Magdalen Tower. The whole town was heaving with people from the university and miles around, though I suspect that had less to do with heralding the arrival of spring and more to do with the pubs being open since dawn.

Having breakfasted on Pimm's and pain au chocolat, I'm now wondering how I'm going to keep my eyes open during Rafe's lecture on Iconography and Symbolism – but first I have to speak to Mom.

'Hello, Mom.'

'Hi, honey, how are you?'

'I'm – uh – good, thanks.'

'Are you sure? You sound a little croaky.'

I glance in the mirror, thinking it's a good job she can't *see* me too. 'Do I?'

'Yes. I hope you're not going down with strep throat. Leah Schulze's niece says it's rife at Brown. Several students have been hospitalized.'

'With strep throat? No, Mom, I sound croaky because I was in the pub at six a.m.'

'In the pub at six! I thought you were meant to be working.'

'I'm about to go off to a lecture but it's May Morning today. The bars open at dawn. It's traditional.'

'Oh . . . well, if it's a tradition, I guess it's OK. Now, I know you're incredibly *busy*,' she says with heavy irony, 'but Daddy has to go to a lunch reception in London on Saturday so I thought you and I could go shopping, or you can show me around some of the museums and colleges,' she says.

'I *am* busy, but I'd like that,' I don't hesitate to reply, realizing that I would, and calculating that I can catch up by working late on Friday evening and getting up early on Saturday morning.

'Then afterwards, when your father gets back, I thought we could go out to dinner.'

'Sounds good,' I say, cheerily.

'I hoped you'd say that because I've taken the liberty of reserving a table for four at the Churchill. I assumed you'd want Alexander to come?'

Assumed? I guess I ought to have expected this, but I still feel a prickle of unease at inviting Alexander along to a family dinner. 'I don't know . . . He's incredibly busy.'

'Well, I think it would be good to return his hospitality, and your father and I would like more time to get to know him. I'm sure he can spare a couple of hours for a meal. After all, he has to eat.'

'I'll ask him,' I say, leaving my mother sounding worryingly cheerful.

To my surprise – and I don't why I'm *so* surprised – Alexander agrees to come along. I have no idea what to expect but I can hardly say no, though I have a feeling it won't be a cosy family dinner.

After a Saturday afternoon of shopping and showing my mother around the Botanical Gardens, I shower and change at Alexander's. He looks so devastating in an inky-blue suit and open-necked white shirt that my fingers are a little unsteady while I'm fastening Granny Cusack's marcasite clip in my hair.

'Want a hand?' He appears behind me in the mirror and deftly fastens the clip into place.

'Thanks.'

His fingers linger at the nape of my neck, sending shivers of lust down my spine. 'You look gorgeous, Lauren.'

'You don't look so bad yourself.'

He trails his fingertips down my neck to the top of my dress. I bought it this afternoon with Mom, from a gorgeous little shop in North Oxford. I'd actually seen it in a magazine and couldn't believe my luck when I saw it on the rail. It's the deepest cherry colour and the fabric drapes in the most flattering way. I knew Alexander would love it. 'I thought I'd better make an effort. You like?'

'Oh, I like very much, as you very well know.' He grins, trailing a hand over my snugly clad bottom.

'Do you mind very much coming along tonight?'

'Not at all but I have the feeling I'm under scrutiny.'

I sigh. 'I'd like to say you aren't but, actually, I think we're both under scrutiny.'

'I'm not what your parents expected. I can live with that.'

'Whatever they say, please don't be offended. It's just their misguided sense that they have to protect me.'

'They should do.' Bending low, he kisses my neck. The warmth of his lips on the exposed skin of my collarbone sends shivers of arousal through me. I close my eyes when he starts to draw down the zip of my dress, kissing his way down the exposed flesh. His mouth is replaced by his hand, resting on my bra fastening.

I open my eyes. 'Alexander, I'm dressed now and we'll be late . . .'

He toys with the strap of my bra a moment longer, then sighs deeply. 'I suppose it wouldn't do to be late, but I'm warning you, I might spend dinner with an enormous hard-on.'

Heat rushes to my cheeks. 'That's an image I am not going to be able to shake off all evening.'

'Well, I can't help it. That dress shows you off so well, I don't think I can cope.'

'But I'm more covered up than I often am,' I tease.

'That's the problem: it leaves everything to the imagination and makes me want to pull up the skirt, take your knickers down and do filthy things to you. I may not last for all three courses, I might have to take you off somewhere and have my wicked way.'

'You wouldn't dare,' I laugh, knowing even as I say it, that of course he *would*.

I turn around to get a better look at the arrogant, teasing smile on his lips.

'Try me.'

Chapter Twelve

'Well, this is going to be fun.'

My mother greets us both with a huge smile and a kiss, and I get a hug from my father while Alexander is treated to the paternal handshake again. Soon, we're seated at a table by the window overlooking St Giles. The restaurant at the Churchill is like a baronial hall, decorated with university crests. While the waiter fetches our aperitifs, we check the menus but I'm finding it difficult to concentrate with Alexander's hand on my knee beneath the tablecloth.

'Gosh, there is so much choice. I don't know whether to have the sea bass or the venison for an entrée, and I really can't decide on the appetizer.'

My father closes his menu. 'I'll have the pigeon breast salad and then the fillet of beef. What about you, Lauren?'

Since I've barely been able to take a word in, I may as well order a burger and fries. Momentarily, Alexander removes his hand from my thigh to turn over the menu and I refocus on the choices. 'Hmm. Tricky when there are so many tempting choices in front of me . . . It's so hard.'

'There are indeed.' Alexander closes his menu. 'Scallops and venison for me, I think.'

He sips his aperitif and seconds later I feel his cool fingers stray to the top of my thigh-highs again.

'Have you decided yet?' My father sounds amused.

'It can't be that hard, surely?' Alexander adds.

'Oh, it is. Very hard indeed,' I say, desperate to grind myself against the chair, but forced to act the demure young lady. 'I'll have the scallops and the sea bass.'

In truth, I've just seized on anything the others have ordered, hoping it will be OK. What I really want is to drag Alexander out of the restaurant and back to the house, much as I love my parents and want to enjoy this last meal with them. That's if I can enjoy it without them interrogating Alexander – or me – on our future plans. My mother was pretty restrained during our shopping trip this afternoon, although she did ask me more about Alexander, Emma and their family circumstances. I said, truthfully, that I know very little about Lady Hunt. Our visit to the Pitt Rivers was a great idea because it kept her distracted.

My mother lays down her menu and speaks to me while Daddy and Alexander are checking out the wine list.

'I forgot to mention to you earlier that Scott's mother emailed me to say I should look him up while I'm in Oxford. Have you bumped into him while you've been here?'

'A couple of times,' I say, apprehensive of Alexander's reaction. Scott's a cousin of my ex, Todd, and my parents know the Schulzes well so naturally the grapevine has been at work.

'Have you met him, Alexander?'

He smiles politely. 'I've had that pleasure once or twice, yes.'

'Really? Well, I did half think of inviting him to join us for dinner this evening, and if I'd known you two were friends, I would have.'

It's all I can do not to heave a huge sigh of relief that my mother *didn't* ask him. I couldn't have coped with refereeing a match between Alexander and Scott in front of my parents. 'Scott's probably far too wrapped up in his work, Mom. He has so much to catch up on after all the time he spent training for the Boat Race.'

'Of course he is. He did so well and his mother sounded so proud of him when we last spoke. He managed to make it back to Washington for a couple of weeks, you know, and I saw him briefly at a charity reception. Leah persuaded him to go along as an added incentive to the guests. I think he added a considerable amount to the fundraising total just by turning up.'

'They *should* be proud, it's a huge achievement. Now, shall we order a bottle or two? What do you think about this French Meursault to start with?' Daddy cuts in.

I'm not sure if my mother is hinting that I should have made the effort to go home too, despite Alexander's injury. Then again, it's not her style to be that sneaky – or at least I didn't think it was, but with

197

Alexander on the scene, I wouldn't put anything past her. I'm sure she must think that Scott's far more suitable for me. Hell, *I* think Scott's far more suitable for me, but the way I feel now, with Alexander's palm on my thigh, I know I'm lost.

By the time we tuck into our appetizers, the conversation has moved on from Scott. On the surface, Alexander is behaving impeccably, acting the diplomat to some of my father's more probing questions – after all he is studying International Relations – and being gentlemanly and interested in my mother's questions about Falconbury.

However, under the table, he's again managed to slip his hand under my dress and is playing with the top of my thigh-highs with his fingers. It's all I can do not to squirm in my leather seat. I just thank heaven for the long cream tablecloths that reach almost to the wooden floor. The arrival of the entrées provides temporary relief because he needs both hands to eat his steak.

I return my knife and fork to the plate, with half the sea bass uneaten.

'How's your sister? Lauren tells me she has some kind of exams coming up?' my mother asks as Alexander finishes the last morsel of venison.

'She's in the middle of studying for her A levels but she has AS exams in June.'

'It must have been very difficult for her, losing your father only a few months ago.'

'Yes, she's had a rough time.'

'You both have. I'm so sorry about your mother too.'

He lays his knife and fork carefully on his plate. 'Thank you and yes, it's been . . . difficult, but we've had no choice but to muddle though somehow. Lauren's been a great help.'

I turn to him, surprised. '*Have* I?'

He smiles. 'Of course you have. I don't know what I – or Emma – would have done without you.'

That's not what he said when we had the row over Henry Favell at the end of last term, but I guess he's entitled to revise his opinion. My cheeks glow and I know that both my parents are studying me intently.

'Lauren has always been a very caring person,' my mother says, but I'm sure I detect anxiety behind the pride in her voice. I think she and Daddy are both taken aback that I've gotten in so deep with the Hunts. 'Do you mind me asking what Lady Hunt was like? Lauren told me she was quite an art connoisseur, like my daughter . . .'

Oh, I wish my mother wouldn't take this tack, but I know she only means well. At least I think she means well, or maybe she's trying to draw Alexander out.

'She loved collecting art and *objets d'art* for the house. Many of the pieces we have are there because of her. I was only a teenager when she died so I didn't appreciate them when she was alive, but I do now, of course. Lauren has taught me more about some of our own pieces than I knew myself.'

'Really?' My mother raises her eyebrows.

'I don't know that much about the period Lady Hunt was interested in . . .'

'Probably a lot more than I do,' my mother shoots back.

I blush fiercely now, uncomfortable with the spotlight full on me.

'There's obviously a lot we still don't know about Lauren,' my father says.

Alexander smiles politely. 'I'm sure there's even more I don't know yet.'

I snatch up the menu. 'I'd really love some more wine.'

Despite having finished our main courses, my father orders another bottle of white and we sip it while the talk, thankfully, turns to anything but Alexander and me. By the time the waiter has cleared the plates and asked us twice if we want to order dessert, Alexander's hand is back on my thigh and I'm finding it hard to concentrate again.

'I'll have to pass. I'm full.'

'You haven't eaten that much.' My father eyes me suspiciously.

'Mom and I had afternoon tea while we were out. I guess it dented our appetites.'

'Are you absolutely certain you couldn't fit anything else in?' Alexander says, in a peeling-off-my-dress-with-a-look voice. My cheeks burn and I wonder, with horror, if my parents have any idea quite how turned on I am and how very much I want to finish what

Alexander has so outrageously started. By the end of the meal, my muscles are aching from the tension. 'Absolutely sure. I couldn't even manage a petit four,' I say.

My mother places her napkin on the table. 'I'm not surprised; the scones at teatime were gorgeous, but maybe we should have passed on them. This meal was wonderful, but I don't think I've done it justice. However, I wouldn't mind a coffee.'

'Just coffee then, I think,' says my father to the waiter.

'Would you like it served in the lounge, sir?'

Daddy gives us a questioning glance and we all nod agreement. 'Yes, that would be good.'

We get up.

'I need the bathroom,' I say, desperate to get some relief from Alexander's relentless teasing. He removes his hand from my thigh, but I can't shake off the warmth of his palm on my skin and the painful knot of desire at my core.

He glances at his watch. 'I know this is incredibly rude of me but would you mind if I made a phone call?'

'Not at all. Bill and I will wait for you in the lounge.'

Alexander holds out his hand behind me. 'After you, Lauren.'

The moment we're out of the room, he takes my hand. 'Right, we have about ten minutes max before they get suspicious.'

'Ten minutes! I can't take that long in the bathroom.'

'Say you saw a friend from college and got talking. Or your hair came down. I don't care.' He sweeps me along a corridor away from the restaurant.

'But we can't just – do it – in here. Someone's bound to see us.'

'Where's your sense of adventure?'

Emerging from a door marked 'Staff Only' is a uniformed bell boy. Alexander hurries over to him and whispers a few words in his ear. The young guy frowns, then his face cracks into a grin. Next thing I see is Alexander handing him what appears to be a bunch of banknotes. The boy scuttles off and the corridor is deserted.

Alexander's back. 'Quick. The porter says there's a store cupboard just on the other side of that door. Apparently we won't be disturbed.'

'We can't have sex in a storeroom.'

He holds up a key. 'Yes, we can and we are. Come on.'

Even though it goes against every rational instinct, all the instincts that *really* matter kick in. My pulse flutters like crazy and I'm already hot for him by the time we've slipped into the storeroom.

There's a click as Alexander turns a key in the inside of the lock.

Actually, it's more like a large closet and the smell of furniture polish and freshly laundered table drapery fills my nostrils. The only light comes from a tiny window with opaque panes high above our heads. Fabric fibres and dust motes float in the air, suspended in a dim shaft of light. He shifts a floor-polishing machine to one side and pushes my dress up to my waist before helping me wriggle out of my panties. As he unzips his trousers, I'm giggling with nerves and the absurdity of the situation. The moment his boxers are down, I'm greeted with a truly magnificent sight.

'My God, you weren't joking.'

He points to his erection. 'I've been in agony all through that bloody meal. I told you what would happen.'

The sight of him has made me even wetter. He grasps me and lifts me bodily off the floor. I press my back against the only spare patch of wall in the closet, and the whitewashed bricks are cold against my exposed back. I throw my arms around his neck and feel his fingers digging into me as he enters me. It must be agony for his arm and I can hear him groaning and breathing with the exertion, but I don't care. I am so ready for him.

'Lauren, you will finish me off one day,' he murmurs, driving up and into me.

I'm not capable of replying, and grip his back tighter as his thrusts grow more urgent. Perspiration breaks out on my back and I squeeze him hard. Behind him, the room is dark and silent but I can see feet and legs passing the window. There are voices outside the door too, laughter, swearing. The staff . . .

The danger only adds to my excitement and I grind myself against Alexander and his breathing grows ragged and fast.

'Oh, Christ.'

With a monumental shudder and a groan, Alexander comes and to my surprise, an orgasm rocks me too, just as I picture the door opening and a group of staff and guests watching us going at it like crazy in the closet.

'That was incredible. I could do it all over again, what's more . . .'

He lets me down to my feet and I stumble as my heel twists.

'Careful.'

We're both puffing with the effort and I'm sure someone must hear us. The air is sticky and still. He holds me and kisses me so deeply I almost pass out.

'We have to get back,' he says. My face is flushed from effort and the fantasy I had of being watched while we ravished each other.

I blow a strand of hair out of my eyes. 'I must look like hell!'

He pushes the strand behind my ear. 'No, you look freshly shagged, which, believe me, is a great look. Now let's get out of here.'

I do my best to smooth down my dress while Alexander unlocks the door and opens it a crack, listening for sounds outside. We slip out and I almost run up the corridor back towards the public areas while Alexander leaves the key in the outside of the door.

I make the fastest visit ever to the bathroom, refasten my hair, slick on some lip-gloss and head for the lounge.

My mother and father are already sipping coffee when I arrive.

'Are you all right, honey? You look a little warm. I was on the verge of coming to find you in the washrooms.'

'I'm fine. I . . . um, bumped into a friend on the way out and I couldn't get away.'

'You do seem flushed,' my father says. 'Are you going down with something?'

'No, I'm fine. It's just a little hot in here.'

'Coffee?' he holds up the cafetière.

'You know, I think I'd rather have some iced water.'

My father signals to the waiter and orders a glass for me, just as Alexander saunters into the lounge.

'I must apologize. My call went on,' he says as Daddy hands him a cup.

'Cream?'

'No, thank you.'

'Everything OK?' asks my mother.

'Yes, I was returning an "urgent" call from my sister but it turns out she's absolutely fine. For once.'

'It's a difficult age, especially with you being on your own. I don't know how you manage.'

Alexander sips his coffee. 'We get by.' He picks up the cafetière and I catch my breath as he grimaces in pain.

My mother frowns. 'Is your arm giving you trouble?'

'The odd twinge. Nothing to worry about.' He lifts the cafetière higher and smiles. 'Blythe, can I pour you some more coffee?'

Ouch. I know exactly why his arm is hurting.

'Are you planning on returning to active service?' my father asks.

I cringe inwardly at the question but Alexander looks completely unruffled and cool as a cucumber. 'I'd like to at least finish my service but when and how I'm deployed is up to the powers that be.'

'I guess you need to be fully fit for your line of work.' Butter wouldn't melt in my mother's mouth.

'They won't accept anyone back to combat operations who isn't up to the job. The army paid for my master's and I at least owe it to them to serve out my term.'

'And what are your plans after that?' my father asks evenly.

I cool my clammy palms on the glass, feeling very uncomfortable with my father's line of questioning, but Alexander seems to take it in his stride.

'I'll make a decision when it comes to it. Blythe, would you like some more coffee?', he repeats.

The smile is warm, the tone polite, but edged with a finality that no one could mistake.

A few days later, I emerge from my room into the sunlight of the Parks, like a mole scenting the outside world for the first time after a long winter's hibernation. The days since the dinner have been a round of reading, research and writing essays, punctuated with a game of tennis with Immy and a few snatched hours with Alexander. We'd both agreed to sleep in our own beds to avoid any distractions, but I succumbed to a hot session with him one evening when I could hardly see straight after spending all day in the Sackler. Professor Rafe would be proud of me.

My parents are leaving later today for a last couple of nights in London before they fly home. We stroll through the Parks, where the willows are all in full leaf and ducklings swim through the ripples. Daddy is in shirtsleeves, his jacket slung over his shoulder, the sun is warm on our backs and Oxford is at its idyllic best. A thud and shouts draw our attention to the cricket match that's taking place on the field by the river.

My father turns at the sound. 'I'll never understand that game.'

'Don't even try. Alexander tried to explain it to me but I just switched off after about five minutes.'

'I don't understand most sports, or at least the time wasted on playing and watching them. Give me a garden or an *objet d'art* to appreciate any day,' my mother adds.

'Don't I know it?' my father says with a shake of his head.

'I guess we'd better have some tea in town because we'll have to leave later this afternoon. Daddy has some work to do and I guess you need to get back to your studies too.'

'I do, but I've loved seeing you.'

'So you didn't mind us surprising you by coming over?' my mother asks.

'A little notice might have been nice, but I guess I'll have to forgive you.'

We stop on a steep footbridge over the river, where the punters have to duck their heads to slide underneath.

'I'm not going to ask you your plans after this term is over. I can see it's complicated . . .' My mother smiles, presumably to soften the blow that's coming.

'But?'

'I was at a lunch meeting with Leah Schulze before we came out here. You know she's on one of my charity committees?'

'I think I heard you say so.'

'Well, Leah also chairs the board of a cultural committee, which raises funds for a major arts foundation . . .'

'I see,' I say, trying to work out where this tortuous trail is leading.

'I hope you don't think it forward of me, honey, but Leah knows you're at Oxford and asked me what your plans were after your master's.'

'And?'

'I had an email from her last night . . . and you don't have to give her a decision now, but she told me there's an opportunity coming up at the foundation, as assistant to the director. It's a lead-in post with a good salary and it would be a fantastic experience. It could lead on to bigger and better things.' She pauses, then adds, 'The director is Donna Ross.'

'*The* Donna Ross?' I say, in awe.

'Yes, honey, how many do you think there are in the arts world?'

'But she's incredible. In fact, I read a profile of her in *Time* magazine on the flight over. Oh my God, the Ross Foundation has an amazing reputation.'

My mother beams. 'Don't get too excited because it's not an absolute done deal, but Leah knows Donna *very* well and has already mentioned how well you did at Brown and how impressed Professor Rafe is with your work. I think we could make it happen.'

I can't help but feel thrilled at the thought of this. 'But would I really be up to a job like that?' I ask, uncertain.

'Don't put yourself down,' my father warns.

'I don't, but I'd hate Donna to think I'm some kind of art-world expert already. I'd have a lot to learn about working in a top organization like that.'

'She'll know that. Everyone starts out somewhere. Your father knew jack about politics and now look at him.'

'Yes, look at me.' Daddy's smile twinkles and my stomach flutters. I am so amazed by this news.

'We really don't mean to pressure you, but the summer vacation isn't that far away and apparently Donna's already looking for someone to replace her assistant, so

Daddy and I didn't think we should waste any time telling you.'

For once, I'm lost for words. Donna Ross *is* amazing and I admire her achievements. It's a brilliant opportunity; it's perfect. But there is a little nagging voice at the back of my head reminding me that it would tie me to the US, away from Alexander. I'm surprised by how much this bothers me. I'm twenty-one, too young to be tied to anyone, and I didn't come here for a romance, I remind myself fiercely.

'It . . . it sounds amazing. *Totally* amazing, but I need time to get my head around the whole thing.'

'We knew you'd need time to take the news in, but if you are interested, I think you should let Leah know in the next few weeks.' Daddy looks at me, kindly, soothingly, proudly, as if I'm still his little girl. I love him, I love my mother, and they're presenting me with a dream opportunity. *But.*

What's wrong with me?

'Thanks. I'll think about it. I really will think very hard about it.'

'I hope we haven't added to the pressure of your exams, but I had to mention it once Leah had made the suggestion. You do understand that?'

'Yes.'

Daddy stands by, almost awkwardly. It's not like him. 'We also understand that there may be other factors influencing your decision. Anyway,' he adds, cutting me off as he sees me start to speak, 'we're sure you'll come to the right decision in the end. You're a smart girl, you know what's right.' Then he softens, and takes my arm. 'I think we should be making our way back to Wyckham so we can say our goodbyes. I can't believe how soon our holiday has gone by.'

And I can't believe how fast my time at Oxford is flying by either, I think. Right now, the future yawns in front of me, a huge abyss that I can't see the bottom of, let alone the other side. We walk back to Wyckham, and with every step I'm fighting unshed tears. The talk of this new job and the reality of life after exams makes me realize Alexander and I really haven't talked at all about the summer, about our plans. I don't think I can bear to, actually, as there is no simple answer, or any answer perhaps?

Alexander has so many decisions to make himself and whatever happens, his future is rooted on this side of the Atlantic. Mine, if I take the job, lies on the other. *It's impossible*, I think bleakly.

No matter how close I thought we'd grown over the past few weeks, today has shown me that we're still oceans apart.

'Alexander, when you said come round for strawberries and cream, I didn't think you had this in mind. Ahh . . .'

I suck in my stomach as a naked Alexander applies a squirt of chilled cream to my nipple.

'Any complaints?'

'No, but . . .'

'Then just enjoy.' He pops a strawberry on top of my creamy nipple and sits back to admire his handiwork. In truth, I have no choice but to 'enjoy' because my wrists are bound with silk ribbon to each side of his bedpost. I could possibly free myself if I really wanted to. But I don't *really* want to. In the weeks since my parents left, we've been studying hard, and college has an air of claustrophobic tension that's finally got to me. We both needed a break and I have to admit Alexander has found a fantastic way for us both to unwind.

'Ohh, that's cold.'

Beneath the pyramid of cream he just squirted on my other breast, my nipple puckers.

'Not bad for a novice artist. Don't you think?' He surveys his creation with satisfaction.

'Don't give up the day job. Oh, my word . . .'

He layers the cream over my mound and nestles a strawberry in the centre. Already the cream is beginning to soften and melt around my nipples.

I test the strength of my bonds, wanting to free my hands to touch myself. I hope he will touch me soon because I can hardly bear the sensation of the cream sliding over my body. Creamy trails have started to run down my breasts, tickling my skin.

'I bet you're going to taste delicious.'

He licks the cream from my stomach before plucking a strawberry from my nipple and swallowing it. A trace of red juice lingers on his lips so he licks it off and then puts his tongue to work on me, lapping up the cream on my breasts as if it's the topping on a sundae. The insistent rasp of his tongue on my skin is sensational, and my nipples tighten until I whimper with frustrated pleasure. Soon, the other strawberry is gone from my other breast and every drop is being licked clean away.

By now, my creamy bikini bottoms are melting too, and I wriggle as the cream trickles between my thighs.

Alexander retrieves the strawberry from my mound and says, 'Open up.'

He pushes the berry into my mouth and the sweet tang of cream-soaked fruit bursts against my tongue.

'Good?'

I swallow the berry before replying. 'My mother told me never to speak with my mouth full.'

He arches an eyebrow, picks up the can again. 'Time for second helpings, I think.'

I think I know what's going to happen but I still gasp with horrified delight when he parts my thighs. There's a hiss, then the shock of chilled cream coating every part of me, outside and in.

'Oh God, Alexander.'

'Really. You don't *have* to call me God when we're in bed, Lauren.'

'You are beyond belief . . .'

'And for good measure . . .' He squirts even more cream between my intimate parts before dangling a strawberry inches from my nose, so its fragrance fills my nostrils. 'You can't have one without the other,' he says and then, without warning, pops the berry right inside me.

'This is . . .' I murmur, wriggling shamelessly while red juice trickles on to his Egyptian cotton sheets.

'Delicious, is the word I think you're looking for.'

Actually, strange, wicked, weird, wanton . . . all come close. My wrists strain against the ribbon bonds cutting into my skin. I try to lean forward so I can watch him while he kneels between my legs, parts my thighs wider and lowers his head. When he surfaces, he has the berry in his mouth and cream smeared all over his lips and nose. I giggle and wonder what his men would think if they could see him now.

He wipes the back of his hand across his face and approaches me, the strawberry held high.

'Open your mouth,' he says.

I can't quite believe where he intends to put the strawberry. 'No, you can't!'

'Yes, I can and you can't do a thing about it.'

The strawberry that was inside me is now right in front of my mouth.

'Open your mouth,' he says, more insistent now.

At first, I keep my lips clamped shut but when the berry touches them, I give in and allow him to slide it between my teeth. I have no choice but to bite it, a fruit that's ripe and sweet with my own juices. Part of me is appalled but most of me is just screaming to have him inside me. But he hasn't finished. He's back between my thighs, licking the cream from every part of me until I'm whimpering like a baby and begging him to take me. I don't think I've ever wanted him so much – I'm almost in physical pain, tugging at the ribbons until my wrists are burning.

'Please, untie me.'

'Only if you promise to do as you're told.'

'I promise,' I say, mentally crossing my fingers so it doesn't count.

He undoes the knots and frees me, leaving my wrists burning a little from the ribbon. It's heaven to finally be able to hold him and urge him inside me. I was so close after his fruit-flavoured foreplay that I come really quickly, helped by the groans of pleasure as Alexander climaxes inside me.

In these moments, the tension between us is so far from my mind I feel as if I could stay like this for ever.

Later, while we sip wine to help ease the pain of essay-writing and revision, I glance up from my laptop screen to find him watching me intently from the table where he's working.

I arch an eyebrow. 'Anything the matter? Do I have spinach on my teeth?'

'No. I've been thinking.'

'Dangerous,' I joke.

He smiles. 'True, but in this case you might enjoy the results. It's halfway through term and I'd hate the Fifth Week Blues to set in. This may be a terrible idea, and I definitely wouldn't suggest telling Rafe or my tutor, but how would you feel about getting out of Oxford next weekend?'

My interest is piqued. 'Where to? Rome?'

'Closer to home. The seaside.'

'To the ocean?'

'Yes. I thought we might drive down to Cornwall on Friday afternoon and come back early Monday morning. It's a bit of a hike for a few days but we could do some work while we're there.'

As if we will, I think, but the lure of a stay by the ocean is way too tempting to refuse. 'I shouldn't leave Oxford. I *really* shouldn't but I must admit college can be very claustrophobic and I've never seen the south-west of England, though I've heard so much about it. I have a tute just after lunch on Friday so I can't leave until then, but Monday is free.'

'Then let's do it. We can go to Tate St Ives and the Barbara Hepworth Museum if it'll make you feel less guilty.'

'I guess I'll have to live with the guilt, but I'd love to go to the Tate anyway. Should we get a hotel booked?'

'No need. I know a little place by the beach I think you'll like.'

Chapter Thirteen

OK. So I had an inkling that Alexander's little place by the beach might not be so little and when he said by the beach, he actually meant *on* the beach. At least that's how it seems now I'm standing on the deck, perched above the waves. It certainly feels as if you could leap straight off the terrace and into the sea that's crashing on to the rocks below. I can almost taste the tang of the ocean and feel the salty spray against my face.

The tiny cove is flanked by cliffs on both sides and the sand is silvery in the dying light from the setting sun. A chilly breeze tugs at my hair. Alexander senses me shiver and puts his arms around me, hugging me from behind.

'Well?'

'Wow! Just wow.'

'A little wild and chilly, perhaps, but I've always preferred the north coast.'

'It reminds me a little of the Cape where we sometimes spend summers.'

'Who's "we"?'

'My parents at one time; university friends more recently. My parents used to rent a house there. It's more austere and rugged here, but it has a wild beauty

I love. How come I never knew you had a house down here?'

He shrugs. 'It didn't occur to me to mention it. Actually, it was my mother's, but since she died, it's largely been let to long-term tenants. To be honest, I had no idea it was vacant until the temporary manager at Falconbury pointed it out to me a couple of weeks ago. He was updating me on some of the properties that are part of the estate and it occurred to me that if we wanted to visit, we'd better do it now.'

'Is it going to be empty for long?'

'The new family takes over in couple of weeks' time. Hence the smell of paint you've no doubt noticed. The place has been refurbished ready for them.'

'Does it have a name?'

'Yes, it's called Spindrift.'

'Spindrift? I like that.'

His hands slip around my waist and the sky glows with a fierce red as the final sliver of sun vanishes below the horizon, leaving only its reflection setting the clouds on fire with coral light. I feel as if I could watch the surf pound the beach for ever, but it is cold, even with Alexander's arms around me.

'Do you want to eat?' he asks. 'There should be some basics in the fridge. The letting agent said they'd stock up so we didn't have to go foraging.'

'Sounds good. It's been a long journey.'

I follow him through the French doors to the sitting room and Alexander disappears into the kitchen. I'm guessing the house is Arts and Crafts, but it seems to be decorated in contemporary 'New England' style, all pale colours and bare boards, an irony that makes me smile to myself.

'You see, I told you there would be essentials.'

Framed in the doorway, Alexander holds up a bottle of Moët and two flutes.

'I like your idea of "essentials".'

He puts the glasses on the table and twists the wire off the bottle.

'I take it you aren't that hungry, then?'

The cork pops softly. 'Starving,' he says, 'but I'm prepared to suffer while I christen the bed.'

'You mean you've never shared it with anyone before?'

'A wet Labrador, once, I seem to remember, and he drooled on my face all night and kept pushing his nose in my crotch. You're not going to do that, are you?'

'Only if you ask very, *very* nicely.'

Later, we're sitting up in bed, sipping the remains of the champagne and eating fresh fruit dipped in dark chocolate. It's hardly dinner, but it seems perfect. I feel guilty about missing my studies, but I've been working very hard the last few weeks and I try to convince myself the break may do me good. Outside, the moon is full, shining a silvery path over the sea and across the bedcover. We made love with the drapes open and the window open a notch to let in the roar of the surf pounding the sand and waves breaking on the rocks.

'This certainly gives a new meaning to the crashing waves . . .' Alexander says.

'Why do they always show that in movies? What the hell has it got to do with having sex?'

'All that relentless pounding and the waves of pleasure? I can't imagine.'

'Alexander?'

The next morning, my shout from the terrace is snatched away by the wind but Alexander has already seen me anyway, and waves back from the beach. He's wearing only shorts and trainers and has obviously been for a run, which must be a sign that he's on the mend. The sky is a glorious blue and I don't think I've ever seen the sun so bright, like a supernatural hand suddenly decided to clean the skylight and let the sunshine in. Yet I'm still cold, despite having pulled on one of Alexander's sweaters. It's definitely what Helen calls 'bracing' out here.

He starts to jog again and then is gone, but half a minute later I hear the front door open and walk into the sitting room to meet him.

Oh, wow! His torso glistens with sweat and his hair is tousled and windswept.

'You got up here fast.'

'There are some steps at the side of the kitchen.' He kisses me. 'We can explore after breakfast if you like.'

'I'd love to.'

After he's showered, he joins me in the kitchen,

where I've laid out the rest of the fresh fruit and set the coffee machine to work. Alexander fries some bacon and makes a towering sandwich while I make do with the fruit and toast. After he's polished off the sandwich, he rubs his hands together and says, 'Ready for a walk?'

'Love to.'

Access to the beach is via steep steps hacked into the cliff face and the moment we turn our faces to the sea, the cool breeze hits our faces. Apart from another couple and a dog, we have the beach to ourselves. Gulls scatter and take off in squawking flight as we run towards them. It's been a long time since I've seen him this relaxed, since *I've* felt this relaxed. It was a good idea to escape the claustrophobic intensity of Oxford for a few days and kick back.

We walk hand in hand towards the surf, past a dog paddling shoulder-deep in a rock pool, bright-green weed trailing from his coat. His owners shout at him and the corners of Alexander's mouth tilt in amusement. 'He'll stink after he's been in there,' he says.

I watch the dog race across the sand towards the couple before showering them in seawater. Alexander laughs as we skirt the line of breaking surf.

'Do you wish you'd brought Benny?' I ask, noting the pleasure light up his face.

'In some ways, yes; but I'd have had to go back to Falconbury to fetch him, and we wouldn't be able to go inside some of the galleries with him.'

'True. You mentioned sleeping with a dog the last time you were here. Was it Benny?'

'No, that was one of our previous Labs, Hamish. He was an old chap by then and it turned out to be his last summer.'

'I still miss Buddy. Maybe we should have gotten another schnauzer after him, but I was almost done at Brown and planning to go away again for my master's so there didn't seem much point.'

We seem to have drifted closer together and I find my hand in Alexander's when we stop just where the breaking waves lap the sand.

Alexander shades his eyes. 'Tide's going out.'

'Or coming in?'

'Definitely out. I know this place like the back of my hand.'

'You said you haven't been here often since your mother died. I guess there are a lot of memories here for you?'

'Yes and no. Mum used to bring us – Emma was tiny then – most school holidays. My father was away a lot, naturally, on some tour of duty or other, so she'd decamp down here with us, sometimes with another military wife and her children. It looks very different from when I last saw it.'

'I love the interiors. Are those your mother's water-colours in our room?'

'Yes. She loved Spindrift, for all kinds of reasons.'

Thick woolly clouds chase across the sky. 'It is beautiful here. I've brought my sketchpad.'

Alexander casts me a stern look. 'I sincerely hope you're not going to draw me again.'

'Why not? I might do my first nude.'

'You'll have to catch me first.'

He races off and, briefly, I play the game, chasing after him, the wet sand sucking at my feet and sapping my strength. I'm not unfit – my jogging and dancing see to that – but I soon realize that the game is purely for Alexander's benefit so I stop to catch my breath.

'Hey, I can't compete with special-forces training!'

He doubles back towards me, breathing hard. 'Neither could I at the moment.'

'But you are feeling much better? I know you've been running again, as well as doing the physio. How's the arm?'

'On the mend, though it'll be a while before it will be passed fit for the kind of duties I'd like to undertake. But . . .' He shoves his hands in his jeans. 'I need to be fit to return to my unit.'

'Do you know where they'll send you?' I ask, keeping my voice light because I don't want to get into any heavy discussions when we're having such a lovely time.

'Wherever they're deployed. Wherever I'm needed. I can't leave until I've served out my commission.'

He takes a step closer to me and my skin prickles when I recognize the wicked gleam in his eye.

'What?' I say, wary now.

He moves like lightning and although I try to dodge him, he's grabbed me and swept me up over his good shoulder. Momentarily surprise robs me of speech, but then I find my voice. 'Alexander! Put me down!'

I'm jolted up and down as he carries me towards the waves. 'Jesus, no!' I shout.

Laughing, he walks straight into ocean, with me holding on to his sweater for grim death.

'No!'

Cold spray hits my face and the waves crash against his thighs. Any moment now I'm going to be swamped. I splutter, 'Don't you dare do this, you bastard. Arghhhh!'

My scream is choked off by the shock of hitting the water. Seawater shoots up my nose and stings my eyes, and I'm pinned to the sand by the breakers. It's not deep but the surf rolls me over until I pop up, gasping for air. My knees scrape pebbles, and I scrabble to drag myself upright, bracing myself as another wave hits my back.

'You bastard!' I shout to Alexander, who's standing in the surf, soaked to the crotch, laughing at me.

He wades towards me and I think he's going to reach out his hand for me but I don't care. Before he can grab me, I lunge forward, toppling him backwards into the sea.

'Arghh!'

The momentum overbalances me but I don't care. I was soaked and frozen anyway and now I'm wading out on to the beach while Alexander struggles to his feet in the surf. It's then I have a stab of panic as I realize that he could have damaged his arm but if he had the strength to lift me up, then he must be fine. I am angry, so angry that he dumped me in an icy ocean to prove some kind of point about how strong he is.

'What the hell did you do that for?'

I stand yards away as he walks, dripping, from the sea. My teeth chatter. 'Me? What did you do it for?'

He grins. 'Because I wanted to see you wet and furious.'

'Because you wanted to prove how strong you are. I'm going back to the house.'

'Lauren, wait. I'm sorry. It was a stupid thing to do. You're right to be pissed off!'

I hold up my hand, the middle finger extended, and stomp up the beach as best I can in sodden clothes.

He soon catches me up, and stands in the doorway to the bedroom, watching while I peel my off dripping T-shirt.

'Much as I've enjoy the sight of you in a wet T-shirt, let me give you a hand.'

I glare at him. 'Don't touch me.'

He's holding his arm but I'm unmoved.

'Where's your sense of humour?'

'I lost it right about when you threw me in the freezing Atlantic.'

'It's not freezing. It's around eleven degrees this time of year. That's warm.'

I snatch up a towel and wrap it around me.

He folds his arms. 'Don't bother with the towel on my account.'

I knot the towel and sit on the bed. 'I'm cold and by the way, you're dripping all over the new carpet.'

He looks down, curses at the dark stain on the rug and walks into the bathroom, leaving the door open. He peels off his sweatshirt and tugs his jeans and boxers down in one. The sight of his butt, dripping wet and a little ruddy with the cold, does annoyingly rude things to me. After tossing his wet stuff in the bath on top of mine, he turns around. Judging by the cheeky smile on his face, he knows his impromptu striptease has had an effect on me.

Rubbing his chest with a towel, he walks into the bedroom. 'I'm sorry,' he says, assuming a contrite expression.

'No, you're not.'

He studies me for a moment. 'OK, I'm not. I just couldn't help myself and it did achieve one aim.'

'Making me furious with you?'

'Getting you naked, wet and cold. I bet your nipples are hard as little beach pebbles under that towel.'

I hold up a warning finger. 'You're not going to find out, Hunt.'

'You think?' He mimics my accent.

'I am going to throw something at you in a minute,' I say, but my resolve begins to crumble at the sight of a naked, wet Alexander advancing on me.

He stops, hands on hips, erection out like a flagpole. 'Go ahead but you know you still want me. Besides, we're trained to know that sharing body heat is the best way of combating hypothermia.'

'Bullshit.'

'No, it's true.' He reaches for the knot on my towel and pulls it open. I let it fall, even though I am still so pissed at him, I could . . . and now I'm standing toe to toe with him, my breasts pressed against his damp chest, my fingers curling around those magnificent and still damp glutes. His erection nudges my stomach and his mouth is on mine.

'You taste of salt . . .' I say when our lips part.

He licks his lips and smiles. 'Ditto.'

We climb on to the bed and his fingers are on me and inside me, caressing me until I'm ready, desperate, teetering on the edge . . . And he lies over me and enters me, all the time looking into my eyes until I close mine and let my orgasm roll through me and over me and under me. I'm a mass of pure physical feeling. I feel him come inside me and then we're both lying side by side. The window is open and it's cold again and the sea is relentless, on and on.

After my unscheduled 'dip' this morning – and the sex that followed – we spent the day in St Ives, visiting the Tate and the Barbara Hepworth Sculpture Garden. The little fishing town is a work of art in itself, with its higgledy-piggledy streets and clotted-cream sand. It's also true what they say about the 'pure' quality of the light there, and the moment we arrived I could see why it has inspired generations of artists. We had lunch overlooking the surfing beach, came home to bed and then walked over the cliffs for drinks in the next bay.

Our planned barbecue dinner on the beach sounded very romantic, but in the end we ate in the house and came down to the sands to have 'dessert' while the sun goes down.

'I'm surprised you haven't gone for the tinder and flint method, just to impress me,' I say as he sets fire to the driftwood pile in the centre of a rock circle with a match.

He shoots me a look and drops more matches into the fire, blowing on it and sheltering it with his hands until it starts to burn.

Once it's alight, I hold out my hands to the flames, grateful for the warmth of Alexander's Puffa jacket. The sleeves are rolled back, of course, but my funnel coat wasn't enough, despite the warmth from the fire.

He hasn't shaved today and the fledgling growth of stubble suits him. I never thought I'd see him toasting marshmallows; I never thought I'd see him so relaxed, so at ease with his surroundings. He hands me a skewer threaded with marshmallows – my idea.

He squats by the fire while we toast them, and the glow of the embers lights his face with a pink glow. I waft mine in the breeze to cool them and then we take the soft sweets from the skewers with mouths and fingers. The sweet smell of the marshmallows blends with the smoky tang of the driftwood fire.

Alexander pulls a hip flask from the pocket of his Barbour and offers it to me.

The alcohol leaves a hot, bittersweet trail in my mouth and throat as it slips down. 'Mmm, nice. What is it?'

He smiles. 'Armagnac. Good?'

I sip some more. 'Uh-huh.'

We sit by the fire, drinking, while we watch the waves rolling up the beach and the sun setting. By now, the combination of Armagnac, the fire and the coat have given me an inner glow to match my outer one.

'It's truly beautiful here.'

'I'm glad you like it.' He picks up the skewer and draws circles in the sand, not meeting my eyes. 'We stayed here the last summer, you know, my mother, Emma and me. When we got back to Falconbury at the end of the summer holidays, my mother had to take me back to school. I didn't want to go, of course. I had to start a new form and I'd been in a bit of trouble before the holidays . . .'

'I can't believe that.'

He gives a wry smile. 'I'd been caught smoking and drinking cider with some other boys in the attics. Lucky I wasn't expelled, but the head told me I was on "licence" and that the staff would be watching me closely. So I was pissed off at having to go back, and upset at my father going away on a tour again and, though I'd never have admitted it, I was going to miss Mum and Emma like fuck. So I . . .' He prods at the sand with the skewer, pushing it down until it almost disappears. 'I took out my frustration on Emma, teasing her until she started to cry. Mum kept telling me to shut up and then she turned round and shouted at us. That's when she lost control of the car.'

He looks at me. 'It *was* my fault; Dad was right.'

'You were thirteen. You were just a boy.'

'I was old enough to know better.' He pulls out the skewer and tosses it on the sand. 'So you see why I have mixed feelings about this place. I haven't been here since my undergraduate days. We came after Finals to have a party and before you ask, I've never brought Valentina.'

'I wasn't going to ask. I already guessed this isn't really her scene. Too cold.' I smile.

'True, but I never gave her the choice either. I don't think she even knows it exists.'

'I'm glad I do. Thanks for inviting me.'

Thinking over his 'confession', I warm my hands over the embers. 'This is like being kids again. Daddy built a fire sometimes, when he had a few days to visit us at the beach house, though it was often just me and my mother and a few schoolfriends, or maybe one or other of the grandparents. When I was at Brown, we rented a house on Rhode Island for the spring break one year.'

'We?' he asks.

'Some of the girls in my sorority house.'

He breaks into a grin that I can scent means trouble. 'That sounds . . . interesting. It is true about the hazing rituals? Is it all enforced nudity and paddling each other like in the movies?'

I roll my eyes. 'What kind of movies have you been watching?'

'One or two. We got hold of them in the sixth form at school, but I'm deeply disappointed that it's all a myth.' He pulls a sad face.

'I wouldn't say it was *all* a myth . . .'

He brightens. 'Tell me more.'

My cheeks warm at the memory of my hazing ceremony, when I ended up naked in a fountain. 'Actually, our sorority did own a paddle, but only for a joke.'

'That sounds worse than my school – or a lot better.'

I shake my head. 'Now I know you're kidding. They haven't done that kind of thing for years at British schools, and I'd have thought the enforced nakedness and harsh treatment were more in your line of work.'

He raises his eyebrows. 'You want to discuss it?'

'No, thanks.'

'That sort of thing turns you on, does it?' he jokes.

I can't tell whether it's the fire, or the brandy or the teasing that's making my cheeks burn.

He tuts. 'I think I'd better get you back to bed for a debriefing, Ms Cusack.'

'Ha, ha. If you're thinking of going into comedy, Mr Hunt, I'd advise you to think again!'

He gets up and throws sand over the fire. 'Oh, what I've got in mind for you isn't funny ... Come on – bed.'

Just before dawn, I'm woken by what I thought was a storm ... and it is, but there're no thunderclaps and lightning. This storm is raging inside Alexander's mind. I kneel on the bed next to him, ready to move in case he lashes out at me again.

'Alexander, it's OK. You're safe. You're here.'

He's quieter now, and his lips are moving but there's no sound. Gradually, his cries have subsided, but the frown etched on his brow and the silently moving lips show the pain he's going through. I keep my distance, wanting to wake him, but still wary. He opens his eyes and looks at me, but I'm not sure if he's fully conscious. My body is as taut as a wire because it was in a semi-coherent moment such as this that he grabbed my wrist so hard my eyes watered.

Slowly, I reach out and touch his bare chest. 'Alexander. Are you awake?'

'Yes,' he says groggily.

'Do you know where you are?'

'Sorry,' he says. Since most of his words are about guilt when he's having one of these terrible dreams, I'm not reassured by his answer.

'What are you sorry for?'

'Making a fool of myself again. Have I hurt you?' He

winces when he pushes himself up the pillows, but at least I know he's properly awake.

'You haven't done either,' I say, noticing the sheen of sweat on his chest. 'You got a little animated, but nothing serious'

'Christ, what was I saying?'

'Stuff.'

'What stuff?' he snaps.

Even though I feel sorry for him, I'm not going to take his brusqueness. 'Hey, don't blame the messenger. Does it matter what you said?'

'Depends. Try me.'

'The usual. That you were sorry and it was your fault. I guess being back here and our conversation about your mother can account for that.'

'Maybe. What else?'

I hesitate, knowing he won't like an honest answer. 'Other stuff.'

'To do with the op?' he asks.

'It could have been, but I have no idea what any of it meant so there's no need to interrogate me.'

Some of the things he said are etched on my mind. They remind me that beneath the polite facade and polished manners is a man who's almost been killed and has almost certainly killed others. Even if it's for some cause he – or his government – think is just, it scares me.

'Fuck.' He slides his hands through his hair. 'I'm sorry you had to hear any of it.'

There's a pause before he goes on, not looking at me again, talking to the wall. 'I've been in trouble before . . .' He laughs tersely. 'But this time was a close shave . . . Some of us were captured and obviously we were where we shouldn't have been, and the people who caught us were *not* happy bunnies.'

So he does want to tell me . . . 'Go on,' I say cautiously.

'Understandably, they wanted to know what we were doing in their neck of the woods and we didn't really want to tell them, so they decided to give us a little encouragement.' So he *was* tortured? My skin prickles at such a horrible idea, but it must be true.

'When it became clear we weren't going to tell them, they tried another tactic and . . .'

He glances up, startled by the window rattling in the wind. I wait, fighting a macabre compulsion to hear the gory details – or to shut my eyes and stick my fingers in my ears.

He gives a smile best described as sardonic. 'Let's just say they weren't setting up the video camera so we could Skype our families.'

I squash down a shudder. 'You mean they were going to *execute* you?'

He shrugs. 'Who knows? It was probably a bluff, and we all knew the score and what to expect. They wouldn't achieve much by actually going through with it, but none of us had any desire to star in our own YouTube video so we decided to get out or die trying. We created a distraction and managed to get free. We were already out of the door when I went back for . . . something I thought could be useful.'

'What? You're crazy.'

'Of course I am. It's a prerequisite. Anyway, one of the guards caught up with me and that's when I got stabbed.'

I don't dare say anything, I don't want him to stop talking. I hardly dare breathe as he continues.

'Occupational hazard. It was my choice to go on the op, and in the end we were incredibly lucky to get away with it.'

'It's a miracle you didn't lose that arm.'

'Good fortune, maybe, but not a miracle. The whole unit is trained in first aid and the medic patched me up on the ride home. But there was a delay getting me back here and the wound started to bleed out by the time we reached the UK.'

I stay silent because I don't know what to say. Maybe he's forgotten – or wants to – that he had to be rushed back into surgery.

'I know this is tough – on Emma most of all . . .' he says. 'But I can't simply up and leave tomorrow, no matter how much attention I need to give Falconbury and how much I want to give Emma peace of mind. The army allowed me leave to do my master's and I have another year to serve after that. Even if I hadn't, how can I leave the regiment when there's still so much work to do? Why should I be the one to be safe at home when others stay on?'

'After this tour, you've done your duty, more than most others will ever do, and you said Emma needs you . . .' I swallow. This is the closest we've come to talking about anything beyond exams.

'She won't believe a word I say after this time.'

'So maybe you should be honest with her from now on. She'll be eighteen at the end of the year and she can do whatever she wants.'

He pulls a face. 'Jesus, what a horrifying thought.'

'She could join the military if she wanted to.'

'Over my dead body.'

'Yes, but she *could* and you'd have to accept it.'

He snorts. 'Emma? In the army? She'd be court-martialled within five minutes.'

'And you're the yes-man who always does as he's told?' I tease.

'That's different.'

'How?'

'Lauren!'

I smile that I've finally made him bite.

'You see what we're up against?' he says, stroking my thigh. 'It hasn't been simple so far and it won't get any easier any time soon.'

'Like I say, simple is vastly overrated.'

What am I saying? What am I doing? Not only have I walked right back into his world, I've done it while waving a big banner saying: 'Bring it on, baby, complicate my life, why don't you?'

The thing is, whenever I get within a yard – a foot – of him, my brain cells seem to sizzle like a moth hitting a candle flame.

'You don't really mean that, Lauren, do you?' he teases, running a finger down my cleavage. Because I don't know how or what to reply, I close my hand around his and guide it slowly down my body, before moving my hand to the part of his anatomy that would distract him even from an earthquake. He's already hard, and he thickens in my hand, uttering a moan of pleasure that makes me just as hot in return. We are soon lost in each other, any thoughts of reality or responsibilities banished.

Chapter Fourteen

All too soon the weekend is over and I'm back in Oxford, my memories of the time at Spindrift already fading. I try to capture them, but they seem to run like sand through my fingers. The Sunday was idyllic, spent reading and drinking wine on the beach in the shelter of the rocks, with the spring sunshine warming our faces. I can understand why Lady Hunt loved to escape to the house with her children, and I can't help wondering if she was relieved rather than unhappy that her husband spent so much time apart from her.

She must have been anxious about him being in combat, as I am about Alexander, though I'd never admit it to his face, but from my experience of General Hunt, I can't imagine she got much affection when he was home. Was there ever a time when the general was like Alexander? They definitely share the stubbornness and emotional repression, which worries me ... but Alexander is also passionate and generous under the cool facade. Is that his mother's influence?

A squall of rain rattling the window snaps me out of my thoughts and when I look down at my laptop, the screensaver has cut in. I guess I should cut myself some slack if my mind has drifted. Since we arrived back on Monday afternoon, we've both been hard at work because Emma is coming over to the Oxford house for the weekend. We're going to a production of *Much Ado About Nothing* in St Nick's gardens. Emma's doing the play for A level and she also wants to check out the costumes.

I close down my laptop and decide to get some air, having been up late last night and working since six a.m., trying to put in as much time as I can to make up for my weekend away. I'm just wheeling my bike from the sheds when I get a text from Scott:

Can we meet? Need to talk. S x

I'm puzzled by the brusque tone but quickly text back.

Of course – meet me at the Head of the River pub?

I'm still wondering about the text as I cycle up the High and turn into St Aldate's. The text was . . . kind of tetchy by Scott's standards and my suspicions are confirmed when I find him already waiting in the street outside. There's a brief but unmistakeable look of tension on his face before he breaks out the usual laidback grin.

'Hi, Scott. Sorry I'm a little late.'

'It's fine. It's really busy on the terrace and I was worried I might miss you so I decided to loiter round the gate.'

He brushes my lips with his, briefly, a sort of semi-kiss that hovers between friendship and something more. I give him a mock reprimanding look but as always he just grins and ignores me.

'Everything OK?' I ask after I've chained my bike to some railings.

'Yeah. Why shouldn't it be?' His voice is light, teasing and yet . . .

'Nothing except that when you say "we need to talk", I start thinking that really means "we need to have a full-scale fight".'

'No need for a fight . . . Let's order a drink first, then we can talk properly.'

Eventually, we managed to carve a path to the bar – and out again. Scott places his pint of Guinness on the end of a trestle table, miraculously just vacated by a couple. It's a cloudy, sticky day but balmy enough to have half of the city outside, with everyone desperate to catch some air. The river next to us seems equally crowded, teeming with scullers and motorboats.

Scott drinks deep of his Guinness. I can smell the malty aroma from here and it makes my nose wrinkle. I'm glad I stuck to a Blackberry Pimm's.

'So, what do you want to talk to me about?' I say lightly.

'Nothing scary, other than I heard that our mothers have been engaging in covert negotiations . . .'

'Oh, you mean the Ross Foundation. It was very thoughtful of your mom to put my name forward.'

'Yeah, I guess, but I want you to know it wasn't my idea.' His words are as close to being curt as Scott ever gets. 'I don't want you to think I'm interfering in your life choices or trying to make you return to the States if that's not what you want.'

'Hold on. I never thought you had anything to do with the job offer and if anyone's interfering, it's my mother. Except I really don't mind the fact that Donna Ross is offering me – *may* possibly be offering me – the chance to work as her assistant. So stop feeling guilty about something that's a) not your fault, and b) nothing to be guilty about. It's an amazing opportunity.'

'Good . . . So if the job is so amazing, I assume you're going to take it?' He looks at me carefully.

'I still haven't decided.' I sigh. 'I really should, if I get offered it. It's not the kind of thing you can turn down, really.'

'Don't be rushed into anything, or feel obliged to take it because you feel you owe it to my mother.'

'Anyone would think you didn't want me to go back to Washington.'

'I don't mean that!' he cries, then, seeing my amused face, says: 'You're winding me up, as they say here.'

'Only a little. I'm grateful to have the opportunity and I promise you, I'll make my own mind up about it. You know me well enough now.'

Seeming mightily relieved that I'm not mad at his mother's 'interfering', he takes a long draught of his Guinness.

'So you haven't kept to the training regime and diet?' I tease when he wipes the froth off his top lip.

'After six months of deprivation? You have to be kidding! Of course, I *ought* to be on the wagon again and living a blameless life because I'm rowing for St Nick's in the Summer Regatta next week. St Nick's just missed out on getting Head of the River last year and the Master is under some kind of misguided impression that I can help us go one better this time.'

'I guess a blameless life with no distractions is vastly overrated . . .' I say, hoping to initiate a conversation about Lia, but not really knowing how to subtly find out if he's still 'seeing' her. *I want him to be happy, honestly,* I tell myself.

'It is.' He looks at me. 'Neither of us is without distraction, I'm guessing, particularly at the moment.'

So, is this *his* subtle way of finding out what's going on with Alexander? 'No,' I say.

'We have to make the most of being bad while we can then,' he says.

'I guess so . . .' I stop myself from twirling my hair. Not only is it a bad habit, it looks suspiciously like flirting. 'How's Lia?' I ask, deciding on the direct approach.

He looks at me hard; he *must* know I'm fishing. 'She's fine. Working hard, of course. She puts me to shame.'

'I'm sure she puts me to shame too,' I say, thinking of all the distractions over the past few months.

'She's planning on going to Africa on an elective as part of her grad medicine degree.'

'Really? That sounds . . . amazing.'

'She *is* amazing.' He grins and I suddenly feel uncomfortable and feel again that pang of something close to jealousy that I know I shouldn't feel. Scott spots my expression, leans across the table and puts his chin on his hand. 'So is Alexander still amazing?'

I laugh. 'If you mean does he constantly astonish me, then yes, I guess so.'

'Still no idea what will happen?'

'None whatsoever,' I say firmly but inside my stomach tightens. It's doing this a lot more as the end of term races towards me, the end of my year at Oxford. No matter how much I tell myself that the wobbles are exam nerves, I can't lie to myself any more. It's the reality of having to leave here; to leave Alexander.

'I love art and I want to make a proper career out of it, earn my own money and make a difference. Alexander and I really haven't talked, but he's got so many ties here,' I shrug, and bat the ball back into his court. 'What are *your* plans?'

'Careerwise? I'm not sure, but I have seen a role with one of the big international charities in East Africa. They need someone to help develop a new fresh-water project.'

'Wow, that sounds awesome,' I say, while also realizing I don't especially like the prospect of him going away so far either. He's been a wonderful friend; he makes me laugh, he's gorgeous . . . Wow, I want to cry; I'm going to miss him – I'm going to miss everyone – and I suddenly realize just *how* much. He looks at me, and I wonder if he can sense the words I dare not say, in case he – or I – take them the wrong way.

With an amused quirk of the mouth, the old Scott is back. 'You see Water Policy isn't quite the walk in the park you think.'

'No,' I agree, grateful for the light tone. 'Saving the world does make studying Klimt feel a little lightweight, although my tutor would probably have a heart attack if he heard me say that.'

He laughs. 'Well, I haven't decided yet. I may leave the Superman costume in the closet after all. Let's just say I'm considering a number of options. Maybe you could visit me in deepest Africa?'

'Yes, maybe I will.' The scratchy feeling in my throat is alarming; why don't I feel more excited by all these plans?

He sips his pint. 'So, you'll come down to support me in Eights Week?'

'I'm not sure if supporting St Nick's over Wyckham isn't tantamount to treason.'

'You could cheer quietly.'

'True, and Immy's already mentioned that Wyckham has a party at the boathouses most nights. I'm sure you'll see me there. Email me the schedule and we can meet up afterwards if you're not too exhausted.'

I register that Scott is looking great today and I notice envious eyes trained on us. 'I'm never too exhausted for you, Lauren.'

I wag my finger at him, enjoying the banter while knowing I probably shouldn't be. 'I know you're testing me, but I'm not going to bite,' I promise.

'Ah, but you'd like to though. Bite, that is,' he says, reaching across the table and laying his hand on mine.

'No.' I shake my head. 'Not even a nibble.'

'Because you know if you even have a taste, you'd want the whole thing?'

I tsk. 'You flatter yourself, Scott. My willpower's stronger than that.'

'Is Alexander's?'

'Now you know I won't go there.' I pull my hand away and seek refuge in my Pimm's, a little warm of cheek. I also glance around to see if anyone heard our conversation and might go telling tales to Alexander, as Rupert did in our first term. Then I feel annoyed with myself for worrying what people might think or say, especially an asshole like Rupert.

Scott drains his glass and points to mine. 'Another?'

'No, I have to get back. I have . . . stuff I need to do.'

'Stuff? Important stuff?' he teases.

I shoulder my bag. 'Maybe I'll bump into you later. A bunch of us are coming to the play at St Nick's.'

'I know. I'm helping out front of house.'

'Oh, really?'

'Yes. One of Lia's actor buddies roped me in to selling programmes and playing usher.'

'Cool.'

'Not really, but at least they didn't get me into a codpiece.' He does a mock shudder.

I laugh and pick up my bag, grateful that we are back on safer ground. 'See you at the play then.'

Back in my room that evening, I've just finished doing my 'stuff' when Immy calls round.

'Hi. You ready?'

'Almost.'

'Hard day working?'

'I had a drink with Scott and I worked on the laptop.'

'Not a completely tough day then. Scott definitely counts as pleasure.'

'You know that job with the Ross Foundation I mentioned?'

'Yes, I do,' she says patiently.

'I've just emailed my application and CV.'

'Well, if it's what you want . . .' Immy looks dubious, which makes me feel a little annoyed with her and annoyed with myself for feeling annoyed. Gah . . .

'Well, I haven't decided what I really want yet but I'd be nuts not to find out more.'

'OK, as long as you're sure,' says Immy lightly.

'I have to take control of something in my life. It scares me that I've even contemplated not taking this chance.'

She flops on to the bed and sighs. 'It scares me that I might commit to anything. I don't know what I want to do so I've decided I'm definitely going travelling for a year.'

'Really? Sounds awesome. Where?'

Immy picks at the cushion my grandma sent over for me. Some of the embroidery has long since unravelled now – we've both given that cushion some angst over the past year. I feel relieved; I was probably reading more into her comments than she intended. We're all tired and edgy at the moment.

'Probably Australia or New Zealand, via the Far East. I've only started thinking seriously about it in the past week or two.'

'It sounds so exciting.'

She hugs my cushion. 'I think so. I'm hoping to make more specific plans but I need to get my degree first.'

'You're still coming to the play though?'

'With all that free Pimm's and the codpieces? Wild horses wouldn't keep me away.'

Alexander picked Emma up from school earlier and has brought her straight to the play. She hugs me. She's still coltish but she looks brighter, her cheeks are pinker and she doesn't look so tired. 'How are you?' I ask discreetly while we're waiting for the play to start.

'I'm fine' she insists. 'By the way, who did you say the guy on the gate was?'

'Which guy?'

'The big blond American who handed out the programmes. He seems to know you very well.'

'Oh him; that's Scott. He's a friend from home.'

'He's lush.'

'He has a girlfriend,' I say firmly, pleased that Emma's moved on from Henry but dismayed that Scott's come on to her radar.

'Serious?'

'I – uh – don't really know.'

She holds up her programme. 'I'll have to find out then,' she announces breezily.

Fortunately for everyone, the production keeps us all quiet for the next hour or so. *Much Ado* is my favourite Shakespeare play; I never tire of the sparring between Beatrice and Benedick, nor the moment they finally fall for each other.

At the end of the play, we all pile out of the temporary stands and mill about by the outdoor bar, drinking. Emma's been allowed a Pimm's and is fizzing like champagne in a glass, probably because Scott has joined us.

Emma turns to him with a flirtatious smile. 'Would you like to introduce us to the cast, Scott? Lauren said you know most of them.'

'Sure,' says Scott. 'Would you like to come, Alex?'

'Oh, he won't want to come. He's not interested in costumes.'

'I don't expect Scott is either,' Alexander says tersely.

'True, but if the girls want to see behind the scenes, I don't mind showing them around. If it's OK with you.'

Alexander shrugs. 'Be my guest. While you're showing the *girls* behind the scenes, I have to make a phone call.'

'We'll see you in a little while then. Come on, ladies.'

He holds out his arms to Immy and me, much to Emma's annoyance, and off we trail to the backstage area. While we're chatting to the cast, Emma is flirting like crazy, but Scott's not rising to the bait. He's friendly, chatty and polite to her but that's where it ends; and there's definitely no way Emma can get the impression he's interested in her. I hope.

Later, back at the house, with Emma in bed, I lie next to Alexander, who's staring up at the ceiling.

'You seem on edge. If it's Scott and Emma, you've nothing to worry about. Scott's been the perfect gentleman and he'd never hit on a girl as young as Emma, especially not your sister.'

'I'm not worried.'

'That's good, because he is gorgeous, and Emma's only human.'

He turns to me. 'Gorgeous? Is that what you think?'

'It's what most women think.'

He snorts in derision. 'I hope you don't say that sort of thing about me.'

'Of course I don't.'

'Good,' he says.

I circle my finger around his nipples and they harden under my fingertip. 'It would be a lie,' I say. 'You're not gorgeous.'

'Thanks.'

I walk my fingers up his chest. 'You're annoying, awkward and borderline rude . . .'

'You flatterer.'

'I'm not flattering you. It's true. You're scary.'

He looks incredulous. 'No, I'm not.'

I smile. 'Would you rather be gorgeous or scary?'

'Neither. I'm just . . . normal.'

I burst out laughing. 'Alexander Hunt, normal is the last thing you are.'

I roll on top of him, delighted to feel the rigidity of his erection against my stomach. I lay my head against his chest, and the hair brushes my cheek.

His voice resonates against my ear. 'So you don't think me at all gorgeous?'

'Not one bit.' I fizz with excitement at what I do find him: Hot, dangerous, knicker-wettingly sexy . . .

My hand moves lower, circling him between my thumb and forefinger and he moans with pleasure.

'As you can see . . .'

Next morning, Alexander went for a run and has now gone up to London for some dark purpose that I assume has to do with the regiment. I've been working all morning and to be honest, will probably be working for most of the day, so I decide to blow away the cobwebs with a quick walk to the Parks and back.

Emma is also meant to be revising but she's already at the door when I walk back up the steps of Alexander's house.

'Lauren. I'm so glad you're back.'

'Really?' I joke.

'Yes.' She hugs me tightly. Too tightly.

'Are you OK?' I ask when she finally lets me breathe again.

'I think so.'

A lump settles in my throat as I follow her into the sitting room and dump my bag on the couch. 'You *think* so? What's happened?'

'Nothing really . . . except I saw Henry.'

'*What?* Here in Oxford?'

'Yes, he texted me and asked me to meet him in a cafe in the Covered Market.'

I resist the urge to scream: 'no, no, and no'. 'What did he want?' I ask nervously.

'To get back together, of course. He said he'd made a "fucking massive mistake",' she says, bracketing her fingers around the words, 'in leaving me and that things would be different from now on.'

I snort.

'Don't look at me like that. Of course I didn't believe him, and I told him where to go.'

'And did he?' I ask, crossing my fingers.

She curls her lip. 'Not to start with. He started grovelling and almost begging me to take him back. It was pathetic, really, so in the end, I walked out.'

She lifts her chin proudly but her eyes are suspiciously bright.

I hold out my arms. 'Oh, Emma, how horrible for you but I'm sure you've done the right thing. It must have hurt to face him again and tell him that.'

She hugs me again, and her tears wet my cheek. 'More than I thought it would, and maybe I shouldn't even have agreed to meet him, but I had to see him face to face. I wanted to prove to myself as much as to him that it was over and he couldn't hurt me any more.'

'So, how did he take being dumped for a change?'

She pulls a face. 'Not well. He turned a bit nasty, in fact, and I was glad we were in the cafe. He said Alexander must be bullying me into doing it, and that I ought to grow up and make my own decisions.'

'My God, he is a prize asshole. He only said that to try and stop you from telling Alexander he'd hit on you again.'

'I know.'

I mime applause. 'Well done you.'

She wipes the back of her hand over her eyes. 'So, I'm glad I saw him, even if it was horrible, because if I hadn't faced him again, and finally seen what a loser he is, I'd always have been wondering what might have been. And it was *sooo* sweet to dump him this time. I think he was only after me to hurt Alexander and get his hands on my trust fund. After the scare I had last term, I wonder if he hoped I'd get pregnant so he could marry me or something.'

I feel sad to hear her say this but also suspect it's possibly true. 'Whatever his motives, you don't need a shit like him. You're gorgeous, Emma; you're funny and feisty and . . .'

'A real pain in the bum at times?'

'That too,' I laugh. 'It seems to be a Hunt trait.'

'I know,' she says proudly, then looks right at me, with the kind of look that slices like a scalpel, the sort her brother does so well, 'But you can't resist us, can you?'

This statement is so accurate I am momentarily dumbstruck, but then I shake my head and say: 'I was thinking of getting out of here and taking you out for tea at Brown's but now I don't know.'

She laughs. 'I'll behave from now on. I promise I won't give you any more trouble. Ever.'

'I doubt it very much, and maybe I'd be a little bit disappointed if you didn't.'

Later that evening, after Alexander has taken Emma back to school, I climb into bed next to him.

'How was Emma?' he asks, knowing we went out for tea.

'OK.' I hesitate. 'She saw Henry earlier today.'

His fingers still and he stares at me. '*What?* Was he here? At the house?'

He shakes his head from side to side, as if can't believe what I've told him. 'If he comes within fifty feet of her again, I will rip off his dick and shove it down his throat.'

'You're too late. Emma has already done it – metaphorically at least.

He snaps up to sitting upright and rakes his hands through his hair. 'Good girl!' he exclaims. 'Was she upset?'

'She's a Hunt, isn't she?' I grin. 'She's proud, like her brother, and she's also smart enough to have seen through Henry now she's not feeling so vulnerable.'

He shakes his head, as if he's lost for words, then looks at me. 'I do . . . appreciate what you've done for Emma; she likes you. I know that occasionally I may seem a little overprotective of Emma . . .'

'Only a little . . .'

He glances at me. 'You're laughing at me.'

'I wouldn't dream of it. But Emma needs to make her own mistakes. We all do it.'

My look lets him know I mean he's my biggest one. Right now, he is a massive mistake because something has changed between us and I feel light-headed. He looks at me, unties the ribbons of my cami, pulls it apart and exposes me.

He kisses the side of my neck. I close my eyes, almost unable to bear the velvet softness of his mouth on my skin. He kisses his way down my throat and down my cleavage.

'Sometimes,' he murmurs, lowering his head towards my breasts, 'I wonder how I'm ever going to survive without you.'

I have no reply. I daren't utter a word. All I can do is focus on the sensation of his mouth because, no matter how hard I try, I can't help wondering exactly the same.

Chapter Fifteen

The following Saturday, there's hardly room to move, let along swing a cat, on the terrace of Wyckham boathouse. The place is jumping, literally, and I half wonder if the boathouse roof might give way. A bunch of us have dragged ourselves away from the library to come to watch Bumps, the traditional Summer Eights Week on the Thames, or the Isis as I must remember to call it, unless I want to attract curled lips. Immy's gone to the bar while I keep a prime viewing spot overlooking the river and slipway.

My mind ought to be on drinking in the sights and sounds, but instead it's on my exams, all the work I still have to cover, and on Alexander, and on the job, and my future . . .

'More Pimm's?'

Immy has picked her way through the forest of boat club boozers to reach me. Pimm's sloshes over my fingers when she hands me the plastic glass but, hey, I already seem to have half of the boat club bar over me, so why worry?

'Eww, cucumber. I hate that in Pimm's.' She fishes out a chunk with her fingers and flicks it over the wall.

'What the hell?'

At this bellow, Immy peers over the edge of the terrace to the crowds below. 'Oh dear, what a shame!'

When I glance over, I see Rupert glaring up at us and wiping a piece of cucumber from his face.

'Sorry, Rupes, I had no idea you were down there!' Immy calls cheerily.

Rupert, holding a bottle in his hand, shakes his head and resumes his conversation with a bunch of guys with bikes.

'Good shot,' I say.

She grins. 'It really was an accident but I suppose you could call it a happy one. Is Alexander still not speaking to him?'

'Other than essentials, no, which is why we haven't been to college dinner much. The de Courceys have been to Falconbury on business but I'm sure they don't know about the video.'

'Rupert's lucky Alexander hasn't ripped his balls off.'

'That's assuming he had any.'

Immy laughs. 'So, where's Alexander now?'

'Working, but he'll be here later. Rowing's not really his thing but he wanted to come.'

We hear a swell of noise from further down the river.

'Oh, Wyckham must be on their way!'

There's a rush for the edge of the terrace and a buzz of excitement. Further down the towpath, I see dozens of bikes racing along and the cheering grows louder. People start shouting behind me as the first boat comes into view round the bend in the river.

'Come on Wyckham!'

The screams are deafening now as the boats chase each other in single file, trying to bump the boat in front without being caught up by the boat behind. It's crazy, really, and there have already been a couple of collisions, one of which ended up with some of the crew in the river. In a minute, it's all over. Someone shouts down my ear and spills his pint on me.

'Look at that! Wyckham have bumped Merton!'

I dab at the lager stain on my dress. 'And this is a good thing?'

'It's awesome. It means that with one more race Wyckham could be Head of the River.'

'Wow.'

'Try and sound more enthusiastic, it matters. They'll burn a boat tonight if we do it.'

'What? Literally?'

'Yes. The Warden has given permission for the boat club to set fire to an old one in the Garden Quad, *if* we do it.'

'But aren't St Nick's up for the title as well?'

'Oh yes, but we can beat them, even if they do have Scott.'

A while later the victorious Wyckham crew arrive at the bank, where their girlfriends are waiting by each college's pontoon with a plastic pint glass of Pimm's for each rower. I find myself alone on the terrace. The crowds have thinned a little but it's still busy up here. Immy had gone to the ladies, but I can see her below on the slipway in front of the boathouse, chatting to the hunky rower she spent the night with at the Boat Race party. There's no way I'm going to interrupt that. Alexander has arrived, but headed to the bar by way of the gents about half an hour ago, and while I don't need to be joined at the hip to him, I'm beginning to wonder what could have kept him. Maybe he's had a phone call from work – or from Emma.

It's then that I spot him outside the boathouse doors below me. He's talking to Rupert, although 'talking' isn't an accurate way to describe their conversation. Judging by his animated gestures, Alexander is laying into Rupert, who has his hands in his pockets and is leaning back defensively. He's obviously trying to act cool, but I can tell he's intimidated. I catch a snatch of sneering laughter. Their voices are raised a little and then Rupert jabs a finger at Alexander's chest before turning his back and stalking off. He glances up briefly, but I don't think he sees me. I hope not; I don't want any crap from him today.

'Hey!' I stumble a little as beer splashes on my dress. It's Professor Rafe.

'Lauren, I am sorry. Here, let me help.'

He pulls out a handkerchief.

'It's OK!' I say through gritted teeth but he's already dabbing at the wet patch on the front of my dress.

'No, really. I'm fine.' I scoot backwards, knocking the arm of the boat club president, who curses.

'I am so sorry. I can have your dress cleaned.'

'No. Really. Please don't bother.' The idea of Rafe having my laundry done makes me want to barf.

'That's very generous of you, Lauren, but I am most awfully sorry.'

He's acting way over the top, even for Rafe, and when I get a strong whiff of beer fumes, it occurs to me that he's a bit tipsy.

'I didn't know you liked rowing,' he says.

'Likewise,' I say coolly, trying to keep some distance between us.

'Of course, I do. I'm here representing the SCR. It's a momentous day for Wyckham. We haven't been Head of the River since 1850, you know.'

I resist the urge to ask him if he remembers the event. 'You don't say?'

He treats me to another beery leer. 'Can I get you a drink? I hate to see a woman empty-handed.'

'No, thanks. Alexander went to get one . . .' I search the terrace, frantically hoping he'll materialize and save me from a prolonged conversation with Rafe. Having to see him in tutorials is bad enough without meeting him at social events. Particularly when I suspect he's had more than a few drinks.

'You seem a little concerned? Has he been gone a while?'

'Not really. I guess there are still long queues at the bar.'

'Not as long as earlier. Maybe someone distracted him.'

'It happens.' I shrug. My skin prickles as it often does when I'm in close proximity to Rafe, and I swear he's just moved a few inches closer.

'I wouldn't get distracted from you, Lauren.' My flesh really crawls now. He *must* be drunk to hit on me like this in a public place. 'You're pretty difficult to ignore.' He leans even closer and I would take a step back but the wall of the terrace is stopping me.

'I'm not sure that's a good thing . . .'

'Oh, believe me, it *is* and I'm glad you've snatched a few hours' respite from essays and revision. In fact, I've been waiting to catch you in a more . . . informal moment. I'm not sure if you've had a chance to think about what you might do after your master's. I'm sure you have many ideas.'

'A few,' I lie.

'Well, I don't want to sound pushy, but I've a friend at another college who's been looking for a research assistant. We'd be able to carry on working in close proximity.'

A friend? Yeah . . . 'Oh . . . That's very considerate of you, Professor Rafe, and I'm flattered your "friend" thought of me.'

'No need to be flattered. I think you'd be an excellent

person for the job and we could continue to develop our relationship while you developed your research skills.'

'The thing is, I've already got a position lined up.' This is more than a slight exaggeration but I don't care.

'How interesting. What is it, if you don't mind me asking?' He looks disappointed. My heart is *breaking*.

'I'd *love* to reveal all, but it's all hush-hush at the moment. I'm meeting the director after exams.'

'What a shame you can't reveal all, but I hope he appreciates your talents.'

'She.'

'It's a woman, is it?' He smirks. 'In the US or Europe?'

'I can't say another thing about it.'

'Hmm. If it's in our former colony, Alexander's not going to be too pleased.'

I plaster a glacial smile on my face, determined to reveal nothing. Damn it, why have I allowed him to provoke me? And *former colony*? What planet is the guy on?

He holds up his hands. 'I'm sorry. I shouldn't have probed into your business.'

Ugh, probe is not a choice of word I care to dwell on. 'Professor Rafe, nothing's absolutely final yet so I don't want to tell *anyone* my plans, until they're definite. You understand.'

He taps the side of his nose. 'Your secret is safe with me.'

'It's not a secret so much . . .'

'I won't say a word but, please, do let me know the outcome. I'm always interested in the destinations of my students and if the job doesn't work out, or you have second thoughts about my offer, do please tell me.'

Never, I think, not if it was the last job on earth and I was living on mud. I'm kicking myself for having been goaded into revealing even as much as I have about my plans.

'You know, Lauren, even if you do leave, I'd like us to keep in touch. You never know when our paths may cross again.' He says this in a low voice, and every word sounds like an innuendo. He's definitely drunk.

'Professor Rafe, you must excuse me . . .'

'What for? You haven't done anything yet, Lauren.'

Damn. I think I may have to actually shove him out of the way but just as I'm about to do it, I spot a familiar face over his shoulder.

'Scott!'

I don't care that I've probably deafened Rafe, because Scott's face breaks into a grin when he sees me.

Rafe's brow furrows – I'm not sure whether that's because he's half cut or annoyed – but he turns round and I take my chance and step away.

Scott hugs me. Never have I been so glad to see his towering frame.

'Professor Rafe, this is Scott Schulze. He was in the Boat Race. Scott, this is my tutor.'

'Your tutor? Pleased to meet you.' He holds out a hand and takes Rafe's in what I think is an iron grip, judging by Rafe's pained expression.

'Yes, very. Well done on the race victory . . .' Rafe mumbles, pushing his specs back up his nose. 'I must go. I'm meeting a friend but I just wanted to have a word with Lauren. Have a nice evening.'

'You too.' I give him a little finger wave.

He scuttles off and I heave a sigh of relief. 'Great timing. Thanks.'

'Purely a coincidence.' As Scott kisses me, his damp hair brushes my cheek. 'Sorry, I came straight out of the shower at the St Nick's boathouse. Was he giving you trouble?'

'Nothing I couldn't handle, but you probably saved me from having to push him over the wall. He's such a creep.'

'You should report him.'

'This close to exams? I don't think so. I've only got a couple more tutes and then I'll never have to be near him again. I really don't know what some of the students see in him.'

'I guess he must hold a dishevelled geeky appeal for some of them.'

'His appeal bypassed me some time ago.'

'Hey, Schulze, you loser!' A couple of the Wyckham Boat Club guys notice who I'm talking to and I stand by while Scott takes the brunt of a few good-natured jibes. Rafe is a sleazeball but the encounter has reminded me that people are going to keep asking me what I'm doing after the end of term. I have no idea what Alexander's up to. I hope he's not thrown Rupert in the river.

The Wyckham boys slap Scott on the back and with a middle-finger gesture at them, which I understand is a sign of respect, he turns back to me.

'Sorry if my fellow Wyckhamites are giving you a hard time,' I joke.

'I can live with it.'

'On this occasion, even I'm glad your team lost.'

'I'll forgive you. Having a good time?'

'Yes, apart from getting drenched with booze and hit on by Rafe, it's been fun.'

'Is Alex around?'

'Somewhere. He went to the bar a while ago. Where's Lia? I thought she'd be here, as she's a rower.'

'She's working on her dissertation, just like I should be,' he grimaces.

I can't resist. 'You mean she wasn't at St Nick's boathouse to hand out the commiseratory Pimm's when you got back?'

'No . . . I had to make do with some hairy guy from our Second Eight. Hey, you could have been there with the drink or would that have counted as sleeping with the enemy?' He raises a questioning – and very cheeky – eyebrow before he adds, 'Metaphorically speaking, of course.'

I wag my finger at him. 'One of these days, you are going to get me into a lot of trouble, Scott Schulze.'

'And why's that then?' Alexander shoulders his way to us, a bottle of beer in one hand and a glass of white in the other.

'Scott was suggesting I – uh – switch my allegiance to St Nick's.'

'Was he now?'

'Without success, so you needn't worry,' says Scott amiably.

'I'm not worried.' Alexander's voice is smooth as silk. 'Here's your drink. I'm sorry I was so long. Emma called me and then there was quite a queue for the bar. She sounded good. Excited over some trip to Paris during the summer holidays and demanding my consent to go.'

'You said yes?'

'Of course! I'm not an ogre.'

To his credit, Scott doesn't so much as crack a smile at this but I can guess he's itching to make a smart comment. Instead, he contents himself with saying, 'I'd better go. I promised to have a few drinks with the crew and then I need to get an early night so I can get an even earlier morning tomorrow. It's non-stop work for me from now on. Nice to see you again, Alex.'

Scott leans down and kisses me, briefly, on the cheek, and the air is so thick with testosterone you could spoon it up.

'See you around,' Scott says, obviously for my benefit.

'If you can spare a moment from your studies,' says Alexander icily.

Scott just smiles. 'Oh, I think I could fit Lauren in.'

'But I'm not sure she could do the same for you.'

The verbal rally flies over my head. Once upon a time, I might have fantasized about having two gorgeous guys competing for my attention and I guess by some twisted logic I ought to be gratified, but it just complicates life.

'Enough, you two!' I explode with a laugh, trying to lighten the mood. 'Do I have any say in this conversation, boys?'

Scott smiles. 'Just our little joke, huh, Alexander?'

'Perhaps Lauren isn't finding it so funny?' Alexander shoots back.

I smile, although like Queen Victoria, I'm not amused. 'Hey, I was thinking that you two should get a room. Excuse me, I need the bathroom.'

'If you want company, you know where I am,' Scott says, ignoring Alexander.

I reciprocate by ignoring them both and heading for the ladies' room at the back of the boathouse. Jesus, I feel like some furry woodland creature being fought over by a grizzly and a cougar.

We got back well before midnight, after going on to a bar but deciding not to bother with a club. Exams start for all of us next week and the partying has to go on hold until they're over.

Now Alexander's dead to the world and the first hint of dawn is creeping into our bedroom when I get up to use the bathroom. That is, to use the bathroom as my office because I couldn't resist hiding in there to check the email that, beeping as it arrived, woke me from sleep. As I'd guessed, it was from Donna Ross's PA, setting up a meeting for the week after the end of term. I slide back into bed next to Alexander, trying not to wake him, and watched the dawn steal into the room.

So. This is it. In just over twelve hours' time, I'll be turning over the page of my first exam essay. To remind me, my subfusc outfit hangs on the back of the closet door, like a cast-off from the Hogwarts costume department. The evening sun shines through the window of my room on to the bizarre combination of black skirt (DKNY), white fitted shirt (J Crew) and graduate gown (Shepherd and Woodward).

The black velvet ribbon I have to wear as a tie lies on the desk top ready for morning, alongside a fresh pack of black thigh-highs. I tried the whole shebang on earlier before texting a photo to my parents and deciding the gown needed ironing. God knows why I'm bothered that it looks right. It seems crazy to be dressed in so many layers on what promises to be the hottest day of the year so far.

Fortunately, I only have three short exams left to do on the methodology I've been studying over the past two terms. I already handed in my option essays and my dissertation.

For encouragement, I look again at the good-luck

cards ranged along the window ledge and tacked to my pinboard. There's one from my parents, of course, from Alexander, Immy and lots of friends from Wyckham and my course. There's also one from Emma, hand-drawn, and a funny card from Letty with a faux Latin message that translates as: 'Don't let the buggers get you down.' They all bring a smile to my lips, for various reasons, even the postcard from Professor Rafe with its creepy Schiele nude and German message: '*Viel Gluck* from Egon!'

I've set my mobile alarm to 'repeat' and Immy and I also made a pact to knock on each other's doors to make sure at least one of us is awake. Alexander has already had one exam and has two more tomorrow; we've agreed to spend the time apart so we can get some work done without further distraction. We've tried studying together but it really didn't work. So we're meeting him in the Lodge at nine a.m. and walking to the Exam Schools together.

Although I try to ease the tension in my neck as I have a quick last look through my notes, the knot in my stomach is back again. Poor Immy, she has eight three-hour papers and was in tears earlier, convinced she's going to fail. Three years of work depend on the next week or so and I know she wants to do well, for her parents' sake as much as her own.

I wonder if I should call round with a nightcap? Or is she trying to get some rest? Should I? One drink won't hurt, will it?

Just as I open the closet to retrieve the bottle of Chase I salted away, I hear her knock at my door.

Vodka in my hand, I open the door and almost drop the bottle.

'*Buona sera*, Lauren. You really didn't have to go to so much trouble for me.'

Chapter Sixteen

FOR a second or two, I consider slamming the door in Valentina's face but I suspect she'd love that and I also have a compulsion to know why she's here, the same one that makes you watch car crashes on YouTube.

'What do you want?' I snap.

She smiles. 'What do I want? I think the question is what do *you* want, Lauren? However, I am happy to discuss my proposition out here if you don't mind everyone hearing.'

There's only Immy up here and an English Lit student who's invariably stoned, I could tell her, but the heaviness in the pit of my stomach makes me less keen to throw her out.

'What proposition?'

'Really, I think it would be better if you invited me inside. Trust me.'

'You have one minute.'

I open the door and stand back. She walks in, her heels click-clacking on the boards. She glances around the room, wrinkling her nose like the place has a bad smell – but the only nasty scent in here right now is Valentina's toxic jealousy.

'Forgive me if I don't offer you a drink after all,' I say, after I've shut the door.

She looks at the bottle I left on the cupboard like it's belladonna. 'Don't worry, I don't drink vodka unless it's Russian and served with caviar.'

'Hey, I'm fresh out of caviar. Now what do you want? I assume you're not here to wish me good luck with my exams.'

'Actually, darling, I do wish you luck. You and Alexander. I understand he has more papers tomorrow?'

I snort in a very undignified manner, but my show of bravado still doesn't stop me from feeling like someone switched on a blender inside my stomach.

'Yes, we both have exams first thing so would you mind getting to the point of your visit so I can throw you out of my room?'

She looks at me pityingly and tsks. 'That is so rude, Lauren, when I've flown all this way to make you a proposition.'

'If it's about Alexander, he made his feelings perfectly plain to you at Falconbury. How is the ankle by the way?'

'I heal very quickly, and it is about Alexander so I would not be so eager to dismiss me.'

'I dismissed you the first time I saw you.' I make as if to move to the door. 'Now, I think your minute is up. Shall I show you back to the Lodge or can you find your own way?'

Her smile dies and her eyes glitter. 'I have tried to be

nice and polite but I can see that I need to be direct. That should suit you, Lauren, being an American. I have come to tell you that I have decided that it is time I shared with the world the treatment I have suffered at the hands of Alexander Hunt.'

I'm stunned momentarily. 'Excuse me, what exactly do you mean?' I ask icily.

She assumes a hangdog look. 'I have tried to be brave and rise above it all, but people should know how damaged Alexander really is. Other women should be warned about his moods and his shameful treatment of me, the way he used me for sex . . .'

'And you think anybody's going to be interested in that?' I bluff, knowing how much the British press seem to lap up any kind of scandal, especially about Oxbridge.

She pouts. 'Yes, I do. I can spice up the details – there's plenty you don't know about, darling – and I shall enjoy sharing that story in the newspapers and posting the sex video to the online gossip sites. The best thing is that Alexander will absolutely hate it, and so will your lovely parents, of course,' she says, clearly very pleased with herself.

The blender in my gut speeds up to max. I am so angry I'm finding it hard to respond. 'You wouldn't dare, and you'd do as much, if not more, damage to your own reputation. Now get out and leave the two of us in peace.'

She studies her talons and smirks. 'Oh, it won't do

me any harm. I'm doing it for your own good too, Lauren. Everyone – including your parents and future employers – will see how you've been duped by Alexander; although sometimes I wonder if it is the other way around, that *you* have lured him into *your* bed. Rupert has told me that you would do anything to be Lady Falconbury and that you even invited your parents over so they could check the place out. While Alexander was at his most vulnerable, you inveigled your way into his life again. I also know what you did to Emma . . .'

'Right, that's it; I'm not going to listen to any more of this. You can get out of here now or I'll call the porters and have you thrown out. I don't know how you got past them anyway.' I step towards the door. 'Go on, out!'

She sighs. 'As you wish, but remember that you were the one who threw away the chance to save Alexander and your family from the embarrassment.'

I pause and instantly regret it, as she's clearly spotted a chink in my armour.

'And remember that I came here to offer you an alternative to having the story of my life and yours all over the gossip magazines.'

'Go on,' I snap impatiently.

She tsks again. 'I would be a little more polite, considering I'm offering you a way out. You see, Lauren, I have a friend – yes, a real friend – who at this moment is just waiting for me to call him and say that I want my story to go live in several magazines – and I don't mean Forbes. And of course the sex clip will probably go viral once it hits the blog sites.'

I still somehow manage to stand my ground. 'If you dare, I'll sue and Alexander will sue.'

'I'm sure you may do that but it will be too late.'

'No decent magazine or site will run the story. They'd be bankrupted.'

'Perhaps not here in the UK or America, but in Italy? In Europe? They are not so squeamish . . . and as you know, nothing can prevent it going viral. I don't think Alexander would enjoy his face – and his dick – being splashed all over the newspapers and the internet. It would certainly ruin his career.' She laughs. 'I also don't think your father and mother will relish your name being associated with such a sordid story either. That kind of mud sticks and can damage a reputation . . . Of course, all of this can stop now if you do just one little thing.'

I know I shouldn't be listening to any more of this but I can't help myself. I have to know the worst. 'How? What exactly is this one "little" thing'? I didn't think even you would stoop to blackmail,' I sneer, more frightened than I want to let on.

She pouts. 'Blackmail is a very serious accusation and I'm hurt you'd even think I would be capable of that. What I'm merely suggesting, as compensation for my hurt and distress, is that you tell Alexander – tonight – that you're ending things. It's the end of term soon, anyway; things would be over between you then, so it's only a matter of "when" not "if".'

'If things are ending between us anyway, why would you go to all this trouble to split us up?'

'Call it a little gentle nudge in the right direction, just in case you were thinking of continuing the relationship beyond the term. Call it my insurance policy in case you have really managed to work your way under Alexander's skin.'

I am furious, but for once the vile creature I thought could never hurt me again seems to have come up with a plan that genuinely could harm us. I have only to picture my parents' faces if they saw any of this, never mind the grief it would give Alexander, to know I can't dismiss her threats out of hand.

She shrugs. 'OK. I should have known you would be stubborn, but think of this when you open up the papers in a few days and see yourself on some sordid gossip site. When your mother is crying down the phone and your father is a laughing stock. Think of how you sneered at me when Alexander is forced to resign from the army.' She laughs. 'Think of that when he blames you for destroying his career which, of course, is the only thing he truly loves.'

I don't speak. I don't even move because the room seems to be spinning around. I grab the edge of the bookcase for support and wonder if I'm about to wake up from some horrible nightmare.

Yet it's not a nightmare, though just as surreal. Valentina has turned up here and threatened to release that sex video and sell her trashy tale to a sleazy Eurotrash tabloid. Even if my name is linked to the story, even if my father is mentioned, I could live with that – but the consequences for Alexander could be disastrous. Valentina's right about that much: it's very unlikely he could keep his job after such a public humiliation.

'You . . . are . . . a . . . witch.' My voice is a whisper.

She looks at me, one eyebrow arched in enquiry. 'Second thoughts?'

'Don't do this,' I say, my mind racing ahead of my mouth, my thoughts swirling like a leaf caught in a whirlpool. 'You can't do this . . .'

'I can and I will unless you leave Alexander.'

'I . . . I . . . How do I know you won't publish this "story" and release the video anyway?'

'You don't, but why would I? If you do as I say and leave him, that's all I want. Maybe then he will understand how little you truly care for him and start to realize who really does.'

'You are quite something, Valentina,' I say bitterly, thinking I've never loathed anyone so much in my life.

She smiles. 'It felt so easy to dismiss me, didn't it? Well, you were wrong. So,' she pauses, 'I take it that you will do as I ask?'

I hesitate, hating what I'm about to do but feeling it's my only option. I nod.

She smiles. 'Then I will tell my friend not to release

the story, but I will need evidence you aren't seeing Alexander. Starting with you telling him you won't be meeting him to walk to your exams tomorrow.'

I frown. 'How can you possibly know that?' I ask.

'I have my ways,' she says, clearly delighted with my confusion. 'You will tell him you don't want to see him and you're going alone.'

'But . . .'

'Nothing. I will know what happens.'

'You mean Rupert will be watching? I see, he's still your little helper and spy, is he? Or is there more to it than that?'

Valentina pulls a face. 'Think what you like but, yes, of course, Rupert is happy to help anyone who has Alexander's best interests at heart.'

'Best interests! My God, the pair of you, you are loathsome.'

'I like to think so. Now I must go. I am meeting a friend for dinner at Le Manoir. Have a nice evening.' And she turns on her heel with a flick of her long hair.

I watch her go, feeling like I've been poked with a cattle prod. I hear her heels tip-tapping down the stair-case, I see her sweep out of the archway and around the quad before disappearing into the Lodge.

I sit on my bed and take a few deep calming breaths. I sit there for quite some time, thinking. Desperately trying to come up with an alternative. After a while, with a heavy heart, I pick up the phone and dial.

*

The next morning, Immy's face is almost as white as her blouse. She fans herself with the black cap we're supposed to wear en route to exams. 'And this thing makes me look like an extra from the *The Tudors*. Subfusc is the most ridiculous thing ever invented.'

'Uh-huh.' I keep checking my phone, half expecting a message from The Witch or her Henchman, saying: 'We're watching you.' And half hoping for a message somehow telling me everything is going to be all right.

'Aren't we supposed to be meeting Alexander in the Lodge?'

I shove my phone to the bottom of my bag. 'He decided to make his own way.'

'Really? You look awful by the way. You OK?'

'I didn't get much sleep,' I shrug. There is no way on earth I am going to burden Immy with my problems today, or any day until she's finished her Finals.

'Me neither, but at least you only have three exams. I've got eight.' And with that, Immy's colour goes again so I grab her arm and manage a weak smile.

'Come on, let's go.'

In the end, we made it to the Exam Schools with a couple of minutes to spare. I don't mind arriving at the last minute as it gives me less chance of bumping into Alexander. Now I scan the crowds anxiously, looking for him, but fortunately there's no sign. Rupert, however, is there, staring at me from the other side of the queue like I'm the spawn of the Devil but, mercifully, keeping his distance. Suddenly, we're called in and everyone surges forward to the stairs. Immy mouths 'Good luck,' but then one of her geographer friends grabs her arm and sweeps her off.

I'm one of the last to ascend the stairs that lead to my exam room. Every step feels leaden and I can't help glancing behind me for a last glimpse of the street, half expecting Valentina to be there, but of course there are only the stragglers running towards the doors.

By twelve-thirty, the first two of my short papers are over, and I wander out of the Exam Schools with a throbbing head and a tongue as dry as Death Valley. While Immy has only finished her first paper by now, I'm more than halfway through. I should be filled with a sense of relief, but instead I feel numb. I have no idea how I did; I answered all the questions; I think I did OK . . . and considering the circumstances, OK is pretty amazing.

It's still so damn stuffy, the thick white clouds holding in the afternoon heat. I take off my gown and stuff the ribbon that was around my neck into my bag. I've already taken off the thigh-highs in the bathroom at the Exam Schools but I long to go back to college and put on my cut-offs and tank top. Except I can't go back, not yet, because I know that if I go now, he'll be waiting outside my room. I don't want to see him until this evening, when he will have finished his exams.

I trudge back along the street, dreading what I will see when I pull out my phone, the missed calls and the texts.

Out of the blue, I hear someone calling my name, a female voice. 'Lauren!' I can't see who it is but then suddenly there's a hand on my arm.

'Letty!' I exclaim, shocked, but oh so pleased to see her.

She looks at me, her expression almost as pained as mine, and her eyes dark. 'I've been looking out for you everywhere. We really need to talk.'

I look at her, not knowing how to take her sudden arrival. 'I'm so sorry, Letty, I didn't know where to turn. I shouldn't have thrown this on you.' Seeing how agitated her usually composed face is, I regret my cry for help last night. What on earth did I think it would achieve?

'You've done exactly the right thing,' she reassures me, seeing my uncertainty. 'I'm shocked, I must admit – I never thought my son would sink to such depths, and I wish he hadn't – but I'm glad you called me. Come on, let's go somewhere quiet. I've lots to tell you. It's sorted.'

'Are you sure you're not angry with me for phoning you? I really didn't want to do it.'

'Sad, shocked, yes; angry – no. Rupert needed a wake-up call and as for Valentina, that witch has been asking for a kick up her bony arse for far too long.'

She ushers me to a table in the furthest, darkest corner of a cafe in the Covered Market. 'Now listen. Before I tell you this, you must promise faithfully *never* to tell Alexander what I'm going to tell you . . .' Letty begins.

'Because this is the only way I could stop Valentina from spreading her poisonous lies.'

My fingers aren't quite steady as I replace my cup in its saucer, my mind conjuring up all sorts of bizarre scenarios. 'Of course I promise, but what have you done?'

'*I* haven't done anything,' Letty says grimly. 'But Valentina has and it's something she never wants Alexander to know, or he really will never speak to her again, although I assume he'll probably cut off all contact with her anyway if you tell him what she's been planning. Have you told him?'

'Not yet, but he's going to want to know why I've ignored his calls last night and this morning, and it's going to be very hard to keep this from him. He's very tenacious,' I say.

She rolls her eyes. 'It's up to you what you say to him but whatever you do, don't tell him what I'm about to tell you now. Promise,' she adds urgently.

'I promise,' I say again, more confused than ever.

I have to strain my ears as Letty whispers. 'I've never told a soul this, not even my husband, but I know my brother and Valentina were together at Falconbury.'

'What? The general and Valentina were together, as in together having *sex*?' I ask, incredulous.

'Shhh. Yes. It was while she was staying at Falconbury. Alexander was due to come back from a tour. I heard them at it in her bedroom.'

282

'Are you sure?'

'Believe me, the sounds that were coming out of that room were unmistakeable. Valentina was wailing like a banshee and as for Frederick, well, the things he was saying would make your hair curl.'

I pull a face, horrified at the idea of Valentina screwing Alexander's father and guessing how Alexander would feel if he knew. It seems incredible, but thinking back to the way Valentina flirted with him at the hunt weekend and how attentive he was to her, I can just about believe there was more to it. The banshee wailing also rings true, having heard Valentina myself on the sex video.

'Frederick had no choice but to admit it when I confronted him,' Letty goes on. 'He said it was all a dreadful mistake, had never happened before and begged me not to tell Alexander.'

She sighs and shrugs. 'I don't believe it was a one-off but I do think he ended it once he'd been caught out. I spent many a sleepless night wondering whether to tell Alexander despite my promise to Frederick, but he swore he'd never do it again. I had an inkling things weren't great between Valentina and Alexander by that stage and a few weeks later they split up so I saw no point in upsetting the poor boy unnecessarily.'

'Alexander would have gone bananas if he'd known.'

'Of course he would. It would have completely annihilated any shred of respect he had left for his father and caused even more trouble in the family, for both

Alexander and Emma. After Frederick's death, of course, there was no way I was going to drop a bombshell like that.'

'So I assume you threatened Valentina with telling Alexander about this now? What did she say?'

'For once in her life, she was speechless, then she gave me a tirade of abuse before finally agreeing to keep her mouth shut and go back to Italy.'

'So you think she will keep quiet?'

'I think so. I was banking on the fact that she's deluded enough to think she still has a chance with Alexander . . . particularly if she thinks you're going to be off the scene at the end of term.'

She looks hard at me but I sip my tea and avoid responding. I'm very grateful – more than grateful – to Letty for her help but I'm not going to be drawn any further than that.

'Then let that work to our advantage,' I say. 'Let her go on thinking that he'd have her back, as you say, so that she carries on living in fear of you telling Alexander about her and his father.'

Letty smiles weakly. 'I'm sorry about Rupert's involvement in this – and that's one reason I've decided to step in, because I feel responsible in a way.'

'You're not, and I am *so* relieved that you've helped us. I'm only sorry it came to this.'

'Well, perhaps not, but I tell you this: if my son gets into any kind of trouble after this, his father and I have warned him he's on his own. We've bailed him out far too many times already and it will do him good to clean up his own mess next time.'

The late-afternoon sun still burns into me as I wait, in shorts and T-shirt now, outside the Exam Schools.

Alexander emerges from the doors. I see a couple of our friends waiting; someone shakes his hand, someone hugs him, but he's on a mission and I know what it is. He strides into the road and jogs down the street, his gown flying behind him. He looks devastating in his army uniform and cap and my heart starts beating faster. I've decided I have to tell him at least the first half of the dramas I've been facing.

Clasping my hands together nervously, I step out from the shade of a storefront and he spots me. His expression changes from determination to relief, then anger. He quickens his pace and rushes up to me.

'Lauren, where the hell have you been? I've been worried sick. I've been calling you last night, this morning and lunchtime between exams. What's going on?'

I take a deep breath. Ever since I met Letty, I've been trying to think of how much I can tell him. He needs an explanation for my terse call last night to say I couldn't meet him today. Besides, now we're out of the woods he ought to know the new depths to which Valentina has sunk. 'I'm sorry I worried you but I've had something to sort out, and you have to promise not to explode when I tell you. You're not going to like it,' I say grimly.

His jaw tightens, his lips press together and I can tell how very hard he's working to keep his feelings in check when he hears what Valentina's been up to. Around us, in the back lane to college, people are laughing and shrieking, corks are popping and party poppers are flying into the air.

'Why didn't you call me last night, as soon as she'd left?' he asks, running his hands through his hair. 'I'd have thought of something.'

'I didn't want to ruin your exams. God knows, you've had enough on your plate this term and I wanted you to have a good night's sleep, and also ... Valentina said the only contact I could have was to break things off. I didn't want to do anything that would make her carry out her ridiculous threats.'

'So you agreed to dump me?' He raises an eyebrow.

'Of course not! Well, yes,' I say, crestfallen, then pull back my shoulders defiantly. 'If I want to dump you, I'll do it on my own terms.' His face darkens and at first I think I've offended him again, before I realize there is another emotion smouldering behind those inscrutable eyes, one that makes me feel quite light-headed. 'And I also wanted to try and deal with things myself and not bother you.'

He seems very surprised. 'You should still have told me. But how have you stopped her?'

'You know I had tea with Letty not long ago. I thought she might be able to exert some influence on

Valentina through Rupert. So I hope you don't mind – I called her for help last night.'

He shakes his head and kisses me briefly, but with such promise, on the lips. 'I can't keep up, so come on, what's Aunt Letty done to them both?'

'Read Rupert the riot act and threatened to cut him out of her will and the family business, told him he's hurt her more than anyone has ever hurt her before.'

'Well, that would have hurt him, being threatened with the prospect of actually having to earn his own living. And Valentina?'

'I have no idea,' I lie. 'I guess she put so much pressure on Rupert, maybe he was able to stop her. I really don't know. She wouldn't tell me,' I end lamely.

He blows out a breath. 'Letty may stop Rupert but I doubt if she – or he – will have any influence over Valentina.'

'You might be surprised . . .'

'Well, anyway, don't worry. Why don't you leave her to me,' he says grimly.

'Alexander, there's no need. I'm sure she'll think better of doing something so stupid, because she'd ruin her reputation too,' I say, worried that Alexander wading in may counteract Letty's strategy. Maybe Valentina will be so furious she'll decide to tell Alexander about her affair with his father after all. 'I'm concerned that you calling her might tip her over the edge and make things worse,' I add.

He frowns and his tone hardens. 'I'm not going to sit back and do nothing after what she's threatened. Now, go back to college.'

Seeing my questioning look, he says firmly, 'I'll see you tomorrow. Go home, and don't lose any sleep over Valentina.' He kisses me to silence my protests.

I wish it was that easy to follow his advice, but it's pointless arguing with him any further in this mood and so I have no choice but to let him go while I hurry back to college.

Once I've gathered my thoughts and tried to put on a brave face, I call on Immy. Despite having exams tomorrow, she's too wrung out to do much revision so I agree to go for a quick drink with her before she gets an early night. There's no way I'm bothering her with my problems and sure enough, despite Alexander's reassurance – and Letty's intervention – I can't completely relax.

The next morning I try to focus on my studies; perhaps it's a blessing in disguise that my toughest paper is coming up and I can't afford to let Valentina distract me. Even so, I can't stop myself from constantly checking my phone, desperate for word from Alexander. What will he do? He is so angry; I hope he doesn't do anything stupid.

It's late afternoon before he finally calls and asks me to meet him at the house. I have to force myself not to run all the way to his place. He must have been looking out for me because as soon as I arrive, he opens the door:

'You don't need to worry about Valentina. I've seen her.'

My pulse rate rises. 'And? What did you do?'

'Something that will make sure she won't be a problem,' he says with a grim smile.

'How can you be so sure? Alexander, what have you done?' I ask, all sorts of scenarios racing through my mind.

'I haven't *done* anything.'

'Then what have you said to her?'

'All you need to know is that she won't ever share that video or her so-called story. So now,' he says, touching my cheek, 'you can relax.'

I let out a sigh, hoping that whatever he's done or said to Valentina is a 'belt and braces' job. He can't know the truth, or he'd surely be devastated as well as angry. 'I don't think I'll ever relax again, not after the past term.'

'I could think of a way of helping you.'

'Really?'

I close my eyes, hoping that – between Letty and Alexander – Valentina is gone for good, and try to surrender myself to the delicious feeling of him teasing my panties down my thighs.

Chapter Seventeen

Standing by the bus stop in the High, I pretend to check my phone as if I hadn't a care in the world. Actually, I shouldn't have a care because my exams are over, yet I've spent the past few days half expecting to see Alexander and Valentina trending on Twitter – and being pissed at myself for thinking such crazy thoughts. As for Alexander, he's remained infuriatingly silent about his encounter with Valentina and my few hints have met with a change of subject. So I've had no choice but to accept his explanation for now. Letty has also sent me a couple of encouraging texts, telling me to 'brace up' and stop worrying.

Today, I'm absolutely determined not to think about her because it's Immy's final exam and a bunch of us are back at the Examination Schools, waiting for her to come out. Trashing was banned years ago, but that doesn't stop people trying to celebrate in the street or the university 'police' trying to catch them in the act. However, there's no way we're going to be put off and, with Alexander's help, I've planned Operation Drench Immy with military precision.

Three friends, Oscar, Chun and Isla, are feigning interest in various storefronts while Alexander scans a bus timetable, not, I might add, that he's been on an Oxford bus for a very long time, if ever.

'Where is she?' I ask.

'I don't know,' he says.

'Well, everyone else is out by now. I hope she hasn't rushed out before the end. She was totally freaking out before this Statistics paper. She hates Stats.'

'Stop worrying. She'll be out in a minute. Look, isn't that her?' He points towards the steps of the Schools, where a hunched dark-haired girl trudges down the steps, her cap in her hand.

'Oh, yes. Poor Immy, she looks worn out.'

Alexander untwists the wire on the champagne bottle in his backpack. 'Get ready because once we've done this, we're going to have to run. There are a couple of bulldogs over there and I don't want to be hauled up before the proctors or end up in one of the tabloids as an example of a dissolute Oxbridge toff.'

'But you *are* a dissolute Oxbridge toff.'

He rolls his eyes as we both pretend to read the bus timetable while keeping a discreet eye on the two bowler-hatted men berating a bunch of guys who have covered their friend in baked beans.

'Hey there, is this a covert mission or can anyone join in?'

'Scott!'

Alexander transfers his attention from the timetable to us. 'It's Operation Drench Immy,' I say.

'I guessed as much. I checked the exam schedules. Permission to join the mission, captain?'

Alexander smiles. 'Lauren's in charge of this one.'

'If you follow orders to the letter, you can join the mission,' I say.

Scott gives me a discreet salute.

Immy has stopped at the bottom of the steps. She wipes her forehead with the back of her arm and glances around her.

'She's wondering where we are . . . Shouldn't we go over there now?' I say.

Alexander shakes his head. 'Too risky. Wait for it . . . It'll be easier to make a getaway from this side of the street.'

'There's a bulldog on this side too, outside the liquor store. What if he spots us?' Scott says.

'He won't. Trust me.'

After looking around her a few times, Immy steps into a gap in the traffic and walks towards us. The bulldog seems to have vanished.

'He's gone inside the wine merchant's,' Alexander says.

'Let's go for it.' I make a 'one, two, three' signal with my fingers to Oscar, Chun and Isla.

Alexander eases out the cork while Immy hurries across the street, dodges an open-top bus and skips on to the pavement.

'Surprise!' I leap out from the bus stop.

'What the –? Arghhh!'

She shrieks as the cork flies out of the bottle and fizz fills the air like a fountain.

'Oh my God! Arghhh!'

Alexander empties the contents over her.

'You idiots! I'm soaked,' Immy shrieks delightedly. 'And Scott! OMG!'

I laugh. 'You'd have been devastated if we hadn't been here.'

Even Alexander smiles and hands the bottle to Immy. Scott kisses her and then I see something rare: Immy actually blushes.

'Congratulations on surviving,' he says, then Alexander curses.

'Shit. The bulldogs have spotted us. Back to college, *now!*'

The bulldogs hover on the kerb opposite, desperately trying to find a gap in the traffic, but we're already off.

We race up the High Street, dripping with champagne, and dart into a narrow lane that leads back to Wyckham. When we finally slow down to catch our breath, Immy heaves a huge sigh of relief.

'Someone pinch me and tell me it's really over. That was the most horrible week of my life and I never ever want to do it again.'

We all laugh and Isla hands over a bouquet of flowers.

'There's more fizz back at college. Everyone's waiting to party. Why did you have to be the last one to finish?'

'I don't know. It's been vile. I don't know how I haven't run out of the exam room screaming some mornings, and I've probably got a third but I don't care. It's over and now I am going to get totally wasted. Will you be joining us, Scott?'

He laughs. 'Much as I'd love to, I have plans for this evening. But I think I can squeeze in a quick one.' He winks.

Later that evening, Immy and I walk back to college together. Alexander insisted on treating a group of us to dinner but has now gone to meet a colleague for a drink. We had planned to go on to a club but after her marathon exam session, Immy's almost dead on her feet so I said I'd walk back with her.

Wyckham looks serene and majestic, its towering gatehouse silhouetted against the indigo velvet of the sky. The knot in my stomach returns and tightens. I still haven't told Alexander about the job interview and the longer I leave it, the harder it seems. Why ruin these final few idyllic days together? I can tell him after the ball on Saturday.

'It was a shame Scott had to go out to dinner with Lia this evening,' I say.

'Story of my life,' says Immy as we enter the Lodge. 'But all may not be lost. Can you wait here while I check my pidge? I've been hoping to get a spare ticket for the ball from one of the committee, and she said she'd leave it here for me this evening if she'd managed to wangle one.'

A few moments later she walks out, waving a white envelope. 'Yes! I got it.'

'Great! So who's going to be your partner?'

'Remember that rower from Jocasta's Boat Race party that I bumped into at Eights Week? Well, he called again last week and said now he'd finished his master's, would I like to hook up?'

'I thought you weren't interested?'

'Well, he did offer to pay for the ticket and it'd be fun to have a partner for the ball, so I thought, why not? He may turn out to be better in the sack when he's not knackered and plastered too. Shall we go and have a nightcap in my room? I've still got half a bottle of Moët from earlier.'

We walk into the Front Quad, where the sky is still twilit, a renewed spring in Immy's step.

'Oh my God, who is that twat?'

On the opposite side of the quad, a clearly inebriated man is climbing out of a window on to the battlements. Shouts and curses from the open casement behind him seem to echo around the walls of the building.

Immy gasps. 'It looks like Rupert.'

'That's because it *is* Rupert,' I say quietly.

Heads pop out of the window behind Rupert, who is wearing a tailcoat and a top hat.

'Come in, you idiot, before the porters get here.'

Ignoring his friends, Rupert starts to beat his chest and howl.

'He thinks he's Tarzan . . .' I say.

'For God's sake, be quiet, Rupert!' Immy shrieks.

Rupert stops howling, puts his hands over the low battlement wall and leans forward.

Immy recoils. 'Christ, he's so drunk he could end up splattered all over the flagstones.'

Even I have my heart in my mouth because no matter how much I loathe the snake, I don't want him to fall.

His top hat falls off and bounces off the flagstones. His friends make a grab for him but he laughs and starts singing – if you can call his drunken howls singing.

'Should we fetch the porters?' I ask.

Immy grabs my arm. 'No need; they'll be here in a minute with all this noise. He is an arse.'

Rupert clearly has a better opinion of himself. 'I'm the king of the world!' His shout is bound to wake someone and, sure enough, a few lights start to pop on around the quad. He also seems to be swaying.

'Shit, we'll have to get someone . . .' Now even Immy sounds worried. She's about to run to the Lodge.

A figure emerges from an archway on Rupert's side of the quad.

'Wait, it's Rafe,' I hiss.

'Oh, the jolly old Bishop of Birmingham!'

At Rupert's drunken shout, Rafe immediately stops,

then stands on the flagstones under the battlements, hands on hips.

'De Courcey? What the hell do you think you're doing?'

Immy winces. 'Oh dear, Rupert really is fucked now.'

'Get down from there at once!'

Rupert starts cackling madly.

'Come back in, this minute!' There are frantic shouts from the window behind him and hands reach out for him, but Rupert's on a roll, drunkenly bellowing out some obscene limerick while Rafe shouts at him from below.

'If you don't get down this instant, I'll wake the Warden!'

Ignoring Rafe, Rupert fumbles with his trousers.

Immy groans. 'Oh hell, I think he's going to moon at Rafe!'

A second later, Rupert's trousers are round his ankles but instead of turning around, he clutches his groin.

Rafe leaps backwards but it's too late to avoid the stream of urine falling from four floors up. He loses his footing and topples backwards on to the lawn.

There is a brief moment of silence before the quad erupts.

Rafe is struggling to his feet as two porters run over the lawn towards him.

'Professor Rafe, are you OK?'

'Of course I'm not OK. That revolting little shit just

pissed all over me. I want him sent down!' He pulls a handkerchief from his jacket and starts wiping his face.

Curses and shouts ring out from the battlements, where Rupert is still cackling madly, waving his dick and singing. He's also swaying alarmingly and seems about to topple forward when he's hauled backwards through the window, his trousers still round his ankles. There's a crash and even louder shouts, then the porters run under the archway to the staircase. The window slams shut.

Immy turns to me. 'Oh Lauren, I really thought he was going to fall off.'

'Me too. Look at Rafe.' The Dean is out now, in his pyjamas and dressing gown, trying to calm Rafe down.

'Serves him bloody right,' says Immy. 'I don't think I've enjoyed myself so much in a long time.'

We both start laughing – I don't know whether it's relief or the booze or just the sheer bizarreness of the evening. Immy is convulsed beside me and I'm laughing so hard my stomach hurts.

'Come on, let's go and have a nightcap. I was knackered, but that's woken me up again. Maybe we should go on to a club after all?'

The next morning – or should I say the next afternoon – Immy meets me in the JCR, brandishing a tabloid newspaper. 'Have you seen this yet?'

'No, I only crawled out of bed ten minutes ago.' For

a split second, my pulse races, thinking that Valentina has gone through with her threat after all, then Immy opens a spread in the middle of the paper. My bleary eyes struggle to focus on the words but the headline is unmistakeable: 'DON GETS A SOAKING FROM DRUNKEN TOFF'.

'Oh God. How did that get in the press?'

'Some hack from *Cherwell* saw it from his room and filmed it on his mobile. The video's on the newspaper site. It's even funnier than I remember. Rafe will go nuts and Rupert's parents won't be too pleased.'

'Oh no,' I moan.

'Why are you bothered? Rupes has been awful to you.'

'Yes, but Letty is lovely.'

'Well, it's not your fault and it serves Rupert right. Apparently he's already been rusticated and banned from the ball! The Warden said he'd brought the college into disrepute.'

'Rusticated? What does that mean?'

'Banned from entering college for the rest of term.'

'Well, technically, term's over.'

'Yes, but they've made him leave his room and he can't come to the ball and he's had a massive fine. I don't suppose he'll care about the fine or being thrown out, but he won't like missing the ball.'

A Rupert-free ball sounds great to me. 'That sounds fair enough.'

'Yes, it does. I also heard from the Sub Dean that the

Warden had to persuade Rafe not to go to the police. He wanted to sue for assault.'

'Does peeing on someone count as assault?' I say, scanning the news report and wincing on Letty's behalf.

'Spitting is, so why not? Rafe's agreed not to press charges but Rupert still has to write a grovelling apology and pay for all Rafe's clothes to be dry-cleaned.'

This news fills me with such childish glee I worry about myself. No more Rupert or Rafe will be one of the few joys of leaving Wyckham.

Immy peers at the image of Rupert drenching Rafe on her mobile. She rubs her finger over the tiny star that's covering his dignity to save the blushes of readers of the 'family newspaper'. 'Of course,' she says, 'he'll probably end up as the next prime minister. Now, if you don't have too bad a hangover, shall we hit the shops ready for the ball?'

The next morning, I've just finished Skyping my parents when Immy stomps into my room and flops down on the bed in disgust.

'Gah!'

'What's up?'

'Can you believe it? After I managed to wangle an extra ticket for Hamish the rower from one of the ball committee, he goes and ruptures his bloody Achilles! How am I going to find someone else at such short notice? Like, who hasn't already left or made plans or isn't a total twat?'

'Oh, Immy, I am sorry.'

'Me too. I was looking forward to having a partner. I know everyone goes in groups now and you, Alexander and the gang will be there, but still, it would have been nice. Poor Hamish.' She sighs. 'And I ordered a gorgeous new dress too, and you know we're booked in to the salon?'

'It'll still be an amazing night. So why don't I take you out for lunch at the Boathouse now?'

She smiles. 'That sounds great, but I'll treat you. The thing is . . .' – she hesitates – 'we don't have much time left do we? Promise you will keep in touch after you leave?'

'Promise you'll make Washington your first stop on your world tour? You'll be welcome any time and I'll be back to Europe at some point.'

'Alexander will make sure of that. Have you told him about the job interview yet?'

I shake my head. 'I'm waiting till after the ball.'

Immy gives me a hard look. 'Are you sure that's a good idea?'

'I don't think there will ever be a good time. Come on, let's go out.'

We're heading into town when we see Scott cycling past the Bodleian. He brakes hard when he sees us and nearly falls off on to the cobbles outside the Radcliffe Camera.

'Whoa!'

'Sorry we startled you.'

'We have that effect on people,' Immy says, seeming transfixed by his cycling shorts.

'We were just off to lunch at the Boathouse. Want to join us?'

'Like this? I'm all sweaty.'

'How awful,' says Immy. 'But we could just sit outside the pub instead. You look like you could do with a nice cool beer.'

'In that case, if you don't mind sitting next to a hobo, it's a deal.'

'I can stand it, if you can,' says Immy.

Scott chains up his bike, and we grab drinks and menus and sit in the sun in the garden of the Turf. Talk turns to what we've all been doing after the exams.

It doesn't take long for poor Immy to start feeling sorry for herself again about the ball and the wasted ticket. 'Oh well, I guess I can get rid of the ticket easily enough at Wyckham, unless you know anyone from St Nick's who wants it,' she says, bravely.

Scott sips his pint before replying. 'Hmm. Tricky, but I might possible know someone . . .'

Immy brightens. 'Really?' Then she pulls a face. 'Is he even vaguely human?'

'Vaguely,' says Scott. 'You're looking at him.'

Immy's mouth literally drops open. '*You?*'

Scott has a hang-dog expression. 'Yes. Although by the look on your face, maybe it's not such a good idea!'

'No, God, no,' Immy says. 'But . . . well, sure, if you

fancy it. I thought you might already be going with Lia?' she says coyly.

'Lia's gone to Papua New Guinea.' Scott says this casually enough but that means nothing. In his own way, he's as good at hiding his feelings as Alexander. Better, in fact. It occurs to me that I think I know him but maybe I've been mistaken.

'She's been planning the trip for a while, and we both knew it was only a fling so we called it a day. Different continents; pretty difficult to keep a relationship going.'

He tosses this comment into the conversation lightly enough, so I can't work out whether he's referring to Alexander and me as well as his own situation.

Studiously avoiding looking at me, he pulls out his wallet. 'So, if you can stand to spend the whole evening with me, how much are the tickets?'

'Oh, forget that – but are you really serious?' Immy says.

'Deadly. If you'll allow me to escort you.'

She sighs thoughtfully. 'Well, I suppose I could lower myself to be seen with a St Nick's person. It would be a humiliation, of course, but . . .'

'I could always wear a paper bag over my head.'

'OK. Done.' She shakes his hand and I am worried her face will actually crack from smiling.

Half a very happy hour later, Immy virtually skips off to the store to pick up her new dress, leaving Scott with me.

I can't help giving him a hug. 'That was nice of you.'

'Not really. She's a great girl and I'd love to experience an Oxford summer ball once before I leave. I've worked far too hard this term. And it may be the only time I ever do.'

I feel a wave of emotion myself at the thought of my precious time here running out. 'Don't upset Immy, will you?'

He frowns hard. 'You're telling me not to upset her? You're telling me how to run *my* love life? Hey, Lauren, look after your own. Immy and I, we're quite capable of taking care of ourselves.'

I raise my eyebrows. 'Hey, that's what I'm worried about.'

Later that evening, I'm sitting on Alexander's sofa after dinner, with my feet in his lap.

He massages my soles with his fingers, and I'm trying to decide if I'm a freak for being so turned on by that. I remember the first time I ended up in this house and he did this to me. That seems a lifetime away and yet only five minutes. Every vow I made then has been blown out of the water, every misgiving I had has been proven true.

He rubs the pads of my toes with his fingers, absent-mindedly. 'Lauren . . . I may be a little late home on Saturday evening.'

'What? But that's the night of the ball!'

He looks at me. 'Yup. I have to go to London on business but I'm sure I'll be back in time.'

'Saturday? On estate business? Surely it won't go on that late, and besides, you're paying the solicitors. Can't they sort it?'

'Not family business. It's work.' He keeps his fingers around my ankle, almost as if he wants to hold me captive in case I decide to leave. I'm trying hard not to overreact. I don't want anything to spoil this final evening, but it's so disappointing I want to shout at him.

'Don't worry. We booked a late dinner sitting and I hope to be home by eight-ish at the latest. If I could get out of it, I would.'

I shrug. 'It's fine. I'll see you when I see you.' I can't help but feel bitterly disappointed – we haven't got long left together and I've been building up to this ball for ages. In my head, it is the last thing to look forward to before reality hits and I won't be able to put that conversation with Alexander off any longer. Earlier today, I had an email from the Ross Foundation about the final arrangements for my job interview. I also booked my flight home to Washington but there's no way I'm going to complicate things by bringing any of that up now.

'I will be here. I promise,' he soothes, seeing my face. 'Now, I don't know about you but I think we've talked enough.' The hand that had been rubbing my feet begins to snake deliciously up my leg with the lightest of touches. I had more to say, but for now I hear Immy's voice in my head, telling me to live in the moment. I can worry about tomorrow tomorrow ... at least that's what I'm telling myself for now.

On the evening of the ball, Alexander's bedroom is lit with the pink glow of the setting sun. Immy has stayed on in her room and Scott is calling for her, but we both did the time-honoured thing and got our hair and mani-pedis done together earlier in town. Just as I'm applying a final coat of lip-gloss and wondering whether to phone Immy and say I'll be late, a key scrapes in the front-door lock downstairs.

'Alexander?'

'Yes, it's me.' His boots thump on the stairs and he walks into the bedroom, wearing army fatigues.

'Told you I'd make it.'

I tap my Cartier. 'By the skin of your teeth.'

'You didn't believe me, did you?'

'Of course I did,' I lie.

With a look that says he definitely doesn't believe me, he kisses me deeply. I am almost dizzy with pleasure when he pulls away. 'I guess I'd better get changed,' he says, 'much as I'd love to get you out of that exquisite dress and ravish you! You OK to wait for me?'

I nod and send him off with a cheeky pat on the bottom, and whilst he's in the shower, I check I have all I need in my silver clutch and add another coat of mascara, though my fingers are shaky with excitement. The hiss of water from the bathroom stops as I'm retrieving the ball tickets from the sideboard in the sitting room. I'm too afraid of creasing my dress to sit down on the sofa. I was going to wear the one he bought me for Rome, but then I saw this gorgeous oyster-coloured one-shoulder silk affair in a boutique, and I couldn't resist it. *It* is *my last Oxford ball, after all*, I kept telling myself, and the silver heels Alexander gave me for the Rome trip *do* go perfectly with it.

I'm also restless with the twitchiness that comes with being ready first and far too early. I'm hyper-aware that this is my last evening with my friends, and I want to savour every moment.

The floorboards creak above me, and there are dull thuds as drawers open and shut. I shuffle the newspapers on the coffee table into a neat pile and throw an empty cookie wrapper into the trash, painfully aware of my need to be on the move – preferably in a big open space where I can keep on going and never have to stop. Because every minute that ticks by brings me closer to the moment when we'll have to part.

The clock chimes. After picking up my wrap from the sofa, I call up the stairs. 'Alexander! It's eight forty-five already. We *have* to go!'

'Coming!'

Half a minute later, he walks into the room, still adjusting his bow tie. That familiar tight feeling constricts my throat. He's in mess dress, of course, and is band-box fresh, from the tight black trousers to the scarlet mess jacket, with its row of miniature medals.

He looks incredible. I've seen the uniform more than once, of course, but every time I'm knocked out by how perfectly it suits him. It's like a second skin for him ... and the kick in my gut reminds me that this interlude at Wyckham has only been a hiatus. Alexander belongs in the military; he lives for the army, no matter what he says. He doesn't belong to me, that's for sure.

He peers in the mirror above the fireplace and rakes his fingers through his damp hair.

'Right. No time for a blow-dry or shave. Will I do?'

The five o' clock shadow at his jaw only adds to his appeal for me. I want to jump on him now but I shrug. 'You scrubbed up OK, I guess.'

He glances down at his jacket. 'You don't seem too sure. In fact, you remind me of my colour sergeant at Sandhurst, although you're a little easier on the eye. Is my uniform not correct? Do you want me to change?'

I try not to laugh. 'No. You look fine as you are.'

'Good.' Then he looks at me again, almost as if he hadn't noticed me when he first walked in, or perhaps as if he's *decided* to notice me now.

'Is there something wrong with *me*?' I ask.

'Wrong? Quite the opposite. You look edible, and I mean edible. In fact, I don't think you've ever looked more beautiful ...' His gaze lingers on me, and my body responds as if he were actually running his fingertips over my bare skin.

'*But* I was hoping you might consider a change of jewellery.'

Instinctively, my hand travels to the Cartier diamond necklace that Alexander gave me in the first term. 'Don't you think this goes with my dress?'

'It's beautiful but I've been meaning to give you something else. Wait here.'

We're already running behind but I'm not going to protest. He crosses to the dresser in the sitting room and opens a drawer. When he turns back to me, he's holding a dark-blue leather box. The lid is plain so I have no idea where it's from, but for that very reason, I'm guessing it holds something special. While I never expect or want expensive gifts from him, I've also learned by now that it's useless to refuse them. Especially tonight.

'For you,' he says, quietly. 'Open it.'

With a press of the catch, the lid flips open to reveal what I think is a choker, glittering within a satin nest. The necklace is made up of what must be diamonds and sapphires, designed as tiny leaves and flowers. The jewels flash with a white fire when I lift the piece carefully out of the box and hold it in my palm.

'Alexander, it's stunning. I can't believe you got me this.' I look up, thinking I might actually cry.

His eyes are alight with pleasure. 'I'm glad you like it. It'll be even better against your skin. Shall I put it on?' And with that, his fingers brush the nape of my neck and the choker tightens briefly around my throat. I want to keep his hand there, to move it down my body, to forget the ball altogether. This man, who looks absolutely fucking gorgeous, never ceases to amaze me and I close my eyes to regain control. We really can't miss the ball.

'Is that OK? Not too tight?' he asks, his voice low and gentle. I'm pretty sure he's had the same thoughts as me.

'No. It's perfect.' I manage to move away from him and walk over to the mirror above the fireplace. The sapphires look sensational with my gown and I have a sneaking suspicion the choker may be a Tiffany.

'I love the art deco style.'

His face appears next to me. 'Good.' I detect a rare glimpse of hesitation in his expression. 'You *do* like it?'

'It's beyond beautiful, thank you, but you shouldn't have.'

He taps his watch. 'Lauren, we have to leave for the ball now, as you helpfully keep pointing out. There's no time for argument and besides, you should realize by now that I won't take no for an answer.'

Under my fingertips, the jewels feel cool and the slightest movement, even my breathing, makes them sparkle with an inner fire. The choker must be the most beautiful piece I've ever seen and it complements my dress perfectly. I can't take my eyes off my reflection and Alexander must have noticed.

'Unless,' he says, kissing the bare flesh between my

shoulder blades, 'you'd rather be late, because if we do wait much longer, I'll decide I'd rather stay here and have you naked except for the choker and heels. I've already been wondering how I'll get through ten hours without getting you out of that dress.'

'Hey, no,' I tease, batting his hand away. 'We'll miss our dinner reservation . . .'

His eyes glint dangerously. 'Who needs food?'

If he touches me again now, I'll never make it to the ball. I steel myself. 'We arranged to meet Immy and Scott at nine. We can't let them down and we need to set off now . . . Come on, we've got all night.'

He heaves in a deep sigh. 'OK, but I warn you, I'll find a way by dawn.'

'I look forward to it,' I tease. How the hell am I ever going to get through this whole evening?

He holds out his injured arm. 'Right then, you'd better take my arm, Ms Cusack.'

'Guess I've no choice, Captain Hunt.'

'Guess you haven't.' Together, we walk out of the house and down the street, Alexander holding on to me while I tease him about the ridiculously old-fashioned nature of it all. Because, if I don't laugh at him – and myself – I have a horrible feeling I'm going to cry.

Chapter Eighteen

I've been to some events in the past year: to a masked ball, a hunt ball – a *Hunt* hunt ball, no less – and even to the opera in Rome, but tonight threatens to knock them all out of the park. There's something magical – even fairytale – about Wyckham tonight, and I don't think it's my wistful mood that's casting the place in such a mellow light.

When we walk into the Front Quad after handing over our tickets and collecting our wristbands, the sun is still bright though the sky is turning a deeper, mellower blue. A string quartet has set up on the hallowed turf of the quad, playing classical themes, and from the Back Quad, I can already hear one of the bands playing.

Immy and Scott are waiting for us.

She is stunning in a shell-pink silk dress with a plunging neckline that makes the most of her curves, and I don't think I've ever seen her look better. The fact that she's on Scott's arm might have something to do with her glow. He looks as if he was born to wear a tux and the perfect cut of it shows off his broad shoulders to perfection.

Immy and Scott both kiss me when we arrive, and

after a kiss for Immy, Alexander even manages a perfectly civil greeting to Scott.

Immy bobs about excitedly. 'So, shall we collect our champagne? I don't know about you, but I am soooo ready to party!'

Yes, I'm ready to party too, and we dive into the crowds of students, admiring dresses, drinking champagne, marvelling at the Ferris wheel that's somehow been fitted into the Warden's Garden. Every corner of Wyckham has been turned over to hedonistic pleasure, with bands playing in a marquee, Pimm's bars in the gardens, a comedy club in the Buttery and a cabaret in the JCR. The sight of fire-eaters and jugglers strolling around the quads is surreal . . . and I can't quite shake off the feeling of disorientation, as if I have stepped into a parallel world that's almost Wyckham, yet slightly offset from the real one.

After dinner, we listen to one of the bands and then head for the mini fairground in the Warden's Garden. We ride the Ferris wheel, then climb into bumper cars. It turns into a full-scale battle, of course, with Alexander and Scott fighting it out with Oscar and a couple of the rowers before Immy and I take our turn at the wheel.

Alexander swears under his breath as we smack into Immy's car. 'Lauren, I am so glad I have never let you behind the wheel of the Range Rover.'

'You should see her in the Cayenne . . . Didn't you get a ticket for speeding last year, Lauren?' Scott shouts.

Alexander raises his eyebrows. 'I didn't know you were a speed merchant.'

I call back, 'I'm not and I was barely over the limit when I got that ticket.'

We drag the guys off the bumper cars and weave our way through the fairground. Immy lets out a squeal of delight.

'Oh, that looks fun!'

We all watch as students – it's exclusively male students – take it in turns to ride a bucking bronco that's set up on the Warden's lawn. The attendant stands by, looking bored while black-tied students swagger up. Most of them last about five seconds before they're dumped on to the foam matting.

'I'd love a go,' says Immy longingly.

'Why don't you?' I urge.

'In this dress? You have to be kidding . . . But you could,' she says to Scott. 'You're American.'

Scott laughs. 'And that means I can ride a bronco?'

'I'm sure you could manage that particular mount,' Immy says, walking her fingers up his tux sleeve.

'Go on, Scott,' I say.

He winces as another guest bites the dust.

'OK, but don't expect much. I've never done this before.'

Immy holds his jacket while he climbs on to the bronco's back and holds on to the rope.

'Don't cheat! One hand only!' Immy shouts.

Alexander drinks champagne from the bottle and

tightens his arm around my back. I have to admit that just watching the 'bull' bucking up and down and round and round makes me feel faintly dizzy, especially on top of the dinner and champagne, but Scott is clinging on manfully. The digital display next to the bronco ticks past twenty seconds, and then thirty, as the bull's speed increases and the angle of its neck grows steeper.

'Ride 'em, cowboy!' Immy whoops and people stand by, watching with admiring glances.

'Jeez!' Scott almost slides off the bull but recovers and stays on as the clock ticks over a minute.

The bull's rotations grow even wilder and Scott's bucking up and down like he's on a stormy sea, then in a flash he's on the crash mat, cursing cheerfully.

'Not bad,' says the bronco attendant, even sounding faintly impressed. 'Best so far tonight.'

Immy grabs his arm as he climbs off the crash mat. 'Well done, Scott You must have thighs of steel . . .'

He laughs. 'They feel more like silly putty after that. You fancy a turn, Alex? Lauren tells me you're a great horseman.'

Alexander smiles. 'She's exaggerated, I'm sure, and this isn't quite the sort of mount I'm used to, but why not?'

Immy exchanges glances with me and I brace myself for another battle, this time between Scott and Alexander.

'Do you mind?' he says, handing me his mess jacket.

He climbs on to the bronco and holds the reins, his

thighs gripping the sides of the bull, and he's off. One arm back in the air, rodeo style, the other gripping the rope as the bull starts its crazy, mesmerizing, dance. Twenty seconds pass and Alexander looks as born to the bronco as he is to his own hunter. Thirty . . . forty . . .

Scott gives a low whistle. 'Lookin' good . . . very good.'

The bull dips deeper and the rotations speed up. The muscles in Alexander's thighs tauten and he starts to use his free arm to balance. Fifty seconds, a minute . . . a few more seconds and he'll pass Scott's total.

'Way to go!' I shout.

Alexander glances over at me – and the next moment hits the mats with a thump.

The attendant clicks his tongue loudly and shakes his head. 'Shame. One second short of your mate's time.'

Alexander is still lying on the mat; at first I think he's just taking a moment to catch his breath but then I see him struggle to get up. I hurry over, followed by Scott.

'Hey, are you OK?' Scott asks as Alexander turns over and grimaces.

'Fine.'

Scott stands by. He doesn't offer to help but there's concern in his eyes.

'Is it your arm?' I ask.

Alexander gets to his feet and manages to clamber off the mat on to the lawn 'Don't fuss,' he snaps.

'I'm not fussing. I only asked what's wrong!'

Ignoring me, he offers his injured arm and hand to Scott. 'Congratulations. You won.'

I see Scott hesitate for a second before grasping his hand. 'Thanks.'

Alexander breaks into a grin. 'Champagne's on me.'

While we walk to the champagne bar, Alexander talks to Scott, and I follow with Immy.

'Is Alexander OK?' she asks. 'I think he landed on his bad arm.'

I'm still pissed at Alexander's curt response so I shrug. 'Who knows? Who cares?'

'*You* do.'

We reach the bar. 'Yes, I do, I guess, but Alexander won't thank me for it. He'd rather die than let Scott see that he's hurt himself.'

'They're hopeless, men, sometimes,' she says.

'Tell me about it.'

We find a table and shortly afterwords Alexander returns from the bar with a bottle of Krug, while Scott carries the glasses. All trace of the pain he felt has been erased, yet I know he was hurt.

The chapel clock chimes midnight and we drift around the ball, checking in on the headline act, attempting a waltz to a dance band in the Great Hall. Alexander and Scott go off to try their hand on the roulette table in the 'casino' set up in the seminar room, while Immy and I spend an ill-advised few minutes on a bouncy castle until another girl tears her ballgown. We cool down with a mojito-flavoured Popsicle on the 'beach' area, and it tastes pretty good, considering it's well past one a.m. Wanting to avoid the crowds in the Main Quad, I visit the bathrooms underneath the chaplain's staircase.

I walk outside and take a few breaths, trying to forget that the night will soon be over. And that I can't put off my conversation with Alexander for ever. It's quiet here in the far corner of the gardens; the jazz group that was here earlier in the evening has packed up and gone, although the temporary stage is still in place, and there are plastic bags of trash tied up and waiting to be collected in the morning. I think I'm the only one here.

The scent of honeysuckle fills my nostrils. Wyckham is just perfect.

I turn to leave, but then I hear a rustling sound from the far side of the Chapel Garden. A leg appears, and the dark tails of a coat. The hedge is in shadow but there's enough light to see the gatecrasher as he struggles to balance on the narrow boughs of a creeper, huffing and cursing. *Hey, he should have paid*, I think, but the ball's almost over anyway and I'm not going to turn him in, and besides, he's lucky he hasn't broken his neck. That wall is eight feet high and if he slips – ouch – I don't want to be the one to pick up the pieces. I think I'll tiptoe quietly away . . .

He glances around, checking there's no one watching, and I revise my opinion about him falling.

'Good morning, Rupert!'

'What the . . . Jesus! Arggh!'

I don't know what actually happened, if my shout caused him to fall, but there's a ripping sound as the creeper parts company with the wall and then he's falling backwards and thumping on to the shrubbery below.

'Owww! My shitting ankle!'

I stroll over to where he's sprawled in the soil between a lilac bush and a tea rose. His tail coat is covered in dirt, he has a twig in his hair and there's a scratch down one side of his face that's oozing blood.

'Wouldn't it have been easier to buy a ticket?'

'I did have a fucking ticket. That tosser the Dean banned me!'

I already know this but I act innocent. 'Oh dear.'

He tries to push himself out of the border and grimaces in pain. 'I think you've broken my ankle.'

'Me? I was nowhere near you.'

'You shouted and that made me lose my balance. You did it on purpose!' He crawls out of the bushes, groaning.

I stand a few yards away. 'You once said you'd like to be on your knees in front me, Rupes. Now you are, I actually rather like it.'

He glares up at me, his face screwed up in pain and fury. 'I suppose you're going to run straight to security and have me thrown out?'

'You know what? I really can't be bothered. Besides, I've got to get back to my friends. They'll be wondering where I am. Have fun trying to climb out of here again.'

He tries to stand and collapses with a curse. 'I really do think I've broken something. Lauren, please, I might need an ambulance.'

'You don't say? How dreadful.' I turn to walk away.

'Can you at least fetch Oscar or Immy for me? I'm going to need help getting out of here.'

'Sorry, you're on your own.' Yes, I know I'm being a grade-A bitch but he deserves it after the misery he's put me and Alexander – not to mention a whole load of other people – through over the past year. 'You'll live.'

He stares at me, his grimace of pain suddenly replaced by a new expression. 'That's a very nice necklace you're wearing tonight.'

I touch the choker without even meaning to.

'Alexander gave it to you, didn't he?'

He says this line with heavy irony, and I know he's going to use the gift to score points off me. 'It hardly takes a rocket scientist to work that out, but yes, as a matter of fact, he did. So what?' I say.

'It's very beautiful. Tiffany, isn't it?'

I'm momentarily puzzled by Rupert's knowledge of jewellery but I shrug. 'I don't know; he just gave it to me.'

His piggy little eyes hold mine. 'Then Alexander really must think a lot of you. An awful lot.'

'It's the thought that counts. I know it must have cost a lot of money but that's not why I like it, or why he gave it to me. You really have no idea what makes me tick, or Alexander. I'm going.'

'You do know it was his mother's?'

My stomach flutters and I know I'm not quick enough with my response to fool him. 'So?'

'He didn't tell you that, did he?'

'Of course he did.'

He sneers. 'Liar.'

'So what if it was Lady Hunt's?'

'So you only have it on loan, just like you only have Alexander on loan. That necklace is a family heirloom. I can remember my Aunt Grace wearing it to parties; in fact, she lent it to my mother once for some do at the Palace. Alexander must have been truly taken in by you if he's given it to you, but I'm surprised he hasn't saved it for Emma. I thought I heard my father say all the jewellery is held in trust for her.'

The choker suddenly feels tighter around my neck, though I know that's purely psychological.

'That's rubbish. Alexander would never have given it to me if his mother had wanted to Emma to have it.'

He whistles. 'Then congratulations on finally getting your man. Even Valentina never got so much as a look at it, and I know how much she wanted to.'

'Alexander is not "my man", I'm not his woman and you are being an idiot – as usual. I'm not listening to another word.'

Even though I've turned my back on him, I can

picture his triumphant, mocking face and no matter how much I pretend not to care, my heart pounds at his revelation about the necklace. Instinctively, I know that what Rupert says about the necklace being Lady Hunt's is true though I'm not sure what bothers me more, the fact that the choker *was* intended for Emma, or the possible meaning of such a 'significant' gift from Alexander. I still haven't even told him I've got a job interview in the States.

'I'll look forward to the wedding invitation!' Rupert calls after me. 'Will the ceremony be a marquee at your folks' or will you just mosey on off to Vegas?'

I raise my middle finger behind my back and hurry across the lawn, only to be intercepted by Professor Rafe, the Dean and a couple of uniformed security guys hurrying towards me.

'Is that Mr de Courcey I can see, making the flower beds look untidy?'

'Yes, I'm afraid he fell off the wall while trying to crash the party. I think he's hurt his ankle.'

'How dreadful,' says Rafe sarcastically and, for once, we're of the same mind.

I spare a glance behind, if only to witness what happens next. The Dean, Rafe and the security guys have reached Rupert. I leave them to it.

I walk out of the garden with Rupert's protests and groans of agony in my ears, but they're only a momentary distraction. In my heart, I know that however malicious and pathetic Rupert is, so many of the things he said are true. He wasn't lying about the necklace. I think I'd guessed it was special, and I half knew it was vintage, but I simply didn't want to admit it to myself. And it isn't right to keep it; it should go to Emma. Already it feels leaden, a burden to wear, however beautiful.

And I'm going to have to give it back.

With a heavy heart, I wander slowly back to the Back Quad, past couples who've already had enough and are meandering towards the Lodge, most of the girls with dinner jackets around their shoulders, a few barefoot, shoes dangling from their fingers. There's a guy flat out on the lawn and a couple asleep on a bench, the girl resting her head on her partner's shoulder while he catches flies.

Alexander is walking towards the archway.

'Have you seen Scott and Immy?' I ask, when he reaches me.

'They seem to have gone AWOL,' he says, trailing his fingers down the back of my neck, touching the necklace. I should say something . . .

'The night's still young,' he says, looking at me in that delicious way of his. So delicious I determine then and there to put off the inevitable even longer. I will not let this night be spoilt by bloody Rupert and all those thoughts he's just put in my head.

The clock strikes two a.m. 'You think?'

He settles his hands on my waist. I should say something, but I don't. The night is still young. Soon – but not now – I'll tell him about the job interview, I really will, and I'll insist he takes back the necklace. Right now I need him one more time before that horrible conversation we need to have spoils everything.

My hand is in his and we're walking, almost running, through the cloisters, up the worn stone steps where I first met him to a door. He twists the iron handle and it opens. It's black inside and then moonlight floods in as Alexander opens another door. He has to duck low under the archway and then we're through into a tiny courtyard, bounded by high stone walls smothered in creeper.

The music from the disco is faint here; the shouts and laughter seem very distant, like we've been tossed high into the air and everything is happening miles below. The scent of honeysuckle fills my nostrils, almost catches at my throat as Alexander kisses me. His lips taste of champagne and I guess mine do too. I push my tongue inside his mouth, desperate to taste him more deeply, grinding my hips against him, digging my fingers into his biceps through the cloth of his mess jacket. Maybe he groans a little, perhaps I've hurt him, but he doesn't seem to care and I'm too selfish to stop.

I back him against the door and pull at the button of his trousers, almost ripping them off as I wrench down the zip. His briefs come down with his trousers, his erection demanding my hand around it. He's hot, silky, hard beneath my circling fingers.

He nuzzles my neck, nips the soft flesh of my shoulder so that I cry out in pain and pleasure. He hikes up my dress and I bunch the skirts around my waist, anticipating the moment when he bares me. Then my knickers are down and his fingers are seeking me out.

'Oh my God. Alexander!' I cry out. I don't think I've ever wanted him this much. I don't even care if anyone can see or hear us.

I'm already so swollen and sensitive under his fingers I can hardly bear him to touch me. Every inch of my skin seems super-sensitized and when he slides a finger inside me, I cry out again, louder this time.

I slide my hands under his shirt and pull him against me; the muscles shift and bunch with the tension. Then suddenly his hands are on my bare bottom, scooping me up and on to him. I cling on to his shoulders, my arms scraping on the wood of the door as he pushes inside me. The oak door shivers with every thrust, my thighs scream and his shake with the effort of holding me up. His fingers dig into my hips – it almost hurts but I don't care. Alexander is rigid beneath me, his eyes screwed shut while I scrabble for my own orgasm, almost fighting for it, frantic, desperate even though this is a moment I should want to go on for ever.

'Hey . . .'

I open my eyes. My arms are still locked around Alexander's neck and he's still holding me, his palms supporting my cheeks, looking at me with a kind of amused wonder.

I come to. Vaguely. 'Oh God, I hope no one heard us.' I feel a little shamefaced, and more than a little shaky.

'I don't give a damn,' he says softly, kissing me before gently lowering me back down to earth. 'I need you to be like that more often,' he says, smiling. The flagstones are cold under my feet. I hadn't even realized I'd lost my shoes.

I smile too, and rest my cheek against his mess jacket, the medals hard and smooth under my skin. Some kind of night bird is chirping from the dark leaves close by, or is it the start of a dawn chorus? Surely it's too early?

'OK?' His voice resonates under my cheek.

'Uh-huh.'

'Lauren?' He pulls back a little so that I have to look at him and his eyes are shining with post-sex euphoria. 'That was pretty spectacular. Did they put something in your drink?'

I smile. 'I know – sorry. I hope you don't have splinters in your butt.'

'Christ, don't apologize. Want to inspect me for splinters?'

'Maybe later,' I say, wondering if there will be a later. I don't have to fly home for a few days. There's still time for more . . . more of what?

And I have to return the necklace.

The door rattles and we hear a raised voice on the other side, cursing.

'Fuck! Quick.'

Still leaning against the door, Alexander tries to pull up his trousers; I retrieve my discarded shoes and smooth down my dress.

'Ready?' he says, and turning, twists the iron ring and opens the door.

A man in chef's whites stands there, cigarettes in hand, then gives a knowing smirk. 'Sorry, mate, just wanted a sneaky fag. Have I interrupted something?'

'Not at all,' Alexander says coolly while I try in vain to stop my cheeks glowing.

I follow Alexander out through the door and the chef winks at me.

'I need to freshen up. Meet you by the breakfast bar in the Back Quad?'

When I get back, Immy and Scott have also made a reappearance so I tell her about Rupert's dramatic entrance while Scott and Alexander queue for breakfast. There are plenty of people willing to wait in line for pastries and hot chocolate. I tug my wrap tighter around my shoulders; Immy has Scott's tux jacket on, with the sleeves rolled up. I *could* be imagining it, but there seems to be a faint lightening of the sky in the east.

We find a patch of grass that's not covered with empty plastic glasses and sit down.

'Scott's jacket suits you,' I say.

She giggles. 'Of course. He's a real gentleman.'

I raise an eyebrow. 'And that's a good thing?'

She tips her head on one side, considering for a moment. 'I'm not quite sure.'

'Go on, spill. You know you want to. You two did a pretty good disappearing act earlier.'

'He's gorgeous and lovely and I've had the best night ever and he said I'm sexy as hell, but as I'm your friend, he'd better not go there.'

'Scott said that?'

'I told him I'd feel weird too, knowing you and he had a thing.'

'Hey, we didn't really have a thing. Don't let me stop you!'

'I'm not . . . We both agreed it would be wrong merely to use each other for sex . . .'

'I sense a "but" here.'

She taps her nose. 'But . . .' She lowers her voice. 'He's a *great* kisser and I'll admit things got a little hot and steamy in my room for a while, but when it actually came to it, it was all a little like snogging someone while my mother was watching. Or George or something. Whatever, we sort of mutually agreed not to go any further.'

'Hi there, ladies.'

We both clam up as Scott and Alexander arrive, laden with pastries and a tray of coffee and chocolate. Everyone's a little weary but determined to last the whole night and we sit and chat until the grass grows damp and the sky turns from slate to grey, and finally the first streaks of pink appear.

'So, what are you doing when you go back to the States?' Alexander asks Scott.

'I've got an offer from the Environment Department.'

'You mean in Washington?' I blurt out, surprised. 'But I thought you were going to work for a charity in Africa?'

'Well, I said I was considering my options. I can't quite believe I've ended up on the Hill but when this job as a legislative assistant came up, it sounded too good to miss. I had a Skype interview last week and in fact I heard I got the offer while we've been here.'

'Congratulations,' says Alexander.

I'm still reeling that Scott's going to be back in the same city as me. 'I never thought I'd see you on the Hill, but wow!'

'Hey, it's only a junior advisor's post. Don't expect me to run for president any time soon. In fact, the most I'll be running for is the Starbucks round.'

'Well done,' says Immy. 'I might have to include Washington on my travels.'

Scott laughs. 'Thanks, you'd be welcome. And the Ross Foundation isn't far away so we could be seeing a lot more of each other after all.'

He directs this comment straight at me and immediately I know it's been said in complete innocence. I also know that its effect is going to be devastating.

For a brief second, I think Alexander has missed the reference, but then after a beat, he turns to me. 'So, the Ross Foundation?'

Scott looks taken aback; Immy bites her lip. They both know what's happened here.

'Well, um, yes, I have an interview with them . . . It's, um?'

'I've heard of it,' he cuts in.

'I'm sorry to spoil the surprise; she didn't get chance to tell you first.' Scott jumps to my defence but I wish he'd drop it.

Alexander manages a cool smile. 'I'm sure Lauren would have got round to it some time. Congratulations to you both.'

'Lauren's done incredibly well to get the offer,' Immy pipes up.

'It's not an offer, only an interview,' I put in, sensing a brewing storm.

'I'm sure she has.' He knocks back the rest of his coffee while Scott and Immy desperately try to move the conversation on to other topics.

Too late. Way too late.

Claiming he wants another coffee, Alexander gets up but walks right past the breakfast marquee and through the archway.

Scott groans. 'Shit, Lauren, I'm sorry. What a jerk I am!'

'Don't be. I should have told him before but I was waiting until after the ball. He had to know sooner or later . . . I need to go after him.'

Almost tripping over my skirt, I hurry after Alexander and eventually find him pacing the far corner of the Chapel Garden, where Rupert fell over the wall.

'Alexander, I'm sorry; I should have told you sooner.' I lay my hand on his arm and he looks down at it as if it might bite him.

'When did you decide? When did you tell him?'

'My parents mentioned it before they left. Leah Schulze had heard that Donna Ross was looking for an assistant.'

'Leah *Schulze*?' He gives me the drill sergeant stare that gets my blood up. 'Any relation or a complete coincidence?'

'Of course it's not a coincidence! She's Scott's mother and she serves on one of Donna Ross's fundraising committees. She knows I'm looking for a career and this is a wonderful opportunity. What do you expect me to do? Ignore it?'

'No, of course not, but –'

'Would it have made any difference if you knew? What was the point in telling you until I'd decided to definitely go for the job?'

'I don't know. What was the point? Perhaps maybe because we're supposed to be close, maybe because we're supposed to . . .' He leaves the sentence hanging, throws up his hands in frustration.

'What? Supposed to *what*, Alexander?'

'Treat each other like fucking adults!'

We face each other down. I force myself to be calm,

because behind the bluster I sense genuine anguish. 'I know I should have told you sooner; it was just with exams and everything going on . . .' I see his face and stop trying to find excuses. 'Look, I've spent a long time thinking it over. It's only an interview, not a job offer, and I'd be crazy not to consider it, even if I did want to stay here.'

'Even *if*?'

He pounces on that one word, like a lion on a gazelle.

'Even *if* you weren't going away to who knows where – for who knows how long. Even *if* you might not get yourself killed, even *if* I stayed . . . how can I throw away this chance? It's like the role was tailor-made for me.'

'How do you know it wasn't?'

'What's that supposed to mean?'

'Isn't it a bit of a coincidence that Scott's going to be back in Washington too?'

So he *is* jealous. 'I had no idea that Scott was coming home too until five minutes ago. My decision has absolutely nothing to do with Scott. Why do you have to turn everything into a conspiracy?'

He turns away from me. '*Why?* I wonder why?'

'What does that mean?' I grab his arm and he winces but neither of us is in the mood for sympathy. My heart seems about to burst out of my chest.

'If you don't know by now, then there's no point us continuing this conversation.' He stiffens, back in military mode, back on duty, and I suspect that I won't get anything from him in his mood. Captain Alexander Hunt, number . . .

'I'm sorry I couldn't be what you want,' he mutters at last.

'I don't want you to be anything other than you are. I never have.'

'Really?' he frowns.

I hesitate. *Have* I? Have I wanted him to be more like Scott? More like me? Am I letting him sow the seeds of self-doubt in my mind?

'I can understand,' he says, holding himself stiffly, bottling everything up, 'that you wanted to take this opportunity, but why not tell me?'

'And that would have made everything OK?' I snap back.

'It would . . .' he begins.

'Well?'

'No, you're right. It *wouldn't* have made everything OK. I don't like the idea of you disappearing off to Washington, walking out of my life just like that.' He snaps his fingers, making me jump. 'Give me some bloody credit, Lauren. But no, I don't relish the idea of you living four thousand miles away, working in the same bloody city as Mr Schulze for one of his mother's cronies.'

'That's not why I'm going! You're being unreasonable!'

He stares at me, glances away briefly, then shakes his head. 'Call me unreasonable if you like but I'm not going to apologize for being pissed off and a *trifle* put out' – he lays sarcastic emphasis on this last phrase – 'that you planned to walk out of my life without so much as a by your leave.'

I'm trembling a little, partly at the injustice of his words – and partly because he may possibly have reason to be upset, but I also know I can't stand the battle any longer. 'If you're thinking of handing me some all-or-nothing ultimatum, Alexander . . .'

'Would that be so bloody terrible?' he demands.

I open my mouth to speak, close it again and hold up my hands in frustration, aware of the stinging at the back of my eyes, at the impasse between us. I expect him to shout, or another bitter retort, but instead of anger, he throws back something else at me: a quiet resignation that's equally ominous in its own way.

He sighs deeply. 'It was unfair of me to assume that any success or opportunity you get is anything other than by your own merits because you're brilliant and beautiful, and you're like . . . Christ, this will sound mad.'

'Try me,' I murmur.

'When you're around, you make me doubt myself and that scares me.'

'*Me* scare *you*?'

'Yes. The way you make me feel, out of control, unsure . . . I hate it and yet I can't seem to keep away because it's not only the sex, though that is pretty bloody fantastic. The thought of you drove me on after

334

my father died, and whenever I'm away on an op, not knowing if I'll ever come home. You're like a thorn in my flesh that I can't remove.'

'A thorn in your flesh? That good, eh?'

He smiles and I melt a little. '*That* good. I know the past year has been difficult. I'm not an easy person to live with – to be with – but, Lauren, I need you around. And please don't underestimate what it takes me to say that.'

I can hardly speak; I'm also digging my nails into my palms to stop myself from trembling as he goes on.

'But I can also see that it's too much for you, the distance between us. So yes, I guess I am giving you the all-or-nothing ultimatum. I want more than you can give me if you're living in Washington. So pick – it's me or the job,' he says, the expression in his eyes dark and unreadable.

I cannot believe he has said this. I know he's hurt, and I know he can be unreasonable. But anger bubbles up in me. I take a moment to compose myself. 'OK, if that's what you want, you leave me no choice,' I say coldly. 'I have my world, you have yours, Alexander . . . and you are not being reasonable'

I don't know what's more painful, watching the struggle in his eyes or fighting my own desperate longing to hear what he has to say. He can't quite bring himself to apologize, and I can see he's not going to back down, but he puts his arms around me, and the wool of his mess jacket is gently abrasive on my tender skin.

He kisses me, so softly that I feel like a candle flame flickering down, sputtering, almost snuffed out.

I push him away, before he can end the kiss. 'Listen, if that's the way things are going to be, if that's how you feel, if that's how we both feel, I'll tell you what's going to happen, right?'

He reaches for me again, holding me lightly. 'What?'

'Before I say, will you promise to do as I ask?'

He frowns. 'Of course I can't do that until I know what it is.'

My heart feels like it's cracking in two but I know that what I'm doing is the right thing. '*Please* listen to me and promise you're going to make this as easy on me – on both of us – as you can.'

'I can't promise that, Lauren.'

'Then I'll have to be strong.' I take a deep breath and reach up to my neck. 'This necklace is the most beautiful thing you've ever given me, but I can't keep it. Shh . . .' I put my finger on his lips. 'I am incredibly honoured and touched that you gave it to me, because I know how much it must mean to you, but you should give it to Emma. Your mother must surely have intended that?'

Without a word, he allows me to lay the necklace in his hands. I'm not sure I can look at him much longer; I feel as if I'm being crushed inside and out and my tears are a hair's breadth away from spilling out.

He slips the necklace in his jacket pocket. 'And what else?' he asks quietly.

'I'll just sit here, and I'll close my eyes and when I open them, you'll be gone.'

He gazes down at me, until I can't bear it any more. 'Is that what you really want?'

'Yes, it is.'

There's a pause, during which my heart thuds wildly, and finally a nod. 'If you really can't bear to see me walk away, then, close your eyes,' he says.

What? No protest? No fight? No battering down of my defences? Just resignation? No 'He who conquers endures' family motto stuff? It seems as if I have finally defeated Alexander Hunt – and victory tastes like ashes and smells acrid and cold.

I close my stinging eyes. I squeeze them so tightly shut it hurts because when I open them, he'll be gone for good.

I wait to hear him walk away; I wait ten seconds and I count one, two, three – then ten – then twenty. I can't hear his footsteps retreating, dying. I hear nothing but the Ferris-wheel music but I dare not look in case he's fooling me, because I know I can never bear this again. I count up to thirty, then forty, stretching the time out beyond a minute. Still I dare not open my eyes, my aching eyes . . .

'Lauren?'

That's Immy's voice, right next to me. I open my eyes and quickly drag one hand over them, while clenching the other hand. I'm trying to defy the tears – to tell them to get the fuck out my life.

'Where's Alexander?'

'Didn't you just see him?'

'No.'

'You must have noticed him walk past you?' I crane my neck, searching the garden for him.

She glances around her. 'No. Maybe he went another way out of the garden?'

'But . . .'

'What's up, Lauren? Where's Alexander?'

'Nothing. He just . . . went home.'

She frowns, and then seems to accept my explanation. 'Oh. I see.'

Soon, I hope, my chest will stop feeling like a giant fist is squeezing it. 'Where's Scott?' I ask.

She nibbles her lip nervously. 'Still beating himself up over the fact that he mentioned the job to Alexander. Has it caused a lot of trouble? Is that why he's gone home?'

'No, he just . . . had things to take care of.'

'OK . . . You've lost your necklace . . .' she says, her face puzzled.

'I know.'

Immy looks at me and in that moment, I know she's guessed what's just happened. She also knows that, for now, one word or touch of sympathy would burst a bubble so huge and so fragile that it would finish me.

So she smiles and links her arm through mine. 'Come on, it's time for the survivors' photo.'

'What's that?' I ask, suddenly feeling so light I could float away.

'Everyone who made it to the end of the ball gathers in the Front Quad and a photographer takes a mass picture. You haven't lived unless you make it to the survivors' photo.'

So I pretend I have limbs that have real bones in them, not Jello, and I stroll with her across the dewy grass towards the Front Quad on this perfect midsummer morning. The sky is a pale blue now, the morning sun bathes the stone walls with a golden light and even the founders seem to gaze benignly down on us.

The photographer shouts: 'Big smiles!'

When Immy and I stand either side of Scott, with his big arms tight around us, I grin like an idiot for the camera and even though I'm dying inside, I tell myself I made it.

Chapter Nineteen

The doors of the Ross Foundation hiss shut behind me and the rumble of the traffic and blast of sirens assault my ears. Heat bounces off the sidewalks and the grey stone facade of the building.

A bead of perspiration slides down my back. It has to be in the high eighties out here in the piazza. I suck in some breaths. The air is hardly fresh, but it's a relief after the chill of the Foundation's offices. Making sure I'm out of sight of the reception, I sit on a wall in the piazza, swap my heels for the ballet flats in my briefcase and sling my jacket over my shoulder. Even in my sleeveless linen shift, I'm too warm, but it's not far to the restaurant where I've arranged to meet Scott.

It's a Latin Asian place, nothing fancy but with a relaxed contemporary vibe, and I order a mint julep while I wait for him. He's only a few minutes late and diners look up as he walks up to my table. He's in a business suit – the first time I've ever seen him wear one – and I catch my breath. He looks serious . . . a little older maybe, but he wears the gravitas very well.

'So, how was the interview?' he asks, kissing me on the cheek before taking the seat opposite.

'Good, it seemed to go well.' I grimace. 'Though for an interview that was meant to be just a formality, according to my mother, I sure took a real grilling from Donna and her HR president.'

He winces. 'Ouch.'

'Yeah, but you know what? I'm glad they were thorough, because if I do get an offer, I'll know I got it on merit.'

'Of course you got it on merit! Believe me, no one makes Donna Ross do anything she doesn't want to, let alone hire an assistant! Have faith in yourself, Lauren, you have a master's from Oxford. And *if* you get the job? Why would you even question it?'

'Well, I won't hear the result for a little while.' I cool my palm on my glass.

'You look the part.'

'I feel a little overdressed after a year at Oxford. I'm used to a mini, skinny jeans or a ballgown. The dress and jacket feel odd.'

'It's the tie I can't get used to. I can see why my father calls his a knot of servitude.' He runs his finger around the knot and undoes his top button.

'Every other time I've seen you, you've been in sports gear, apart from at the ball, of course.'

'Did I scrub up?' he asks.

'Pretty well.'

'Good. So, apart from post-interview trauma, how are you?'

'Good, I'm good. So how's life on the Hill?' I ask.

'Interesting . . . Who knew Water Policy could stir up so much intrigue?'

'Mmm. So, have you been sent to spy on *me*?'

He taps the side of his nose and whispers, 'Of course. Keep it under your hat, but I'm the new recruit for the WMA. Washington Mothers Agency.' He picks up the menu. 'Have you ordered? I don't know about you, but I could eat a horse.'

The rest of lunch is a mix of gossip, about Scott's department, rowing, mutual friends and foes. It's so great to be able to relax after my morning of interviews. I hadn't realized how tense I was until now; I can feel my shoulder blades tangibly sinking from somewhere around the top of my ears. Arranging to meet Scott for lunch was such a great idea; he knows me so well, and in no time an hour has gone by.

Scott glances at his watch.

'Do you have to get back?' I ask.

He smiles. 'Not yet. My boss is out of town and I had a meeting nearby this morning, which is why I suggested this place. I can say I was with Senator Cusack's team if any one complains, but they won't . . . Say, if you don't want to order coffee, why don't we get out of here?'

We go halves on the check, and Scott pulls off his tie, before we stroll out towards the park across the street. The shade of the trees is welcome as we meander around the pathways.

'So, what's the story with Alexander?' he asks.

I think I was prepared for this; in fact I'm a little surprised he didn't bring up the subject sooner. Even so, I take care with my words. 'Do you know, it's been so hectic since I've been home, I've hardly had time to think about him. Which is good. We've gone our separate ways. He couldn't handle me coming back here.'

'Really? Have you not talked at all?'

'No, and I don't expect to. We left things on a sour note – it was just impossible. We're both tied to opposing sides of the Atlantic, and he gave me no choice but to end things cleanly.'

'Hmm,' he muses. 'That's a great statement for the press, Lauren, but is that how you really feel? I'm still beating myself up that I put my foot in it by mentioning your job offer. It wasn't deliberate, though you may not believe that.'

'I *do* believe you – I know you'd never play games with me, Scott, which is why I love you to bits.'

'You love me to bits?'

I stop under the shade of a maple, slightly regretting my choice of words. 'You know how much I think of you, and as for Alexander, you did me a favour. I had to tell him sooner or later.'

He looks at me. 'Still, I'm sorry I messed up.'

'No worries,' I say brightly. 'The whole thing had a time limit on it from the start and maybe shouldn't have even begun, and it's over now. In fact, can we not talk about Alexander today? I wanted to make it a beginning, not an end.'

He grins. 'Absolutely delighted not to.' His attempt at Alexander's aristo accent is pretty good but I roll my eyes anyway.

We walk on a little more until we reach the other side of the park. A siren wails.

'You know, I ought to call a cab and get home. My mother will be dying to hear how I got on. I'm amazed she hasn't called me by now.'

'I guess I should go back too.'

'Shall I call you a cab? Or we could share part of the way?'

He glances at the gates of the park and then back at me.

'I can't do this any more.'

'What do you mean?'

'This. Pretending it's all OK, that I'm happy just to be a shoulder for you to cry on and a little light relief from the angst of fucking Alexander.'

'Scott, I don't understand.'

'You're just about the smartest girl I know but you must be blind not to see what's in front of you.'

I'm too shocked to speak.

'And this is the craziest, most stupid thing I've ever done. It's too soon, you're still mad about Alexander and I know I'm going to crash and burn . . .' He holds up his hands and groans. 'But, hell, Lauren . . .'

*

'Lemonade, honey?'

Two days later, my mother places a tray containing a jug and two glasses on the table on the deck. A drop of condensation slides off the base of the glass and on to my cut-offs but I don't wipe it off. Since my interview, the thermometer has inched up another few degrees. Even in the shade of a parasol by our pool-cum-summer house, the heat burns through the fabric until it's almost unbearable. At least, I tell myself, it makes me feel alive.

My mother sits down at the table and fans herself with her straw hat. 'Can you believe this heat? I'd jump in that pool myself if I hadn't got to go to Karen Amster's Fourth of July ball committee meeting. How's it going?' She nods at the pack of information the Ross Foundation sent me, which includes my contract of employment.

'Good . . . it's all good.'

'We're so proud of you, sweetheart. We thought you might not want the job as it came via a friend but you got it all on your own merit. Donna must have been seriously impressed to have the contract couriered over.'

'I guess so. Thanks, Mom.' My stomach stirs a little at the memory of that day and the revelation that turned my world upside down once more.

'Any luck in finding an apartment in town?' she asks. 'Because I can get one of the girls at the trust on to it. A couple of them are realtors and have some great connections – and you don't have to worry about the rental costs; your father and I can cover it if you want somewhere that's more than your salary.'

'Thanks, Mom, but I haven't had a proper look yet . . .'

My mother pats my hand. 'I know you want to be independent. I would too, in your position, but you'll always be welcome here with us.'

'Thanks. It means a lot to me to have yours and Daddy's support.' I sip the lemonade carefully, focusing on the bittersweet tang against my palate.

'Forgive me if I'm prying, but Leah called me this morning.'

I lick my lips. 'Did she?'

'Yes. She's thrilled she was able to help you in some small way. She told me you had lunch with Scott the other day, after your interview. Of course, I already knew that, but for some reason, Leah acted like it was some kind of big secret so I pretended to be surprised.'

A bead of perspiration slides down my back. 'Thanks.'

'So how is he?'

'Good. Buzzed about his new job.'

'He should be. Your father thinks he'll do very well in the Environment Department. He could be a policy advisor in no time and after that, the sky's the limit; he could do anything. Look at Ronan Farrow.'

I force a smile, but I might have known that Mom is only lulling me into a false sense of security.

'Tell me to mind my own business but I have to ask. Leah said Scott was acting a little weird when he called in to see her after he met you, and that's not like him. You know how laidback he is, even the Boat Race thing didn't seem to faze him, so she was a little concerned. I know she fusses over him, but he is her only son.'

I almost laugh at this – as if my mother doesn't fuss over me. 'So she asked you to try and find out what was going on?' I say lightly.

'You can't blame her. How *are* things between you two?'

'They're fine. Why wouldn't they be?'

'No reason . . . I did wonder when she said that he seemed agitated, but she may simply be hyper-sensitive. I do hope everything's fine because Scott's a great guy. Your father and I both like him a lot, and I probably shouldn't say this, but he's ten times the man Todd was.'

'I agree.'

My mother narrows her eyes; I know exactly the word she's about to say and it only has three letters but a whole lot of meaning.

'*And?*'

I smile again. '*And* you're perfectly right. Scott is ten times the man that Todd is.'

Narrowing her eyes at me, she sighs and stands up. 'I think I should have minded my own business. When you're ready to share, I guess we'll hear soon enough.'

'I love you, Mom,' I say, looking up at her gratefully.

She kisses the top of my head. 'You too, honey.'

A while later, the parasol is no longer any match for the fierce heat of the sun. My biography of Modigliani lies abandoned on the pool tiles and I can't seem to focus on anything. It could be the anti-climax after the past term and the fact I've been running like a hamster round a wheel for the last few months.

I turn over on to my stomach, watching Hockneyesque ripples on the pool, wondering whether to fetch my watercolours and try and capture the scene, or whether it will only leave me frustrated at my own inadequacies. Besides, the glittering blues and the sun sparkling on the water only remind me of the sapphire necklace. A pang stabs at me unexpectedly; I can't forget Alexander's face when I gave it back to him, or how much it hurt me to return it.

As for Scott, I can't decide whether he's made my life way more complicated – or much simpler.

I turn over on to my back, replaying his words, the look on his face.

'I know I'll regret this – I already do – but I want you to know how I feel about you. You've really got under my skin this last year.'

'Scott. You mean the world to me . . .' I said, knowing that deliberately misunderstanding him was the coward's way out. Knowing that dancing around his meaning was cruel.

'Ah, but I mean more than that and you know it. I've liked you – more than liked you – for a long time. Even back in the Todd days.'

I didn't pull away when he took my hand. I tried to let him

348

down gently, because I'm selfish and I wanted things to stay the same between us, to cling on to that fragile balance of friendship and something more.

'And I really do love you to bits too, Scott.'

He smiled and let go of my hand. 'You love me to bits.' I know, you told me that already today. Oh, Lauren, how I wish those two little words didn't exist. The first three would be plenty for me; the final two tell me all I need to know.'

He shook his head and I fought back the tears.

'Scott, I'm sorry. I can't give you what you want. Not right now, not at this moment. I'm really a mess after Alexander.'

Why was I the one in anguish? Why was I the one crying and feeling like my world had fallen apart? Because Scott means so much to me; his pain is mine, and the fact I inflicted it sliced through me like a knife.

He kissed me, on the lips, lingering, just like he did in the street last winter, and it still felt the same: lovely, delicious, warm and comforting.

Scott will always be all of those things to me, even if he never wants to set eyes on me again. He walked with me to the gates of the park and called me a cab. I didn't want him to, but I couldn't bear to add another act of rejection to the one I'd already hurled at him. His final words are burned on my conscience for ever.

'You'd better take a long hard look at what you really want from life, Lauren. It might not be what you thought. It might not fit neatly into your plans, it might even scare you, but if you don't take the risk, you might always regret it.'

Then he kissed me goodbye. 'I don't regret telling you how I feel about you — remember that.'

349

And then . . . and then I came back home.

Now, I shove my fist in my mouth, biting back the tears. I know this: I can't lie by this pool for ever, however much I want to. I have to do something and stop this awful limbo.

I can't dodge my parents for ever either, and even now I'm anticipating the rattle of the electric gates opening and my mother's Cayenne pulling up on the drive. My father has said he'll try to make it home for a family supper this evening, so I guess I'd better take a shower soon and get ready for the fray.

You see, I made a big decision today – a huge one. I just hope they don't think it's all too hasty and impulsive, but now I've made my mind up, there's no reason to wait. I hope they understand; Alexander too, though I don't know why I'm worried about how he'll feel. It has nothing to do with him any more. Nothing I do will ever have anything to do with him, ever again.

Maybe I should tell my parents *before* dinner and get it over with?

I get up and dive straight into the pool, hearing, feeling, smelling water, trying to blot out everything *but* water. My eyes sting when I open them. Everything is blurry and the shapes are distorted but the peace is profound. No one can get me; I'm free, safe. If I could only hold my breath long enough so I didn't have to face the world again . . . My lungs are almost bursting as the blue of the tiles at the end of the pool come into sight. I stretch my arm out, fingers inches from the wall.

What the –?

My mouth opens in shock as a shadowy figure appears and water rushes down my throat. I break the surface, spluttering, my nose burning with pain, eyes blinded by chlorine.

A hand reaches down to me. 'Are you OK? I'm sorry.'

'You . . . idiot. My God!'

I tread water, flailing while my eyes try to focus on the man crouching at the edge of the pool.

'Do you need a hand to get out?'

His shadow shields me from the sun.

'No . . . I . . . do . . . not!'

As my eyes start to focus properly, I catch my breath for a different reason because no photograph on my phone and no memory, however seared into my brain, can ever match up to having Alexander Hunt here in the flesh, those intense blue eyes looking down at me from that arrogant breathtaking face.

Chapter Twenty

I lean on the edge of the pool, glaring up at him. 'What are you doing here?'

'I flew over to see you,' he says simply.

'What for?'

He looks down at me coolly. 'Why do you think?'

'Making an educated guess, I'd say it was to fuck up my life again.'

He gives a wry smile. 'That's about the size of it, and because you should know by now that no matter what I might have said to you, I never ever give up. Here, let me help.'

His muscular forearm is gilded by the sun and I don't have to take it but I can't help myself. I need to feel his flesh on mine again, if only to convince myself that he's actually here in Washington, in my garden, invading my territory.

It's an impulse of the moment, and I don't know why I do it or why I'm so angry that he's landed back in the middle of my life again but I really can't help what happens next. Just as he rocks forward on his toes, I jerk my arm back and kick away from the poolside as if my life depends on it. My arm is almost wrenched out of its socket but it's worth it as he overbalances face-first into the deep end.

'What – ?'

His shout is swallowed by a huge splash that has me spluttering. I know I'm for it and even before he's surfaced, I'm striking out for the shallow end like Michael Phelps is after me. The pool's not big but I can already hear Alexander carving through the water behind me. Heart bursting, I'm almost at the first step in the shallow end when his hand clamps around my ankle.

'Get off!'

I barely have time to clamp my lips shut before I'm dragged under the surface, kicking and struggling. He has me round the waist now and seems to be underneath me, holding me against him but I'm thrashing and struggling. I open my eyes and think I can see his white shirt billowing, his face a blur a foot from mine. My lungs ache, I'm starting to panic and then, suddenly, I'm thrust upwards into the sunlight.

I gulp in air, water burning my eyes again. Alexander breaks the surface next to me, shaking droplets from his head, and grabs me.

'How could you do this to me!' I try to break away from him, but he holds me against his chest.

'*Me?* Look at my bloody clothes!'

And, oh my word, I do. His shirt is moulded to every contour of his broad chest and abs, his nipples are tight dark shadows under the cotton.

'Serves you right. You scared me half to death. I thought you were an intruder! In fact, where's my mother? Did she let you in?' I say, knowing that the momentary thought that he was an intruder isn't half so intimidating as him just being *him*.

He grimaces in apology – I think. 'I'm afraid not.'

'You mean you broke in here?'

'Not exactly. I was a little more discreet than that. By the way, your father really should rethink his home security.'

'Discreet . . . Do you mind telling me what you want, Alexander?'

The moment he releases his hold on me, I wade towards the steps and climb out of the pool.

'I suppose I should have called first,' he says, following me up the steps.

'*Suppose* you should have called?' Water pools on the terracotta tiles around his feet. His shorts cling to his thighs like shrinkwrap.

'I was afraid you might not want to see me, so I took a chance on you being in.'

'You're right, I don't want to see you but as you're here, a little notice so I could have prepared myself might have been nice.'

'Oh, I don't know. I think you look pretty good as you are.'

His gaze licks my body, reminding me I'm still wearing only my bikini, and an itsy-bitsy one at that, and instinctively I hug myself. This may be my territory but I feel utterly defenceless.

He reaches out for me and all of a sudden the fight goes out of me. I look at him, I look at those eyes that devour me, and I know I am helpless. I'm so mad at myself I could weep but I know it's something I can't defeat, and wordlessly I move closer to him. He pulls my wet arms around his back, and presses my soaking half-naked body against his shirt, and I can do nothing but abandon myself to the molten slide of his mouth against mine.

He pushes away the strands of hair sticking to my cheeks. 'You are very, very hot, Lauren.'

I look up at him, almost drunk with my need for him. I'm wet, he's wet and I'm already virtually naked and I can't help myself. I bunch the sodden folds of his shirt in my hands and press the fabric into the muscles of his spine. 'We'd better seek some shade, then.'

He follows me into the pool house; I close the door. In the sultry shadows, our mouths meet again, devouring each other in a chlorine-scented kiss that's one of the best I've ever tasted. Alexander pushes his hands down the back of my bikini bottoms, rests his hands on my bare butt and crushes my pelvis on to his erection. His shirt is dripping wet but I manage to drag it out of his waistband.

The door rattles on its hinges and my pulse skitters. 'Oh God, Mom could come back at any moment.'

Alexander pulls the little catch across. 'Then we'd better get on with it.'

Thrumming with desire, I watch him unbutton his shorts. He strips them off and I toss them over the rickety Lloyd Loom chair in the corner of the hut while he deals with his shirt. Water drips off us both, tiny rivulets running down the grooves between the wooden floorboards.

I'm trembling with lust when he slips the strap of my bikini top over my head and lets it fall to my waist. I flatten myself against him, my breasts sticking to his damp skin.

'I've missed this so much. I've missed you so much,' he whispers.

I take refuge in the solidity of his chest because I don't trust myself to reply. I'm afraid of showing how much I've missed him . . . I don't want to admit it to myself or to him. His fingers fumble with the damp ties of my bikini bottoms and, muttering an oath, he pulls them down over my hips.

The wet bottoms fall on to my feet and we're both naked. Heat beats down on the tiled roof; the place is like an oven, ramping up the sizzling heat from our bodies.

'Oh . . .'

The first touch of his fingers on me sends me heavenwards. I grasp his back while he strokes and flicks at me.

'You bad, bad girl.'

I tighten around his finger, around both of his fingers.

'Here.' My voice is tight, raw, as I guide him to the discarded hammock mattress on the floor of the pool house. My mother still hasn't got round to throwing it out. Oh my God, if she could see what we're doing on it now!

I pull him on top of me, and feel his erection brush against the inside of my thighs before he enters me, quickly and smoothly. Stifling a whimper of ecstasy, I wrap my legs around his ass and dig my heels in hard. The friction of him inside me, against me, and the sheer physical presence of him drives me wild. With his hands planted either side of me, he looks right into my eyes, watching me gasp and writhe and try not to scream out loud. My fingers slip in the sheen of sweat and water on his back, as his thrusts speed up, harder and stronger. I can't hold back any longer, I don't want to – but I'm scared of letting go, of shouting, of my mother walking in on us.

He comes, gloriously hard inside me, and I lose it . . . crying out, coming so hard, every muscle tightens like wire.

I open my eyes, eventually, and the dusty dark roof of the pool house comes into focus. There are cobwebs in the corners and the air feels thick enough to stir with a spoon.

I turn my head towards Alexander. He's on his back next to me, half on, half off the mattress, breathing hard, eyes closed.

'Did I make a noise?'

'I . . . have . . . no idea.'

'It's so hot in here.'

He turns his head and looks at me, smiling and more at rest than I've ever seen him in my life before. 'You can say that again . . .'

I touch his arm. 'Alexander?'

'Shh.' He eases himself up on to his elbows, chin lifted. 'Is that a car?'

My heart rate, only just returning to normal, speeds up again at the distant sound of an engine at the front of the house. 'Oh God! It must be Mom.'

He holds up his hand. 'Wait . . . I can't hear anything now. They must have driven on.'

I scramble to my feet anyway. 'I hope so, but she will be home soon. Jesus, how am I going to explain this to her?'

'Why don't you tell her the truth?' Alexander gets up.

'That we've been screwing each other in the pool house? She'd have a coronary.'

I begin a frantic search for my bikini.

'Because we'd had sex in the pool house or because you'd had sex with me?'

'Both.'

I knock over a plant pot while I'm trying to find my bikini top. 'Shit.'

Alexander plucks the top from under the mattress and holds it out. 'I know I'm not the American dream in your parents' eyes, and I don't blame them. I'm trouble, I keep on hurting you and they must think I'm hell-bent on taking you halfway round the world.'

'No, you aren't. I make my own choices. I don't stay here for their sakes.'

'Or Scott's?'

Suddenly, and without warning, I burst into tears. I snatch my top from him and wipe my hand over my eyes, ashamed of how quickly I've rushed back into his arms and how emotional I feel. 'Just get right back on the plane to London and leave me alone. This isn't going to help either of us.'

'There are no flights until tonight,' he says with a patience that makes me want to hit him.

'I don't care. You can't parachute in here and lob a grenade into my plans. You can't.' I pull my top over my head, getting tangled up in the strings.

'All I've done is call in to say hello.'

I almost trip over while trying to put on my bikini bottoms. Alexander smiles at me.

'It's not funny!'

'I'm simply enjoying the view of your delectable arse, Ms Cusack.'

'I don't care! Aren't you going to get dressed?'

'What's the point? My clothes are soaking.'

'And my mother could be home any time. You *have* to get dressed and leave.'

He holds my shoulders. 'Not until you listen to me.'

'There's nothing to listen to. I asked you to walk away from me at the ball and you did. That was the end of it.

I have a new life now . . .' I stare at him, tears pouring down my cheeks. He picks up his shirt and offers it to me to wipe my face. 'That's not much use, is it?' I mumble.

'It's the thought that counts.'

'Please, don't do this to me again. I can't stand it after the last time. Just leave?'

He puts his fingers on my lips. 'Shh.'

My heart pounds and I strain my ears while Alexander cracks open the door of the pool house.

This time, the engine note is unmistakeable and my hand flies to my mouth. 'Oh my God, it's the Cayenne.'

A rattle from the front of the house tells me that the gates are opening. 'You have to leave *now*!'

'How? Climb back over the wall? I nearly broke my neck getting in here.'

'Good. Now go!'

'Like this?'

I pick up his shorts and throw them at him. 'Yes. My mother can't find you here.'

He holds on to the shorts. 'Lauren, it's too late.'

I hear the engine rev as the car drives up the short slope through the gates. 'What the hell are we going to do?'

'I'll think of something.'

'You're naked!'

'Wait.' Alexander pulls his wet shirt over his arms as the gates grind shut behind the car.

'What are you *doing*?'

'Stay calm.'

'Calm? She'll be out here by the pool in two minutes tops.'

From the driveway, the engine noise grows louder and then, finally, there's silence.

Alexander buttons up his sodden shirt. 'Go outside. Quickly.'

Pushing open the door, I screw up my eyes against the sunlight. A car door slams shut.

Alexander walks out behind me, still buttoning his shorts.

'How do we explain this?'

He puts his finger to his lips and slips on his Havaianas.

'Look shocked and horrified,' he hisses, jogging over to the pool steps.

'That won't be hard!'

Half a minute later, I'm still holding my theatrical pose, hands over my mouth, eyes wide, as my mother appears in the French windows.

'Alexander!'

At my shout, her first reaction is to freeze, and then her jaw drops. She hurries out to the poolside.

'Lauren? Alexander? What's going on? Why is Alexander in our pool?'

'He tripped over the hose and fell in . . .'

My mother glances from the pool hose snaking its way across the tiles to Alexander, then back at me.

Shaking water from his head, he wades to the shallow end, where my mother waits, still looking like someone dropped a bomb in the pool.

He walks up the steps and holds out a dripping hand. 'Good afternoon, Blythe. How lovely to meet you again.'

A short while later, Alexander emerges from the house, in dry shorts and T-shirt, rubbing his hair with one of my mother's guest towels.

'Is there anything you need?' she asks.

'No, thank you, and I'm sorry for soaking your carpet.'

'It's no problem. I loaded your wet things into the machine while you showered.'

'That's very kind of you, Blythe, and I must apologize. It's incredibly rude of me to simply drop in on you like this, and I really should have called first, but I was sort of passing by, so I thought I'd pop in.'

No matter how shocked my mother is to see him, the full hostess training kicks in. 'Are you on business in Washington?'

'Of sorts.' He gives her a mysterious smile.

'I see. When did you fly in?'

'Not that long ago,' I say. 'Alexander decided to call round on his way to his hotel.'

'As soon as he landed? Well, it's such a shame he had a damp start to his visit . . .' She directs this comment at me; while she can't possibly know what we've been up to, she knows something weird is going on. 'Where exactly are you planning on staying while you're here?' she adds.

'One of the big hotels in the centre,' he says.

My mother eyes him sharply, then looks at me suspiciously. I hope she puts my flushed face down to the sun. 'So have you fixed our visitor a drink yet, honey?'

'Not yet, Mom. I haven't, uh – had a chance, as you can see.'

'Well, it's very hot out here. If you just got off a flight, you must be dehydrated. Can I get you some lemonade, Alexander?'

'I don't want to put you to any trouble, but that would be lovely, thanks.'

'It's no trouble as you've made a detour to see us. Would you prefer tea? I have some Earl Grey in the kitchen. Lauren seems to have acquired a taste for it while she was away.'

'Lemonade will be fine, thanks, Blythe.'

'Why don't you sit down here while I fetch it? I've asked your driver into the kitchen for a cool drink; he must have been baking out in the car, despite the air conditioning.'

He settles his big, lean frame in the deckchair at the table, while I collapse into the seat opposite, grateful for some solidity under my watery limbs. My mother is halfway around the pool when, out of the corner of my eye, I see her turn her head and give me an open-palm gesture of total confusion.

He rests his hand on the table, inches from the envelope containing my contract. 'What a lovely garden. I had no idea you had a pool,' he says innocently, then starts to toy with the envelope. It has the Ross Foundation logo on it, my name on the front. It doesn't take a genius to work out what it is.

My mother comes back with the drinks on a tray. 'Here you go. If you need anything else, Lauren will sort you out, I'm sure. Now, I need to get changed out of this suit and I guess you two have a lot to catch up on.'

She leaves us alone. Alexander taps the envelope.

'That's the job offer,' I say, almost defiantly.

'I guessed as much. Congratulations.'

I stay silent.

'You asked me why I was really here, so I'm going to tell you.'

I stiffen in my seat. 'Oh.'

Despite the lemonade, my mouth is dry.

'You remember when Valentina threatened to share that video?'

My heart rate picks up. I can't deal with any more of her crazy antics now. 'How could I forget?'

'We both thought she wouldn't go through with it, but nonetheless I had to take it seriously. I could have spoken with the count and contessa. I could have told them what she's been up to and how it would have hurt my mother and father, if they'd known, but I didn't. I told Valentina to go ahead and share it.'

'You did what? Why?'

'Perhaps it was a risk, a huge risk, but I know by now that you have to take risks to survive and get what you want. I told her that posting that video and her story would be pointless. I told her to go ahead and do it, that if I got kicked out of the army for it, I'd accept that, but nothing and no one would ever be able to force me into doing something I don't want to – *stop seeing you.*'

I swallow hard at the implication of his words. I don't know whether to laugh or cry, knowing he was prepared to risk his commission for . . . me.

'And I didn't mean it, the all-or-nothing thing. I was just upset,' he says simply.

Now I am really lost for words; I wasn't expecting any of this. Alexander keeps going.

'Listen, I've made another decision too. Assuming Valentina doesn't carry out her threat and the army don't chuck me out, I've no choice but to complete this year. I owe them, and I owe it to myself to finish it. But then I'll leave. I know I can't carry on with it.' He sees my questioning look but stalls me. 'So it's only for a year that we can't be together. I know you are tied here, I know our jobs make things bloody difficult. But I'm not giving up, Lauren.' He looks at me fiercely. 'I need to have you in my life, in whatever small way. I probably *will* fuck your life up, and you mine, but I don't care. Seeing much less of you is a hell of a lot better than not seeing you at all. You know I *have* to keep fighting.' He finishes his long speech and takes a deep breath.

'Fighting each other?' I whisper.

'Yes, each other if we have to, because anything is preferable to the nothing I've suffered over the past two weeks. Fighting each other is better than lying down and giving in. I *don't* give in. I don't lose. Do you?'

I flail around for a response. I can hardly breathe, let alone speak rationally. 'You didn't say any of this at the ball.'

'I was upset – shocked about the job. And then, before I knew it, you made me promise to walk away – you demanded I left – and for your sake, I did it. I didn't tell you how I felt because I didn't want to hold you back, and you didn't want to hear it anyway. Well, you're hearing it now and I don't care what it does to you. I'm a selfish, single-minded bastard, you know that by now. I'm not asking you to come back. I know that isn't going to happen.'

I look up at him, still unable to speak.

'But, like I say . . . even if you can't be with me physically, I'd like to know – I need to know – that you'll be with me *somewhere* . . . unless it's too late, of course, and someone else got there first?'

'No . . . No, they haven't . . . but . . . Look, I don't need you or any other guy. I love my parents too, but I don't need them to find me a career. I can make my own decisions about my life, my love life, my career, even if' – I take a deep breath – 'they're very, very stupid ones.'

He looks at me questioningly, as if he can't believe what I'm implying. 'What are you saying?'

I take a deep breath. 'I've decided not to take the Ross Foundation job. My parents don't even know this yet but I emailed Donna this morning to say thanks, but no thanks.'

'Why?' He doesn't move a muscle.

'Like I said, I make my own decisions. The job, it felt too "set up" for me – almost *too* perfect.'

'So you're turning it down because your parents arranged it?'

'Not only that. It's . . . I'm not ready to settle into the whole career thing just yet. I've had a taste of freedom, with all its joy and pain . . .' I smile at him. 'A *lot* of pain at times but going it alone seems to have given me a taste for adventure, so I've decided I want to travel, like Immy. I'm hoping I can join her, wherever she is.'

He swallows hard. 'Immy and you let loose on the world? That *is* an adventure . . . And your decision has nothing whatsoever to do with me?'

'Would it hurt your ego if I said it didn't?' I smile, I hope enigmatically, while my heart does a slow thump, thump against my ribcage.

'Not even a little?'

'Well, maybe a teeny tiny bit.' I pinch my fingers together to show him just how little, while inside I have the strangest feeling, like I'm as light as a helium balloon and if someone cut my string, I'd fly off into the sky.

'Listen, that's fine,' he says quietly, and I feel like I really have stunned him. Then he looks up, giving me a guarded look. 'Though it won't be nearly so easy for me to visit you when I'm on leave,' he says ruefully. 'Christ, I don't know how I'll cope – I'll be in Britain and God knows where else. You'll be halfway round the world. It'll be a form of torture seeing so little of you – seriously,' he adds when he sees my face. 'But,' he sighs, 'in a year's time I'll be back at Falconbury for good and things can be different – if you want them to be.'

I start to speak but he stops me. 'It's not just about you; it's time I did my duty to Falconbury and to Emma, no matter how much she thinks she doesn't need me. Maybe I can still have some kind of role, in training or intel, but I need to go home and take up where my father left off, and hopefully, if I try very hard, make a better job of things, of everything, than he did.'

Now this really takes me by surprise. I know how much he's struggled with the idea of being tied to Falconbury, but I guess his father's death changed everything, and I admire how he's facing up to his responsibilities. Seems content to do so. And then, just as I think there can be no more surprises, from the pocket of his shorts, he pulls out the necklace. It sparkles in the sunshine, way more dazzling than the sunlight on the water.

'But it *is*, partly, about you too. My mother didn't leave this for Emma; she set it aside for me.'

'It wouldn't suit you,' I say, yet my voice sounds wobbly.

He laughs but doesn't let me off the hook, his gaze burning into me. 'You know what I mean. Are you going to wear it?'

'With my bikini?'

'I can't think of a better outfit.'

Every rational cell in my brain, every smart one, is saying, solemnly: no. Yet my instincts are not rational when I hear his next words.

'Lauren, I know I'm rubbish at this sort of thing but please take this. Keep it with you, treat it like it's a piece of me while we can't be together. I really want you to have it – *need* you to have it. And if in a year's time you want to give it back, if we can't survive this year apart, I'll accept it back then, if that's really what you want. I'm in this for the long haul, and I want to give you this to show you I mean business. I want a future for us when we've both got through the next year.'

You know, he looks so agonized that I almost feel sorry for him.

Almost.

I could say anything at this point. I could tell him it's not going to work, that we'd better walk away from one another now. That we will both move on and forget all about each other. I do none of these things. It takes all my resolve not to tell him I'll come back to Falconbury with him, that all I want is to be with him, because right

369

now, that's exactly what I long to do. But I can't, I know I can't.

I look down briefly at the choker before looking up into those eyes again, almost blinded by the intensity of their gaze, and I give him a barely perceptible nod. I hold out my hand, and I take the choker, my fingers clumsy and awkward.

I hear his soft intake of breath, of astonishment and relief, and then he lifts my chin and something shifts in those dark, beautiful eyes. He moves to clasp the necklace round my neck and I almost think I can feel his fingers shaking as he does it, but then maybe it's me shaking.

He pulls me to him roughly and kisses me like he's never kissed me before, his still damp hair brushing my face. His hands exert a firm and totally delicious pressure on the back of my bikini bottoms. I don't know what to think, I really don't, but right here, right now, I can only let myself enjoy the feeling of him against me and take one day at a time.

'My mother must be watching,' I whisper.

'I don't doubt it . . .' he murmurs. 'And if mine is watching too, I should think she's a hell of a lot happier than yours.'

OK, I can feel the tears threatening now and yes, I'm wearing the Hunt family heirloom along with my bikini, and my mother is definitely watching because I can see her in the French windows, one hand over her mouth like she's waiting for Daddy's results on election night.

Alexander sees her too, but neither of us cares.

Something has shifted in both of us and he gives me that slow, lazy smile I can never resist. 'So, um, Lauren, I have a week before I have to rejoin my regiment.'

'Only a week?' I moan, instinctively leaning in closer to him. How on earth am I going to say goodbye in a week's time?

'I'm sorry.' He pauses, then adds, 'So how do you propose we fill it?' He really is outrageous. One minute you can almost hear the sound of my heart cracking in two and the next I could rip all his clothes off right here in front of my mother. I shake my head and take a moment to steady my thoughts before grinning at him helplessly and walking my fingers up his chest. 'There's a lot that can happen in a week . . .' I whisper.

'That's what I'm worried about. I don't want to go back to my unit in a worse state than I just left it.'

Every inch of me is fizzing and now I really don't care what my mother sees or thinks. I slip my hand down the back of his shorts, revelling at the look on his face as he closes his eyes and I reach up to kiss him. 'Like what could I possibly do to hurt you?' I whisper.

He gives me such a look. 'Severe mental trauma? Physical exhaustion?'

'You think?' I tease.

'Oh, I *know*. And frankly, I can't bloody wait.'

Acknowledgements

There's probably a statement at the start of this book, reminding people that the contents are purely a work of fiction, but I'd just like to add my own 'disclaimer'. While I have done a lot of research into many aspects of the worlds I've been creating, I've also – shock horror – made a lot of it up. So I apologize to all the generous people who've helped me gain insight into military life, horsey things, hunting etiquette, American culture, etc. If I used some of your information while changing other aspects to suit my story. While many of the places mentioned in the book are real, all the people and the events are pure fantasy. Actually, no one would believe it if I did include some real stuff, but that's another story . . .

So now I've got that out of the way, I can have the pleasure of thanking all the people who helped and supported me in writing the series. It has been a total joy as well as an exciting challenge. I'm sure I'll miss someone out, but here goes, in no particular order: Janice Hume, Liz Hanbury, Nell Dixon, Lizzie Forbes, Mike V., David I., James T., Hannah T., Catherine Jones, Debra Ross, Leah Larson, Karen Markinson-Ambrose, and a bunch of great students, who had better remain nameless.

At Penguin, a huge thanks goes to my ed, Claire Bowron, for her skill and forbearance, and to Alex Clarke for making me laugh in a good way and giving me this wonderful chance. Also thanks to the copy-editing team, especially Emma Horton, to Charlotte Brabbin and Viola Hayden, and the fantastic sales and marketing gurus, in particular Katie Sheldrake and Anna Dercakz.

To my agent, Broo. You are a legend. 'Nuff said.

Finally, to my parents and my family, ILY. John and Charlotte, you are amazing and I genuinely couldn't have done this without you.

Follow the love trials of Lauren
and Alexander in the sizzling and
seductive Oxford Blue Series
by Pippa Croft

Available from Penguin
in Paperback and eBook

He just wanted a decent book to read ...

Not too much to ask, is it? It was in 1935 when Allen Lane, Managing Director of Bodley Head Publishers, stood on a platform at Exeter railway station looking for something good to read on his journey back to London. His choice was limited to popular magazines and poor-quality paperbacks – the same choice faced every day by the vast majority of readers, few of whom could afford hardbacks. Lane's disappointment and subsequent anger at the range of books generally available led him to found a company – and change the world.

'We believed in the existence in this country of a vast reading public for intelligent books at a low price, and staked everything on it'
Sir Allen Lane, 1902–1970, founder of Penguin Books

The quality paperback had arrived – and not just in bookshops. Lane was adamant that his Penguins should appear in chain stores and tobacconists, and should cost no more than a packet of cigarettes.

Reading habits (and cigarette prices) have changed since 1935, but Penguin still believes in publishing the best books for everybody to enjoy. We still believe that good design costs no more than bad design, and we still believe that quality books published passionately and responsibly make the world a better place.

So wherever you see the little bird – whether it's on a piece of prize-winning literary fiction or a celebrity autobiography, political tour de force or historical masterpiece, a serial-killer thriller, reference book, world classic or a piece of pure escapism – you can bet that it represents the very best that the genre has to offer.

Whatever you like to read – trust Penguin.

read more
www.penguin.co.uk